"As always, however, Ms. Thayne's writing is emotional, riveting, and keeps you hoping all turns out well."
          —*Fresh Fiction* on *The Sea Glass Cottage*

"This issue of the Cape Sanctuary series draws the reader in from the first page to the gratifying conclusion."
          —*New York Journal of Books* on *The Sea Glass Cottage*

"[Thayne] engages the reader's heart and emotions, inspiring hope and the belief that miracles *are* possible."
          —#1 *New York Times* bestselling author Debbie Macomber

"Thayne is in peak form in this delightful tale… A warmly compelling and satisfying work of women's fiction."
          —*Booklist* on *The Cliff House*, starred review

"The heart of this sweet contemporary story is in the women's relationships with each other, and it will suit readers on both sides of the blurry romance/women's fiction divide."   —*Publishers Weekly* on *The Cliff House*

"RaeAnne Thayne is quickly becoming one of my favorite authors…. Once you start reading, you aren't going to be able to stop."   —*Fresh Fiction*

RaeAnne Thayne

Christmas
at *Holiday House*

HQN

ISBN-13: 978-1-335-45998-5

Christmas at Holiday House

First published in 2020. This edition published in 2021.

Recycling programs
for this product may
not exist in your area.

This edition published by arrangement with Harlequin Books S.A.

For questions and comments about the quality of this book,
please contact us at CustomerService@Harlequin.com.

HQN
22 Adelaide St. West, 40th Floor
Toronto, Ontario M5H 4E3, Canada
www.Harlequin.com

Printed in Lithuania

MIX
Paper from
responsible sources
FSC® C021394

For my daughter, Kjersten, and all other teachers everywhere who work so hard to impact young lives under sometimes impossible, difficult conditions.

Christmas

at Holiday House

CHAPTER ONE

ABBY POWELL DROVE through the downtown area of Silver Bells, Colorado, fighting the odd sensation that she had somehow slipped onto the set of a Hallmark movie.

This couldn't be real, could it? No town could possibly look so festive and charming and...perfect.

On this day before Thanksgiving, Christmas seemed to have already taken over the ski resort town. Snow was lightly falling, dusting everything with a soft, pearly powder. The holiday season was in full view, from the brick storefronts adorned with colorful Christmas lights twinkling merrily in the dusk to the wreaths on every door in sight to the crowds of shoppers in parkas and coordinating beanies who made their way out of the stores, arms heavy with bags.

If she rolled down her windows, would she hear Christmas music chiming through the early evening? She was tempted to check it out but glanced in the rearview mirror and decided her five-year-old son probably wouldn't appreciate a sudden ice-cold breeze.

This snow-globe perfection seemed like a different planet from Phoenix, where her apartment complex manager at least had made a bit of an effort to get into the spirit of things. Before they left, she had noticed a new string of lights on one of the saguaro cacti in the common area near the barbecue.

"Are we almost there, Mommy?"

She shot another glance at Christopher. "Nearly, honey. This is the right town. Now I only have to find the address."

"Good. I'm tired of the car."

She smiled at his overly dramatic tone. No one could sound more long-suffering than a five-year-old. "I know it's been a long drive, but you have been such a good boy."

"Course I have. Santa's watching."

Christopher had been obsessed with Santa since before Halloween. She wasn't exactly sure what had flipped the switch this year. If someone could figure out the inner workings of a five-year-old boy's brain, she wanted to meet that person.

Maybe her son was finally old enough that the concept of a benevolent gift-giver made more sense. Or maybe his friends at preschool had discussed it at length.

"If he is watching," she said now to her son, "I know he has seen a boy who's been a big help to his mom on this drive."

This trip, nearly eight hours, was their longest road trip together. Christopher really had been wonderful. She hadn't been sure how he would be able to entertain himself for the journey. This would be a good test for the longer trip from Phoenix to Austin in a month's time, when she would be hauling a trailer full of some of their belongings.

The only other long road trip they'd ever taken together had been in February when they had driven the six hours from Phoenix to Southern California. They had spent a long weekend there playing on the beach and spending an unforgettable day at Disneyland, just the two of them.

Everything was just the two of them these days.

Abby ignored the pang that thought always stirred in

her. She did her best. She and Christopher took many trips to the zoo, the aquarium, local museums and festivals. She made certain her son had a rich life, filled with swimming lessons, playdates and educational opportunities.

She never felt like it was enough. Did every single mother worry she wasn't hitting some mythical benchmark that defined good parenting?

Probably. Single or not, likely every parent, regardless of relationship status, stressed about the same thing. Why hadn't anybody warned her worry was part of the job description?

Her navigation system instructed her to make a right at the next street. At the stop sign, she signaled, then obeyed and was struck by how the business of the downtown area seemed to melt away, replaced by a serene, tree-lined road bordered with older homes behind iron fences, each more lovely than the one before.

Where was Holiday House, her destination?

She peered down the street through the soft, swirling flakes that had begun to fall harder, obscuring her view.

Navigation system or not, she expected she would know the place when she saw it. During the two years they had been college roommates, Lucy Lancaster had shown her plenty of pictures of the huge, graceful mansion where her friend had spent the happiest moments of her childhood.

Abby could picture it in her mind: three stories, with a wide porch across the entire front, a smaller porch on the second level and three thick Doric columns supporting them.

She drove slowly, peering at each house.

"Will the lady like us?" Christopher asked, his voice worried, as they continued on their way.

Christopher had been a precocious, adventurous toddler but since Kevin's death, he had become more nervous around other people.

That was another reason she was moving to Austin—for herself and for her son. Both of them needed to reach outside themselves and embrace the beautiful world around them. Kevin, who had spent his entire career trying to help others, wouldn't have wanted them to be insular and withdrawn.

Abby smiled in the mirror. "How could she not like us? We're adorable."

Chris giggled, his dimple flashing. The sound chimed through the interior of her small SUV, warming her heart. He was a complete joy. How dark and dreary her world would have been without him these past two years. In the early days of grief and shock, he had been the only thing dragging her out of bed in the mornings.

"Don't worry," she said now. "Winifred Lancaster is wonderful. She's our friend Lucy's grandmother, so you know she must be awesome."

That connection seemed to reassure Christopher. "Lucy's funny. She's my friend."

"I know. Aren't we lucky to have her in our life?"

"I like it when she sends me stuff from other countries."

That wasn't an infrequent occurrence. Lucy had lived in a dozen countries since they lived together at school, always trying to make a difference in the world. It helped that Lucy had a freakish facility for languages and probably spoke eight or nine by now.

First she was in the peace corps in central Europe, then she worked for a nongovernmental organization in North Africa, focused on improving educational opportunities for girls. For the past two years she had taught English in Thailand. Wherever she traveled, she stayed in touch with Abby, often sending local treats or games or toys made by her students to Christopher.

Her life seemed exciting and fulfilling, though Abby wasn't entirely sure her friend was as happy as she said she was.

"In one hundred feet, your destination is on the left."

The disembodied voice of her navigation spoke through the car, making them both jump.

"Is that it? That big house?" Christopher asked, a new note of excitement in his voice.

Abby swallowed. Holiday House was vast, easily the biggest house on the block—the biggest one in town, from what she had seen driving here. The house and large garden took up almost half a block at the end of the road.

"Oh, my."

It was gorgeous, everything Lucy had said and more, illuminated with tasteful landscape lights as dusk gave way to night. How was it possible that she and Christopher were lucky enough to be able to spend a few weeks here? Abby wanted to pinch herself.

"I really hope she likes us," Christopher said.

Abby's cell phone rang with a FaceTime call before she could even turn into the driveway. When she saw it was Lucy, she pulled over to the side of the road and shifted her car into Park so she could safely take the call.

"Do you have spies watching for me or something?" she asked, only half joking when her friend's face flashed on the screen.

"No. I was just checking in, wondering how close you are."

"We couldn't be any closer." She turned her phone camera around so Lucy could see what Abby was looking at out the window—the beautiful pale house that gleamed in the snow.

"Are you just getting there?" Lucy's relief was obvious in her expression. "Oh, I'm so glad. How was your drive?"

"Mostly uneventful. We learned that Mr. Jingles isn't a great traveler, but we made do."

Their cat had thrown up in the first hour then yowled about every hundred miles, requiring a stop. She hadn't minded too terribly, since Christopher always seemed to need a stretch and bathroom break around that same time.

"Hi, Lucy," Christopher called from the back seat.

Abby turned the phone in that direction, where her son waved enthusiastically.

"There's my favorite dude."

"We went on a long car ride, only now I want to be out of my car seat."

"You're there, kiddo. I can't wait for you to meet my grandmother. I think you two are going to love each other."

"Okay." That seemed to put the last of Christopher's worries to rest and he put his headphones on to watch the rest of his show.

"Thank you so much for doing this," Lucy said to her. "I honestly don't have words."

"Really?" Abby teased. "With all the languages you speak?"

Lucy rattled off a bunch of words that Abby assumed all meant *thank you*. She picked up *gracias* and *merci*, but that was it.

"Seriously, I can't thank you enough. I still can't believe

you agreed to drop everything to help out Winnie. You're going to love her, too, I promise."

Abby shrugged. "The timing was right. My last day at the hospital was Saturday and we were only going to spend the month kicking around Phoenix before the move to Austin."

The past twenty-four hours were a blur, really, from the moment Lucy had called her, frantic, to tell her that her beloved grandmother had sustained a serious fall. She was in the hospital with a broken wrist, sprained ankle and bruised ribs. She needed home care in order to stay in her house, and did Abby have any friends from nursing school in Colorado who might be looking for work?

She wasn't sure if Lucy had asked her to come out or if Abby had offered. It didn't matter, she supposed. By the end of the phone call, she had agreed to travel to Colorado for a few weeks to help Winifred, until Lucy could finish her school term and make it home to Silver Bells herself.

It would be a lovely adventure for her and Christopher, she told herself again, as she had repeated about as often as Jingles and Christopher had needed bathroom breaks.

She wanted to give her son the best Christmas ever and couldn't imagine a better place to do that than Silver Bells, a beautiful historic winter resort town tucked into the Rocky Mountains. They weren't staying the entire month and expected to be back in Phoenix for Christmas itself. Two weeks should be enough to enjoy the holiday spirit in this beautiful town.

"You know I love your grandmother," she said to Lucy. "We'll all be fine."

Lucy hesitated. "There is one tiny complication I should probably mention."

Her friend was going to offer a complication *now*, when Abby was a hundred feet from her grandmother's door? "Please don't tell me I just spent eight hours in the car with a five-year-old and a dyspeptic cat for nothing."

"No. Not for nothing. But..." Lucy paused again. "I may have misled you about how desperate the situation was. Not on purpose, I promise. I was only going on the information I had."

"Misled me how?"

"When Winnie called to tell me about her accident and asked me to find a home nurse, she led me to think she was in dire straits. She told me Ethan, my brother, was insisting she go into a rehab facility."

"That's often the best place for older patients after a fall, so they can receive supported care."

"She absolutely refuses. Winnie wants to be home and I'll admit, I don't blame her. She loves Holiday House, especially this time of year."

It was not hard to see why, Abby thought, looking at the grand house on display in front of her.

"Where is the part where you misled me?"

"She led me to believe that if I didn't find a nurse, Ethan would have her carted straight from the hospital to a rehab center."

"Have things changed?"

"Not really. But kind of." Lucy looked apologetic. "I thought Ethan was going to be out of town until next week, and by the time he got back you would be there and it would be a done deal. I had arranged with Winnie's friends to get her home from the hospital and for someone to stay with her until you could get there. Unbeknownst to me, my brother rearranged his schedule and ended up flying back to town this morning instead of next week. I had no idea he would be there, I swear."

Okay. So she would have Lucy's brother to deal with, too. No big deal. She had been a nurse for years, with plenty of experience dealing with arrogant doctors and demanding family members. How hard could Ethan Lancaster be?

Unless he had already arranged for Winnie to go to assisted living, in which case she *had* just traveled eight hours in a car with a five-year-old boy and said dyspeptic cat for nothing. "So do you need my help or don't you?"

"We do. Definitely. Winnie and I need you more than ever. She really can't be alone at the house, especially now with a broken wrist. If you're not there, Ethan is sure to move her out of her house."

"If she is in her right mind, he can't make her go."

As much as Abby adored Lucy, her friend's brother sounded like a jerk. During the two years she and Lucy had been roommates at Arizona State University, before she graduated and married Kevin and Lucy left to work overseas, she had never met Ethan. She knew *of* him, though, and knew he had been living overseas, managing one of the family's hotels in Dubai. She wasn't eager to meet him now.

"He might not be able to force her, but Ethan can be persuasive. He says this is the perfect opportunity, while she is recovering from her accident. He's been saying for years that Holiday House is too big for her and too much work. This latest accident will only reinforce his opinion. My brother can be stubborn. Like all the Lancasters, I guess. Once he makes up his mind, he can be immovable."

The whole thing sounded tangled and ugly, the kind of

family drama Abby had always tried to avoid and of which she had zero personal experience.

She glanced behind her and saw that Christopher still had his headphones on.

"Are we going to have to barricade ourselves inside Holiday House with your grandmother and fight off your brother like that kid in *Home Alone*?"

Lucy grinned. "As much as I would pay to see that, no. Just be your amazing self, that's all. I talked to Ethan earlier today and told him the cavalry was on the way— namely you—that you were a nurse and amazing and would be the perfect one to stay with Winnie while she recovers, until I can get there. He's not happy about it, but what can he do?"

What had Lucy dragged her into? She hadn't said anything about her brother throwing a wrench in things during any of their previous conversations over the past twenty-four hours.

"I don't want to referee a fight between you and your brother, with your grandmother in the middle. I can find a hotel for tonight and go back to Phoenix tomorrow."

"I need you there. So does Winnie. Please, Abs. You'll love her and you'll love Holiday House."

Abby had no doubt she would love the house, which might just be the most beautiful structure she had ever seen in real life.

She wasn't crazy about the rest of it. She wasn't good at family squabbles and didn't want to be caught in the middle.

"Everything will be fine. I'll be there in two weeks. At that point you can decide whether you want to stay and spend Christmas with Winnie and me, or go back and finish packing for your big move."

She was here not only to help Lucy with her grandmother's medical needs but also for Christopher, she reminded herself. She wanted this Christmas to be perfect for him.

Oh, she knew her hopes were probably unrealistic. No Christmas could be perfect, but it would have to be better than the past two she had been through.

Two years ago, she had spent the holidays still reeling from Kevin's death, only ten days before Christmas, battling her own grief as well as that of a confused, sad toddler.

Her days had been busy dealing with the police investigation, paperwork and the hospital's hollow apologies for their egregious security lapses that allowed an unstable patient to bring a loaded weapon into the facility and shoot the very resident who had been trying to help him.

The previous year, the hospital where she worked—across town from the one where Kevin had died—had been short staffed in the middle of a local influenza outbreak and she had been forced to work overtime through the entire holidays.

This year, she had vowed things would be different. Christopher had turned five the previous month, old enough to begin forming long-term memories. She wanted those memories to be good ones, not of a frazzled mom working long hours and too tired the rest of the time to have fun with him.

"I don't want to battle your brother, Lucy."

"You won't have to. Ethan isn't unreasonable. He might seem overbearing and bossy. Part of that is his personality and part of that is from his position as president and CEO of Lancaster Hotels. But underneath his gruff, he's a reasonable guy. He adores Winnie and wants the best for her. We just differ a little right now on what that is."

The man wanted to move his grandmother out of her home against her wishes. That didn't exactly endear him to Abby.

"I guess we'll see how reasonable he is," she said, more determined than ever to stand up for Winifred Lancaster now.

Lucy's face lit up with relief. "You're staying. Oh, yay. I could hug you right now. I owe you big-time. Seriously. Anything I own is yours. I mean that. Which, okay, isn't much, but I offer it freely."

She smiled. Lucy had never been one to care about material possessions, which was one of the things Abby loved about her. Someone meeting her for the first time would probably have no idea her family owned an entire luxury hotel group.

"I will pay you that back in spades, I promise. Thank you. I'll check in tomorrow to see how you're settling in. Bye. Bye, Christopher."

She turned around. "Lucy says bye," she said, loudly enough for him to hear beneath the headphones.

He waved but didn't look away from the screen.

Okay. She could do this. Abby turned to pull onto the driveway. Someone inside must have seen Abby's SUV approach. The black iron gates slid open smoothly before she reached them.

Her stomach jumped with nerves as she continued up the long, winding drive and pulled up to the house.

When she climbed out to unbuckle Christopher from

his car seat, her son gave her a winsome smile of thanks while their cat meowed from his carrier.

"Can we take Mr. Jingles?" Christopher asked.

Like the rest of them, the cat was tired of traveling, but she didn't want to toss a rascal of a cat into what might be a volatile situation.

"We had better leave him here for a moment until we check things out. He'll be okay in his carrier for a few more moments, since he has his sweater on and we won't take very long."

To be safe, she set a quick alarm on her watch to remind her about Jingles in twenty minutes.

The cat seemed content for now in his carrier. Abby left the dome light on as well so he wouldn't be nervous, then walked up the big steps to the front door, Christopher's hand held tightly in hers.

A few pine boughs decorated the window on one side of the front door but not the other, as if someone had started the job of decorating for the holidays and become side-tracked. Winnie must have been in the middle of it when she was injured.

Maybe Abby and Christopher could help her finish. It would be a fun activity for them, in between helping Winnie.

"Can I ring the bell?" Christopher asked eagerly.

"Go ahead."

What child didn't love ringing doorbells? she wondered as chimes sounded in the November air.

A moment later, warmth rushed out as the door was opened by a tall, dark-haired man in a white dress shirt and loosened tie. She had a quick impression of sculpted features and blue eyes much like Lucy's. This could only be Ethan Lancaster and he wasn't happy to see her, at least judging by his scowl.

"Hi. I'm Abby Powell. I'm a friend of Lucy's. This is my son, Christopher."

He didn't smile a greeting. "I know who you are. Come in. Maybe you can talk some sense into my grandmother."

He didn't wait to see if they followed before heading back down the hall. After a moment, Abby walked into a grand foyer dominated by a sweeping staircase.

She didn't know what else to do but close the door behind them and follow him, trying not to notice how his tailored shirt clung to a strong back and tapered to lean hips, or the way his hair curled just so at the nape of his neck.

She was exhausted. That was the only explanation she could find for the instant attraction curling through her.

She gripped Christopher's hand as Ethan Lancaster led her down a hallway lined with artwork she would love to examine in closer detail at a later time.

After what felt like forever, he reached an open doorway where she could hear a game show playing on a television.

Ethan Lancaster led the way into a huge bedroom decorated like something out of a Victorian bordello, with flowered wallpaper, fringe-edged red satin curtains and large dark furniture pieces. Dominating the room was a giant four-poster bed with a canopy that matched the curtains.

In the middle of the bed rested a petite woman with wrinkled features and hair the pink color of cherry-flavored cotton candy.

Perched around her were three little corgis, who lifted their heads long enough to yip a quick greeting in unison, then promptly closed their eyes as if they couldn't be bothered to care.

"Abby. Darling. So wonderful to see you. How long has it been?"

"At least a decade," she answered, walking closer to kiss the woman's cheek in greeting.

She had only met Winifred Lancaster a few times, when the woman came to visit Lucy.

Winnie was unforgettable. Though small in stature, she was the kind of woman who commanded attention wherever she went, mainly because she seemed intensely interested in everyone around her.

Winnie had insisted on including Abby whenever she would do anything with Lucy. They had gone to dinner at several of the better restaurants in the Phoenix metro area. She had even met Kevin when he could break away from his med school classes.

Abby immediately sat down on the side of the bed and took the older woman's free hand in hers. "Well, I have to say, you look better than I had feared," she said, which made Winnie break out in raucous laughter.

"I'm not quite knocking on death's door, you mean."

"Not even walking up the sidewalk, from what I can see. Lucy tells me you had a bad fall."

"She tripped on one of the blasted dogs and tumbled halfway down the stairs," Ethan Lancaster said darkly. "How long did you lie there in pain, Winnie?"

His grandmother sent him an annoyed look. "Not long. Only an hour or so, until I was able to get to my phone and call for help."

An hour. It sounded like an interminable time frame. She couldn't even imagine it, though she knew the woman's injuries could have been much worse.

"Things aren't as bad as my darling grandson is making them sound. I only broke my wrist and sprained an ankle."

"Don't forget the bruised ribs and the pulled muscles in your shoulder," Ethan said darkly.

Winnie pulled a face that made Christopher giggle from halfway behind Abby.

"How can I forget them, when they insist on reminding me every time I breathe?"

She peered around Abby. "And who is this handsome young man? This can't be Christopher."

"Yes, it can," Abby's son answered rather defensively, which made Winnie smile. "My name is Christopher Kevin Powell. I just had a birthday and I turned five."

"I am Winifred Elizabeth Johnson Lancaster. My friends call me Winnie and I regret to say that I am much older than five."

"I like your dogs," Christopher said. "They're cute. What are their names?"

She grinned with delight, though Abby didn't miss the twinges of pain in her eyes. "Thank you. I like them, too. They are Holly, Ivy and Nick. See, Ethan? This is a young man of taste and refinement."

"No doubt," Ethan said, his tone mild and without inflection. He didn't roll his eyes, but he might as well have.

"I'm so glad you're here, my dear," Winnie said. "Thank you so very much for coming to my rescue."

"I'm happy I could help," Abby said.

"I feel so much better knowing you can be here to help me."

Ethan's glower seemed to deepen. "You need to be in a facility where they can care for you properly. You can't even shower yourself here."

"This is my home and exactly where I want to be. Now I can be, since Lucy found a solution all the way from Thailand. Abby is a highly qualified nurse and, with her help for the next weeks until Lucy can make it home, I should be fine. Problem solved. She can help me get around, and you can go back to running your empire."

"I had everything arranged with that nice new facility by the hospital."

"Well, you can unarrange it. You ought to know better than to make plans for me without asking my permission. I might be old, but I'm not senile yet."

His laugh sounded more frustrated than amused. "I'm well aware. You're the sharpest old bag I know."

Winnie didn't appear to be offended by this, at least judging by her hoot of laughter.

Ethan reached for her hand and the sight of that wrinkled, age-spotted hand in his made Abigail's knees feel a little wobbly. Probably just hunger, she told herself.

"I just want what's best for you. You know that," Ethan said.

Winnie turned her fingers over and squeezed his. "I know that, darling. I appreciate it. I do. But right now, spending Christmas in the house that I love is absolutely the best medicine for me."

His sigh held capitulation and annoyance in equal measure. "We need to have a serious talk after the holidays. You live in this huge, crumbling heap by yourself. It's not safe."

"Watch it, young man. This is your family's legacy. Before you call it a crumbling heap, maybe you should remember that without this house, you wouldn't have a hundred hotels spread across the globe, including three right here in Silver Bells. Your ancestor mortgaged this house to buy his first hotel after the silver mines ran out. Without that, we all would have been bankrupt."

She had a feeling this wasn't the first time they had had this exact same conversation.

"Now, Abby," the woman said, turning to her. "You and Christopher have been driving a long way. Ethan can bring in your luggage and help you to your quarters. There's a two-room suite just down the hall, so you'll be close to my room if I need you."

"That sounds perfect."

"Ethan can show you everything."

"Are you sure you'll be okay?" her grandson asked, undeniable worry in his eyes.

"Fine. Just fine. The dogs will keep me company. When you're settled, come back and talk to me," she ordered Abby. "Ethan, darling, I'll see you tomorrow for Thanksgiving dinner. I'm planning a late one, five p.m. You can still make that, can't you?"

He sighed again. "Again with Thanksgiving. I thought you agreed to forget about it. I can bring you a meal from the hotel."

"I didn't agree to any such thing. Don't be silly. A big Thanksgiving dinner here is a tradition."

"Traditions don't matter in this situation. You're injured. The last thing you need to worry about is Thanksgiving dinner."

"I won't be worrying about anything. It's all been arranged. I won't have to lift a finger, trust me."

"I can help," Abby offered.

"I can, too," Christopher said, though he obviously had no idea what he was volunteering to do.

"There you go." Winnie beamed at her. "I have ready-made helpers. We'll see you tomorrow. Five p.m. sharp. Will you help Abby with her bags now? Christopher, do you mind staying here and keeping me and the dogs company?"

"I don't mind one bit," Christopher said, plopping into a chair next to his new friend's bedside with an expression of delight.

After another charged moment, Ethan walked out into the hall, all but vibrating with frustration.

Left with no choice, Abby followed him. The man looked even more stern and forbidding up close, his mouth set in a tight line.

He was gorgeous, she couldn't deny that, with blue eyes, lean features and an appealing afternoon shadow along his jawline. He also smelled delicious, some intoxicating mix of expensive leather and a pine-covered mountain.

Not that she noticed or anything.

She had to clear the air between them or she was in for an uncomfortable few weeks. "I'm sorry. When Lucy asked me to stay with your grandmother, I had no idea I was walking into a family disagreement."

His rigid expression eased slightly. "It's certainly not your fault. This is an old argument, I'm afraid. I've been trying to convince Winnie to move for years, but she insists she's fine here. Recent events have proven otherwise."

"Because she fell?"

He nodded. "I can't imagine how terrifying that must have been for her, all alone here. Next time, she might not be able to make it to the phone to call for help. I wish I could convince her she would be safer in a one-level condo somewhere."

She didn't know Winnie well, but Abby was still quite confident that would not be an easy sell. At the same time, she couldn't entirely fault the man for wanting to look after his grandmother.

"Do you want me to leave? I told Lucy we could go to a hotel tonight and return to Phoenix first thing tomorrow."

"That's not my choice. Winnie and Lucy want you here, so obviously I've been outvoted."

"Sorry."

"Again, not your fault." His rigid expression softened further until he looked almost approachable. "You've had a long drive. Let's get you settled for now. You're going to need all your strength to keep up with my grandmother."

CHAPTER TWO

ETHAN WOULD RATHER deal with a labor strike, political strife and an economic downturn than have to try persuading his grandmother to do something she didn't want to do, even when it was in her best interest.

He didn't want to be a jerk about it. He adored Winnie and wanted her to be happy. She was the closest thing to a stable, loving parent that either he or Lucy had ever known.

He loved Holiday House, too. This place, despite its quirks and problems, had always been a port in the storm for two lost children. Winnie and Clive had opened their home to him and Lucy whenever their parents had needed time away from the pressure of parenting. Which had been often, unfortunately. Divorces, new relationships, personal crises. Rick and Terri Lancaster didn't need much of an excuse to drop him and Lucy off with their grandparents.

The rest of their world might be filled with chaos— fighting adults, slamming doors, angry words. Here at Holiday House, he and Lucy had been free to be children and all his very best childhood memories had taken place here.

That did not change the fact that Winnie was approaching eighty years old. This house was too vast for her and she refused to accept help maintaining it, other than the cleaning crew she let in twice a month.

He had tried to convince her to hire a companion, but

she said she refused to have her space invaded by an unnecessary babysitter.

At least she had allowed Abby Powell and her son to stay. Maybe this would be the impetus she needed to change her frame of reference. If she wasn't going to move out of Holiday House, at least she could have someone here to keep an eye on her.

He wasn't entirely sure Abby was the right person for the job, though. She looked almost elfin, with red curls and green eyes, as if she would blow away in the first hard Colorado wind. She was petite, probably no more than five feet three inches tall, and she seemed too slight to even help Winnie back up if she fell again.

Likely she was tougher than she looked. She was a nurse. He knew that much. According to Lucy, her former roommate had been working at a hospital in the Phoenix area but had left the job only days earlier in preparation for a move to a new city after the holidays.

He still wasn't sure why she would make the trek all the way to Colorado to stay with a woman she didn't know. Ethan had plenty of good friends but wasn't sure he would be comfortable asking any of them for such a favor.

"The timing couldn't have been more perfect," Lucy had told him when she called to tell him she had figured out a way to care for Winnie after her fall, with help from her friend. "Abby is totally free to come and stay with her for two weeks, until I can get there. And don't worry, though I think she would have come anyway, Winnie insists on paying her a nice salary. You won't have to worry about a thing."

Only that a strange woman was coming to live with his grandmother in a house filled with valuables. No problem.

His sister never thought about things like that. Lucy went through life without considering the consequences. So did Winnie.

He wanted to think Abby Powell's motives were entirely altruistic, but he didn't know the woman. He had to view everything with suspicion.

She was a widow. He knew that much. Her husband had been an ER doc killed by a patient. Lucy had been pretty broken up about it and had flown home from somewhere—Estonia, maybe—to attend the funeral. Was it two years ago? Three? He couldn't remember, and it didn't seem the sort of thing one just bluntly asked about.

"Are you sure this won't be a problem?" Abby asked him now. "I would rather not even unpack our suitcases if you're only going to come back tomorrow and tell me my services are no longer needed."

She had a slight Southern accent, almost imperceptible, like a teaspoon of honey mixed into iced tea.

He didn't want to find it charming. He also didn't want to find that combination of auburn waves and wide green eyes so alluring.

He wanted to tell Abigail Powell to jump back in her car and drive away, but doing that would risk alienating both his sister and his grandmother, something no sane man would willingly do.

That didn't mean he wouldn't be keeping his eye on the woman while she was here at Holiday House.

"My grandmother's mind is apparently made up, which is basically the last word on the subject around here. I hope you know what you're getting into."

She smiled slightly. "I've dealt with worse, I can assure you. I've spent the past five years working in a pediatric unit. Your grandmother is nothing compared to a four-year-old having a meltdown."

He was willing to bet she would find strong similarities.

"Is your car unlocked? You can wait inside while I carry in your suitcases."

"I can help."

He decided arguing would just be a waste of breath so he walked with her outside. She drove a small pewter SUV that looked to be about three or four years old, serviceable but nothing fancy.

The hatch was loaded with two large suitcases. He grabbed both of them as she went to the back seat and pulled out a couple of backpacks, as well as a pet carrier. Great. Was it another corgi?

A meow from inside told him otherwise. He frowned. "Does Winnie know about the cat? Her corgis aren't always the most gracious to newcomers."

In the exterior lights of the porch, he could see a worried expression cross her features. "I told Lucy and she said it would be fine. We can keep Mr. Jingles in our room."

He shrugged. "I never know how they're going to behave. They might love, er, Mr. Jingles."

After she closed the hatch of her SUV and locked it, he carried the suitcases upstairs. "You can probably park in the garage. There should be plenty of room since Winnie only has her old Cadillac, which she won't be driving for a while. I can give you one of the remote door openers."

She looked surprised by the offer. "That's very kind of you, but I don't mind parking in the driveway."

"You will when you have to clear a foot of snow off your windshield. If you want, I can move it for you after we drop your bags off."

"I… Thank you. That's very kind of you."

He wasn't being kind, it was simply good manners. He was in the hospitality industry, trained to be polite.

He led her back inside to the guest room his grandmother had told him would work for Abby and Christopher. It was a set of two connected rooms that shared an en suite bath, just down the hall from Winnie's room.

With no idea about the condition of the room or when it might have last been used, Ethan opened the door somewhat warily. To his relief, it smelled of vanilla and apples, and he could detect no obvious signs of neglect. His grandmother did have a good cleaning service, at least.

"Oh," she exclaimed. "This is lovely."

"There is another room connected to this one, through that door. I think it was designed as a sitting room originally. There's a foldout bed in there. If you wanted, you could use that as a bedroom for your son or keep it as a sitting room."

She gestured to a daybed alongside the main bed. "This should work for Christopher. He likes to be close to me, especially when we're in a strange place."

"Whatever you decide is fine." He set the suitcases in a corner of the room.

"Thank you very much, Mr. Lancaster."

"Please call me Ethan."

She offered a tentative smile. It wasn't much of one, but it still sent heat sneaking through him.

He frowned, uncomfortable with his reaction, which made her smile slip away.

"I'd better go rescue Winnie from Christopher."

"Or the other way around," he said.

Her son beamed when they reentered Winifred's bedroom. "Guess what, Mommy? Winnie told me there's a train set in one of the rooms upstairs and I can even play with it sometime."

"That sounds like fun."

"It belonged to my son first and then *his* son played with it."

Ethan shifted, uncomfortable with the appraising look Abby sent him, as if she couldn't quite imagine him as a child.

"I have to go to the bathroom," Christopher informed his mother, jumping up from the floor where he had been playing with one of the dogs and dancing around in a way that indicated the need was rather urgent.

Abby looked alarmed. "Hold on. I'll show you where our rooms are so you can use the bathroom there. I'll come back to talk to you shortly," she told Winnie.

"Take your time," his grandmother said with a wave of her hand.

"Did you want me to move your SUV into the garage?"

She looked a little disconcerted but handed him the keys. "Thank you. You can just leave the keys inside."

When they disappeared through the door, Ethan felt strangely as if the light in the room seemed to dim a little.

"So. What do you think of my guests?"

"They're not guests, Winnie. Abby is here to help you."

"I know that. But she's lovely, isn't she? And it's so nice to have a child in the house again. Heaven knows, neither you nor Lucy are going to give me great-grandchildren anytime soon."

As soon as the words were out, she winced. "I'm sorry. I shouldn't have said that. It's the pain medicine. This month would have been your anniversary, isn't that right?"

Yes, and thank you for the reminder.

He gave a cool smile. "Is it? I guess I've been too busy building my hotel empire to pay attention."

He was lying, of course. How could he forget the grand wedding that had been planned for the previous November at The Lancaster Silver Bells, the crowning jewel in his family's hotel group?

He also couldn't forget the ugly implosion of his engagement just a month before the celebration.

"Brooke was never the right woman for you," Winnie said. "I knew it from the beginning. The two of you never acted like an adoring couple, more like you were finalizing a pesky contract clause of some multimillion-dollar merger. You'll find the right woman someday. A woman who can see beneath that all-business attitude to the sweet boy inside you."

Perish the thought.

He did *not* want to talk about his broken engagement or his nonexistent love life with his grandmother right now.

"Get some rest. I'm going to move Abby's car and then take off. If you need me, just call."

"You're coming tomorrow, right? You can't miss Thanksgiving."

"I'll try. Don't overdo."

"When have you known me to overdo?" she asked rhetorically.

"I think we're both too tired for me to start going through the list. I love you."

"Love you, too."

With one more kiss on the cheek, he left the room. Abby's door was still closed. He was glad he didn't have to deal with this inconvenient and unwanted attraction, he told himself as he headed out into the lightly falling snow.

After moving her vehicle, he walked back out into the night and was almost to his SUV when his phone rang that he had a video call coming in. He recognized his sister's distinctive ringtone and quickly answered just as he slipped inside the driver's seat, out of the snow.

Bright sunlight filtered across her features and she looked to be dressed for the day. Chiang Mai was thirteen hours ahead of mountain time, which meant it must be early morning there.

"Are you furious with us?" Lucy asked.

"Why would I be?"

"Oh, I don't know. The high-handed Lancaster women are at it again, arranging things behind your back."

He shrugged. "What else is new?"

Lucy made a face, looking more like the baby sister who used to follow him around when he would hang out with his buddies. "Don't be mad. I know you want Winnie to move into a rehab center while she recovers, but she would have hated that so much, especially over Christmas. You know how much she loves the holidays. They're kind of her jam."

Anyone who had ever looked through the rooms at Holiday House would know that, since each room was packed full of Christmas-themed knickknacks.

"I'm not mad. The two of you act like I'm some kind of tyrannical monster who is going to stomp around destroying everything if I don't get my way."

She winced. "You know we don't think that. You just… like to have your own way."

Because his way was usually the right one. "I'm not

completely unreasonable. I'm willing to give your friend a chance."

"I trust her with my life. And with Winnie's, for that matter. You won't find anyone more compassionate or kind. Didn't you find her nice?"

"I spoke with her for possibly five minutes total, so it's a little soon to make a final decision on that. But, yes, she seemed nice."

"She is. If I had the kind of hard knocks in life she's had, I would be a bitter old crone by now, but Abby just seems to have more love to give everyone. You'll adore her, I promise."

Ethan was careful to keep his expression clear. "It doesn't really matter whether I like her or not, does it? The question is whether Winnie will listen to her and take better care of herself. Our grandmother is getting older, Luce. Like it or not, she's not as strong as she used to be. This tumble banged her up pretty good. The next one will likely be worse."

"I know. I want her to be around forever. I know she doesn't have that many Christmases left. That's why I wanted her to be able to stay in her house for this one."

"I get it. Again, I'm not completely heartless. I said I was willing to give Abby a chance. But you know as well as I do that Winnie won't be the easiest patient. Nice or not, I hope Abby can be tough enough to stand up to her."

AFTER ETHAN HUNG up, Lucy shoved her phone into the pocket of her trim sundress and opened the door to her classroom, where the students of her first class of the day were already waiting, though school didn't start for another half hour.

"Good morning, Miss Lancaster," they all said in perfect unison, and she couldn't help but smile at their cheerful, eager faces.

Of all the positions she'd held, paid or otherwise, since leaving college, this was by far her favorite. This was her second year teaching English in Thailand, which was definitely a record for her.

"Good morning," she said. "Until class starts, your vocabulary is on the board. I want you to have a conversation with a partner using all the words listed there. We have fifteen minutes. Go."

She walked through the classroom, correcting pronunciation and verb conjugation while her mind was busy thinking about what was happening right now at Holiday House.

Abby really had saved the day for her. While it would have been possible for Lucy to find a substitute to finish her classes until her Christmas break, it wouldn't have reflected well on her. She liked this job and wanted to at least finish the school term in March, after she went home for the holidays.

A sudden longing for Silver Bells hit her hard, probably because she had been on the phone so much to her family and to Abby, who was now there. She could picture the town now, the picturesque downtown, the soaring mountains, the stately Victorian homes.

And José.

Her heartbeat quickened a little at the thought of him.

She had numerous pictures of José Navarro on her phone but did her best not to look at them obsessively every day. She didn't need to look, anyway. She could picture him perfectly. The high cheekbones, his wavy dark hair that he sometimes let get a little too long, the thick-lashed brown eyes that could sparkle with laughter one moment and just as quickly become intense and passionate.

He had been Ethan's good friend and trusted executive at Lancaster Hotels for years. She had been friends with him, too, but more casually, until about five years ago, when he was traveling for Ethan more as a troubleshooter and location scout.

Whenever he was anywhere close to where Lucy was working, they would meet up and spend a few days sightseeing.

It started when she was working with refugees in Albania. He had been traveling to a Lancaster property in nearby Greece, so it was a relatively easy thing for the two of them to meet up and travel the countryside for a few days.

After that, they began to email or message each other frequently until she now considered José among her closest friends and her strongest single connection to home outside of Winnie and Ethan.

Or at least he had been among her closest friends.

She thought it was only friendship. That's what she had been telling herself, anyway. In retrospect, she could see she had been fooling herself, ignoring the growing attraction that seethed just under the surface of their friendship.

Three months ago, everything between them had changed.

José hadn't traveled much for Ethan since his father died a few years earlier, but had made an exception to check on one of the company's newest hotels, in the resort area of Koh Samui on the stunningly beautiful Gulf of Thailand.

Because it was a quick plane ride from her teaching gig, she had flown down to meet him and they had spent three days together after his business was done. They had snorkeled, hiked, even visited a secret Buddha garden hidden away in a jungle containing dozens of statues.

They had laughed together, talked together, shared dreams. And finally on their last night, José had walked her to her villa and shocked her by kissing her.

It was a kiss unlike anything she had ever known before and had rocked her to her soul.

Even now as she walked among her first-year students, listening to their sweet voices, when she closed her eyes she was immediately back in those lush tropical grounds at the Lancaster Koh Samui. She could smell the flowering jasmine, almost taste the sea air.

José had drawn away, those beautiful eyes blazing with emotions she wasn't ready to see.

"I have feelings for you, Lucy. You have to know that. I love being your friend, but I want more."

She should have smiled politely, wished him good-night and slipped into her villa. That's what she would have done with every other man who might have expressed any serious kind of feelings for her. She couldn't. Not with José.

She might have been a little bit tipsy. That still didn't explain how she had wrapped her arms around him and kissed him, her body tight to his, aching inside for more. "Why did you wait until the last night to tell me this? We could have spent three days in bed instead of snorkeling and visiting every temple on the island."

They kissed again, the warm breeze swirling around them, tantalizing and seductive. She wanted to tug him inside to her villa, even though warning bells were sounding that everything between them would change if she did.

She didn't want to listen to those bells. She wanted to live in the moment, with him, this man she…cared about.

José was the one who stopped, who stepped away, breathing raggedly. "I won't be one of your short-term flings, where you run off as soon as things start to get serious. I want more than that. I need to know that you are as committed as I am before we go any further."

At his words, she had felt as if he had dunked her into the ocean without warning, as if she was drenched and sputtering and fighting for air.

"That's not fair," she had finally managed. "You know that's not what I want right now."

"Then I'll wait until it *is* what you want."

She had felt perilously close to tears. Again, probably because she was a little tipsy. It couldn't have anything to do with the line he was drawing in the sand at this tropical paradise. A line she would never cross.

"That's stupid. Why not just sleep together now? We both want to."

He had gazed at her for a long time in the moonlight, his features shadowed, inscrutable.

"I am thirty-three years old, Lucy. I don't want another meaningless relationship. I'm looking for something deeper. Something that will last beyond the sunrise. And I want that with you."

She didn't remember everything she had said in response but was fairly certain none of it showed her in a good light.

He had kissed her one more time on the forehead, leaving her achy and hungry, then had gone into his villa.

The next morning, they had barely spoken on the way

back to the airport as she prepared to fly back to Chiang Mai and he on the first leg of his long journey back home.

Her head had pounded, her throat had been tight and her eyes had felt gritty and sore, as if the entire beach had poured over her in her sleep. Finally, just when they would have separated at their respective gates, he had kissed her again, holding her for a long time. "Goodbye. I love you, Lucy. When you're ready to say those words back, I'll be waiting."

"Don't bother," she had snapped. "I'll never be ready."

It had been completely unfair of him to throw that at her. He knew what her childhood had been like. Her parents' marriage had been a nightmare. They loved and hated each other with equal passion, and had divorced and married twice that she could remember. Each had had affairs, marriages, divorces, remarriages.

It had been chaotic and horrible, and had convinced her she was genetically incapable of a long-term relationship. She would never put someone she cared about through that kind of turmoil.

She had decided when she was about thirteen years old, listening to her mother sob after yet another relationship disaster, that she wasn't ever going to be vulnerable like that. She refused.

Yes, she preferred short-term relationships where both parties knew the ground rules. It wasn't like she slept around. She'd had a grand total of four relationships. It was completely unfair of José to make it seem like she was the kind of woman who loved a man and then left him.

Everything had changed between her and José after Thailand. And yet... He still texted her a couple of times a week and they had video chatted a few times, usually at the request of his brother Rodrigo, who José knew was Lucy's one and only true love.

José never referred to the ultimatum he had given her, but it was always there simmering just below the surface. He wanted a relationship with her but only on his terms, which were exactly the terms she couldn't accept.

She would see him again in two weeks, when she returned to Silver Bells for the holidays. It was inevitable. He worked for Lancaster Hotels, his mother was one of Winnie's best friends and the two families were close.

How would she handle it?

Easy. She had told him how she felt, and she wasn't about to change her mind.

No matter how much she might ache to be in his arms again.

CHAPTER THREE

ABBY WOKE UP in that strange netherworld of semiconsciousness, not knowing for a few moments where she was.

She blinked and opened her eyes to a room she didn't recognize at first. The walls were painted a soft sage green and the furniture was much nicer than anything she and Kevin had been able to afford while he was in med school.

For a moment, she thought she was back in the hotel in Austin where she had stayed when she interviewed at the hospital there. Somehow that didn't feel right. Why would she be there again? She and Christopher were leasing an apartment not far from the hospital, near one of the best schools in the city.

She blinked again and a few more elements came into focus. She wasn't in Austin, she suddenly remembered in a rush. She was in Colorado for a few weeks helping Lucy's grandmother.

The events of the day before flooded back. The long drive. Arriving at the beautiful Victorian mansion. Meeting Lucy's brother.

Ethan Lancaster's handsome features danced across her memory. Oh. That must have been why she dreamed of blue eyes and a smile that left her breathless.

The bed was warm and luxuriously comfortable. She didn't want to move. If she wasn't mistaken, she had enjoyed a much more sound sleep than she had known in a long time. She wasn't sure if that was due to the snug bed or simply because she had been exhausted from the drive.

"Hi, Mommy."

She sat up and saw Christopher beaming at her from the slipper chair in the room, his favorite action figures beside him.

She cleared the sleep from her voice. "Good morning, bug."

"Happy Thanksgiving."

"Oh, that's right." With a jolt, she sat up. It was Thanksgiving, and she was supposed to be cooking dinner for Winnie and her guests.

"The lady is awake. She's in the big kitchen."

Abby was the worst mother ever. If Christopher knew that, then he must have arisen before she did and wandered out of the room. Why hadn't she woken up? They were sleeping in the same bedroom!

She was usually a light, uneasy sleeper but had to assume exhaustion from their drive had played a part in her negligence.

"Oh, man. I had an alarm set, but I must have slept through it."

"She told me to let you sleep so I took your phone in the other room. I played with Mr. Jingles and watched TV on the phone."

How could she have slept in, leaving her son to entertain himself by wandering around for who knows how long in a strange house?

"Give me five minutes. Stay here and play on my phone a little more, then we have to go help Winnie with dinner."

"I haven't even had breakfast yet," Christopher said.

She kissed his forehead. "We'll take care of that, too, I promise."

"Okay." He returned to his action figures, and she thought again how very blessed she was in the child department. Her son was sweet, kind and excellent at entertaining himself. He usually never minded finding something to keep him occupied when she had to do other things.

She dressed quickly, washing her face and yanking her hair into a ponytail, before hurrying into the kitchen with Christopher close behind her.

She did indeed find Winifred Lancaster there. The woman was standing at the table trying one-handed to knead what looked like bread dough.

"Good morning," Winnie said with a sunny smile that didn't completely hide her pain.

Abby winced, feeling terrible all over again. "I am so sorry."

"You've got nothing to apologize for."

"I'm supposed to be your nurse, but instead I slept in and here you are in the kitchen working on Thanksgiving dinner. Please stop. You should be resting."

"I'm fine, really. And I haven't been here long."

Abby stepped forward. "I told you last night I would handle Thanksgiving dinner for you. I'm sorry I overslept, but I'm here now and can take over."

"No need. I've got this covered. You should go back to bed. You had a long day yesterday."

Abby moved closer and drew on all the experience gained over the years of dealing with recalcitrant patients. "No. You should step away from the dough and let me take over whatever you're doing there."

Winnie chuckled, though it sounded a little strained to

Abby. "I wanted to prep the dough for the rolls so it would have plenty of time to rise. Turns out kneading dough is a little trickier than I expected one-handed, but I think I'm getting there."

Abby crossed to the sink and lathered her hands, speaking as she rinsed. "Lucy asked me to come to Silver Bells for a few weeks so I could take care of you in her place. That includes helping you knead dough for rolls. You have to let me do my job, or I'll feel like I'm failing you *and* Lucy."

Winnie sighed. "I don't feel good about dumping everything on you. You're not the one who invited a dozen people over for dinner."

"A dozen? I thought there were only ten."

"I'm counting you and Christopher now. I can't just expect you to do it all."

"You have to. I insist, Winnie. This is the whole reason I'm here."

"To help me take my meds, not to feed my friends."

"To do whatever you need, and that includes Thanksgiving dinner," she corrected. "We talked about this last night when I helped you get ready for bed. I might be a little late to the party this morning, but I think we can still make it work."

She sensed Winnie wavering, probably because she was struggling to knead the dough with only one hand.

Abby pressed her advantage. "As I told you last night, I'm not the greatest cook in the world, but I take direction very well. I've already made a list of what I need to do."

"That might be a problem. I've never been very good at delegating. You can ask anyone."

"There's a first time for everything," she said cheerfully. "Christopher and I will bring in a comfortable chair for you, and you can oversee the entire proceedings from there. How would that work?"

"I don't know. I feel guilty about just handing it all over to you. On the other hand, I won't lie, this ankle is biting at me."

"Ankles can't bite," Christopher informed her knowledgeably. "They don't have teeth."

Winnie chuckled. "I just meant it was hurting me. I would like to know why my broken wrist hurts less than my sprained ankle and bruised ribs. It makes no sense."

"Your wrist is supported by the cast. It's still going to hurt, but it's not being jostled like your ribs every time you breathe. Also, you're putting weight on your ankle, which you're not supposed to do. Of course it's going to hurt. You'll feel better once you sit down, I promise."

The older woman sighed. "Fine. I suppose there are still plenty of things I can do while I'm sitting. Snap beans. Fold napkins. That kind of thing."

"Excellent. Teamwork. That's the way to get the job done. Now, what chair would be most comfortable for you, and where can I find it?"

Winnie pointed to a seating area next to the kitchen, dominated by a gas fireplace that glowed merrily in the room. "My favorite chair in the house is that big red thing next door."

Abby headed in that direction, where she instantly found a thickly padded club chair and matching ottoman tucked into a comfortable corner near the fireplace. Several books, magazines and notebooks were neatly stacked on the side table. This must be Winnie's own cozy retreat. She could definitely see why. Next to the fire, a little Christmas tree decorated with antique bobbins and spools of thread twinkled brightly.

Fortunately, the chair was sturdy but not heavy, and she was able to slide it on an area rug across the hardwood floor of the sitting room and the tile floor of the kitchen.

As soon as she found a space for it in the kitchen, Winnie settled into it with a sigh of relief that told Abby all she needed to know about Winnie's pain level.

"Christopher. Help me move the ottoman."

"Okay, Mommy."

"I think we can use the same rug and slide it."

"Can I have a ride?"

She couldn't think of any reason why not. Her son giggled like they were at Disneyland as she tugged him the short distance between the sitting area and Winnie's new corner in the kitchen.

"That looks like fun. When my ankle is better, maybe you can pull me around," Winnie said to the boy, which sent Christopher laughing again at the idea of trying to pull an almost eighty-year-old woman through her grand house on a makeshift sled created out of a throw rug and an ottoman.

"All right. Thanksgiving. Where do we start?"

Abby had never cooked dinner for more than a few friends before. She had to admit she found the idea of being in charge of serving twelve people beyond daunting, though Winnie seemed certain she could handle it.

"I've found it's best to write out a schedule for what needs to be done when. The turkey doesn't need to go in for another hour," Winnie said. "I think the two of you should find something to eat first. You need your strength."

"I'm starving," Christopher said dramatically.

"We can't let the boy starve. A friend of mine brought cinnamon rolls over yesterday. They're delicious. I bet you wouldn't have to twist his arm to convince him to have one. There's plenty for you, too."

Abby wasn't a big breakfast eater. She usually only had coffee and sometimes added a slice of avocado toast. Christopher, on the other hand, was a pretty avid lover of scrambled eggs with feta cheese and her buckwheat pancakes.

He would have to make do today with straight carbs.

"I love cinnamon rolls," he declared.

"You're in luck, then. These are the best around."

Winnie pointed to a tray on the counter, and Abby pulled out a gooey, sweet-smelling pastry that she set on a small plate for him.

She settled her son at the island with the roll and a glass of almond milk from the refrigerator, then pulled a chair closer to Winnie's.

"All right. Where do we start? Also, I need to find a notebook so I can write a list. I was thinking I should run to the grocery store first thing. Don't they usually close early on Thanksgiving?"

Winnie shook her head, pink locks flying. "No need for that. First of all, our Thanksgivings here at Holiday House are always potluck, so you don't have to do everything. We've had crowds of up to twenty-five and everyone brings something. My guests have already told me in advance what they wanted to bring so I could make sure everything is covered. Here's the list so you can see the plan."

Ah. A woman after Abby's own heart. She loved lists and plans. Sometimes she thought being organized had been the only thing keeping her sane after Kevin died.

Winnie handed Abby another piece of paper, and she

saw that Winnie had written the names of her guests and what they had agreed to bring to dinner—yams, salad, cranberries and pie.

"I am only taking care of the turkey, the mashed potatoes and gravy, the rolls and a pumpkin pie. The turkey doesn't have to go in until noon, since we're eating late this year. Which means we only have to do the pie and maybe prep the potatoes this morning. I already bought everything we should need last week, and the turkey has been thawing for days. I'm usually not this organized, but some crazy instinct told me to get ready early this year. I had no idea why. Boy, I'm sure glad I listened to that inner voice, right?"

"Definitely."

"Isn't it funny, how the universe sometimes tries to give you a warning that your life is about to be shaken up?"

Abby could certainly relate to that. She had been getting signals from the universe for a year now, ever since the initial shock and overwhelming grief over Kevin's death began to wear off and her life began to fall into patterns that would become her new normal.

Something else had been calling her, a whisper on the wind telling her maybe it was time to make a new start.

She had lived in Phoenix for nearly a decade, but it wasn't really her home. She didn't have any family there and neither had Kevin. He had moved there for med school and she had followed him.

Over the years, they had built a strong network of friends, wonderful, cherished people who had supported her throughout the ordeal of losing him so violently. She would be forever grateful to all of them for helping her these past two years.

Lately, though, she had grown weary of the role everyone had assigned to her. To all their friends, she would always be the grieving widow. She could see it in their sympathetic looks, hear it in the cut-off conversations when she would walk into a room.

She didn't want to wear that badge for the rest of her life.

That didn't mean she would stop grieving for Kevin's bright light, extinguished too soon. He had been a wonderful man and a dedicated, caring doctor. He had already been offered a position at a teaching hospital in Austin when he finished his residency. They had researched the town and thought it would be a good place to raise their son and any other children they might have.

He hadn't accepted the offer yet but had been on the brink of taking it when a patient who should never have had access to a gun because of his mental illness had barged into the ER that fateful night and extinguished that bright, cheerful light.

She had spent the first year after his death in limbo, lost and grieving for the future they planned to build together. Six months ago, she had decided the time had come to emerge from that cocoon of pain and begin figuring out the rest of her life with her son.

As soon as she made that decision, a hundred different things came at her, telling her it was time to make a new start and to do it before Christopher started grade school.

She had started making lists of all the possible places they could go. As she and Kevin had already researched Austin, moving there seemed the logical choice. It was scary and overwhelming and exhilarating, all at the same time. She still wasn't sure if she was making the right decision, but the alternative was complacency and even stagnation.

"I always worry about what signals I might be missing because I'm too busy to pay attention," she said now to Winnie.

The older woman nodded enthusiastically. "Exactly. I'm so glad Lucy asked you to come help me. We're going to have such fun. Now, have you ever made a pumpkin pie?"

She had tried once, but Kevin had always preferred pecan pie like his grandmama and mama used to make.

"I'm not an expert at it, but I'm more than willing to learn."

Winnie's laugh sounded more like a cackle.

"I like your grit, honey. Let's do this, then. I like to gather all my ingredients and measure them all first, like they do on cooking shows. That way if I've run out of ginger, I don't have to run to the neighbors in a panic halfway through the recipe. They call that mise en place."

"That's a funny word," Christopher said from the table. He tried to repeat Winnie's phrase in an exaggerated French accent that made the older woman laugh.

"Close enough. Why don't you finish your cinnamon roll, and you can help your mother find everything she needs for the pie?"

She could do this, Abby told herself. She was already tackling much harder challenges in her life than making a simple pie.

ETHAN DREADED HOLIDAYS.

Oh, he didn't mind the actual celebrations themselves. It was hard to live in a place as relentlessly festive as Silver Bells and actually hate the holidays. But as someone who worked in the hospitality industry, he knew holidays could be headaches for a hundred different reasons. Supply chains, staffing issues and overall guest satisfaction, to name a few.

By two on Thanksgiving, he had put out as many fires as he could. Everything else could wait until the next morning, he decided.

He walked down to the lobby and was surprised to find José Navarro at the concierge desk, talking to a guest.

"I didn't expect to see you working today," Ethan said when their conversation finished and the guest left satisfied. "Are you running the concierge desk these days in addition to managing our three hotels in town?"

"Pinch-hitting. We're shorthanded with the holiday, and I just sent Stacey Delacorte home to have dinner with her family."

That was one of the reasons José made such a great operations manager—and also why Ethan planned to some day make him the chief operations officer for the entire hotel group. He cared about each employee and wanted the best for him or her.

José was an invaluable partner. Together, he had helped Ethan expand the Lancaster brand into new markets. Ethan missed his leadership and his business acumen, though it was now focused closer to home running the company's flagship hotel and ski resort along with two smaller properties in town.

"What about your own family? Shouldn't you be with them? I don't want to get on Sofia's bad side."

"Who does?" José said with a laugh. "No worries. My mother would never blame you for anything. You know you've always been her favorite."

He adored José's entire family. He could even admit now that at one point in his youth, he had been jealous of the loving, squabbling, hectic *normalcy* of it. He had loved hanging out there during visits with Winnie and Clive.

"Don't worry about it," José went on. "My sisters are at their in-laws' today, so we're doing our family Thanksgiving celebration over the weekend. And my mom and Rodrigo are heading to Holiday House shortly for dinner with Winnie."

"That's right. I forgot they were on the guest list. Winnie is stubbornly insisting she's still doing Thanksgiving, despite a broken wrist and a sprained ankle."

"She and my mother are cut from the same cloth, bro. I told Mama the restaurant here is open, and she and Rod should just come here and grab something to eat, but she wouldn't miss dinner with Winnie."

"My grandmother is all about tradition, even if she has to cook the turkey from a hospital bed."

José smiled. "Your grandmother is quite a character. Good thing you've got Abby there now to help you keep her in line."

He couldn't quite hide his surprise. "You know Abby?"

José was suddenly busy stacking papers on the desk that already seemed neat enough. "Not really. Only through what Lucy has told me over the years and I went with Lucy to her husband's funeral."

He hadn't remembered that, which wasn't really a surprise. He tended to avoid any reminder that his sister and his best friend had a friendship independent of Ethan, one he didn't like to examine too closely.

Ethan had often wondered if there was something between the two of them, something more than friendship, but he *really* didn't want to think about that. Whatever it was, he knew it couldn't be too serious. Lucy was fiercely independent, determined above all else not to become their parents.

He worried that she was shutting herself off from a happy future with someone who adored her above all else. Lucy could be as stubborn as their grandmother. Even if she cared about someone, she seemed to do her best to maintain that careful distance so no hearts were involved.

He hoped José didn't end up with his broken by Lucy's obstinacy.

But then again, Ethan wasn't exactly in the best position to even offer an opinion on someone else's love life. Not when his own was such a disaster.

"You really should join your mom and brother for dinner at Winnie's. I know she won't mind one more."

José looked undecided for a long moment and then finally nodded. "That would be nice. My mom's taking her famous cherry pie, and I would walk barefoot across the ski slope for some of that."

"Dinner's at five. I'll let Winnie know you're coming so she can set an extra place for you at the table."

"Thanks."

Ethan walked away, grateful someone would be at the table that he could always trust to have his back.

"I CAN'T BELIEVE we pulled it off."

"Correction. You pulled it off," Winnie said firmly. "I sat here on my keister doing absolutely nothing while you worked away all day long in a hot kitchen."

"Not true. Your list was perfect and you supervised me

wonderfully. Plus, you kept Christopher out of my hair so I could work. I can't believe he fell asleep."

A few hours earlier, Winnie had moved to the sofa in the sitting area next to the kitchen. Her sprained ankle and her wrist were both elevated, and she had even agreed to take a pain pill.

Christopher had plopped down beside her, ostensibly to be close to run errands in case she needed anything. It had only taken him about fifteen minutes to fall asleep curled up beside Winnie, his feet resting on her lap.

"He's a darling boy, Abby. I've had so much fun hanging out with him today."

The two seemed immediately smitten with each other, which Abby found so heartwarming. Christopher didn't have anything resembling a grandmother in his life. She loved that he had found that with Winnie, even if it was only for a few weeks.

"What else do I have to do?"

"I think everything's done. Our guests will be arriving soon."

"Ready or not, right?"

Winnie smiled. "It all looks wonderful. You've been such a dear to jump right in and throw everything together, even though I'm quite sure that wasn't in the job description when Lucy talked you into doing this."

"I said I was available to do whatever you need. I mean that."

"Well, thank you. I suppose I could have canceled, but I didn't want to waste all that food I had already bought for Thanksgiving."

"It was no trouble, really." She paused. "I'm not sure you really needed a full-time nurse, do you? I haven't done much to help you in that department, other than getting you a drink of water and helping position your ankle. It appears to me you're handling most things just fine on your own."

"Not everything." Winnie looked suddenly uncomfortable. "I do have something else I need to talk to you about. Something I probably should have mentioned before now. I suppose the time has come for total honesty between us."

Abby raised an eyebrow. *Now* was the time for total honesty? After nearly a day together? Honesty would have been nice before she drove eight hours to come here to Silver Bells.

"The truth is, I'm in a pickle and need help, and not just someone to hand me pills and find me a clean nightgown."

"That's good, as you haven't let me do either of those things since I arrived," she said tartly.

Winnie looked abashed. "I'm a stinker. I know. I'll be the first one to tell you that. I'm also the last one to ask for help unless I'm really desperate. I'm really desperate."

Abby sank down onto the adjacent chair at the sincerity of Winnie's words.

"What can I do?" she asked immediately.

Winnie gave a heavy sigh. "I may have gotten in over my head with something and need somebody to help pull me out of the mess I've made."

"Now you're scaring me," Abby said, only half joking. "What's going on?"

And why hadn't Winnie mentioned any of this earlier, when they had been working together all day on Thanksgiving dinner?

"How much of the house did you have the chance to see when you came in last night, before you went to bed?"

She frowned a little at what seemed an unrelated question. "Not much. The great room, your bedroom, my bedroom. Today I've seen this room, the kitchen and the dining room where we'll be eating. Oh, and the outside, which is beautiful. It's a gorgeous house, Winnie. I can see why you love it. It's obvious this is a house that has been lived in and loved."

"Holiday House is historic here in this region. A treasure, really. One of the truly great leftover estates from the silver boom."

"Maybe I'll have time tomorrow to walk through and see everything."

"I hope so. And I hope you love it as much as I do."

"What's this about, Winnie? Why do you want to know how much I've seen of the house?"

"That's a bit of a long story." Winnie again shifted in her chair. Abby couldn't tell if she was physically uncomfortable or trying to avoid answering.

"I belong to a choir that has existed in one form or another since the first miners' wives used to sing together over their laundry. We're called the Silver Belles. Belle with an *e*."

"Cute," Abby said, though she still had no idea what any of this had to do with her.

"We now have about thirty members. It used to be all women, but we decided about five years ago we were being discriminatory so we opened up to men, too. We now have twenty-three women and seven men to hit the low notes for us."

"That sounds like fun. Do you put on concerts?"

Winnie nodded. "We do four main seasonal concerts a year, usually. In the summer we perform in the concert at the park series, and the rest of the time we use the high school auditorium. But we often do other events through-out the year. Church services, club meetings. That kind of thing. Do you sing? We can always use another strong voice."

"I'm afraid not. If you were after another voice for your choir, you won't find it here."

She enjoyed singing but was well aware that her voice and range, while adequate, would never earn her a celeb-rity coach on a TV reality show.

"None of us is terribly gifted. There are a few who think they are, but most of us are amateurs. Still, we have fun together and it's always for a good cause. At our concerts, we usually ask for donations of food for the local food bank in lieu of admission, that kind of thing."

"That sounds nice." She was still baffled about why Winnie was telling her this. Hopefully, the other woman would work her way around to it.

"This year instead of the food bank, we decided on our most ambitious project yet."

"What's that?"

"A couple of our members have children with disabili-ties. One is my best friend Sofia Navarro, who is coming to Thanksgiving dinner with her son Rodrigo. He's amazing and funny and kind and happens to have Down syndrome. Another member of our choir has a daughter, Haley, who is nine years old with muscular dystrophy. She's the great-est kid, with the biggest heart."

"That's wonderful." As a pediatric nurse at a major uni-versity hospital, she had a great deal of experience with differently abled children and always loved having them as her patients.

"We wanted to do something for Rodrigo and Haley and

other people with disabilities in our community, so we're trying to start an adaptive outdoor recreation program."

"What a great idea!"

"Isn't it?" Winnie beamed. "Other places have them but we have never started one here, and it's a real shame. We certainly have a large enough population who could use it. We were able to get a grant to buy adaptive skis and sleds, but need a place to store them and also a small accessible lodge at the ski resort where differently abled skiers and their families can hang out if they need a quieter environment than the main lodge."

"That sounds ambitious."

"Yes, well, we've had a few corporate donations to help get it off the ground. It's going to take much more, of course, but it's a start."

She paused to take a sip of water.

"Do you need something more for the pain?" The nurse in her had to ask.

"No, I'm fine. Where was I? Oh, yes. This year we had the idea of combining our talents and offering an evening of music but more, too. We wanted to create more of an event, really, which we hope becomes an annual tradition around here."

"That sounds intriguing."

"Oh, it's going to be wonderful. We're calling it Christmas at Holiday House. It's an exclusive evening of history, music and food, and all the holiday spirit you could ever want."

"Christmas at Holiday House. You're talking about having it here?" Did Ethan know what his grandmother was cooking up?

"That's the big draw. People have been dying to see inside this house for years. You wouldn't believe the people who just drive by and ring the bell to ask if they can walk through. I figured, why not give them the chance?"

Why not, indeed. Did Lucy know about this? If she did, she hadn't bothered to mention it when asking Abby if she could come and stay with Winnie.

"The tour will run for just over a week, and we're only selling a hundred tickets a night. And guess what? We're already sold out!"

"Wow. That's terrific."

"I know. One of the women in the Silver Belles has a catering company in town and another one owns a bakery. They're handling the refreshments, which will be pastries and hot cocoa, mostly, and there are others who make handicrafts, needlework, homemade soaps and lotions, that sort of thing. They're all donating their work for the gift shop area, which we plan to set up in the room I call the blue drawing room."

"This sounds great. You seem to have everything figured out. Where do I come in?"

Winnie sighed. "Holiday House just isn't in the state I would like it to be for visitors. I have a cleaning service and they do a fine job of keeping the dust away, but I need someone to spruce up the collections, arrange furniture, put out my holiday decorations. That kind of thing. I thought I could handle it myself, but that was before, well, before I fell down the stairs."

Winnie needed a Christmas decorator, and she was actually looking to *Abby* for that? She wanted to laugh but had a feeling this wasn't a joke.

"I am the least qualified person you could find to help you with this, Winnie. I don't know what Lucy told you, but decorating is definitely not my strong suit. In our dorm, her side of the room was gorgeous, with handwoven rugs, a couple of art-glass lamps she picked up at a thrift store, a landscape she found at a flea market. I only had a tacked-up poster of the human anatomy I bought at the campus bookstore."

She had to smile at the memory. Lucy had taken one look at her side of the room and begun to subtly interject color and style. First she bought a few throw pillows, then a colorful quilt she found for cheap in vivid colors. By the time their first year ended, Abby's side had been as cozy and warm as Lucy's.

Fortunately, Kevin had had a much more highly developed interior design style than Abby, so she had left all the furniture decisions for their apartment up to him.

"That doesn't matter," Winnie insisted now. "You said yourself what a good team we made fixing Thanksgiving dinner today. This can be the same thing. I can supervise and tell you just what to do. I just can't do it myself with this stupid arm in a sling."

"Surely you have friends who have skills better suited for what you need," she said, hearing the slightly desperate note in her voice.

Drat Lucy Lancaster for dragging her into this without giving her the full picture.

"Yes, but they're all doing other things to make Christmas at Holiday House a success. I already told everyone I could handle getting the house ready."

"That was likely before your accident. They can't expect you to put up a Christmas tree in your condition."

"Will you at least think about it? After dinner you can take a tour of the house and see what most needs to be done to spruce things up a little. It's not really all that much. Maybe Christopher can even help you. What kid doesn't like decorating a Christmas tree? I have a dozen of them."

A dozen Christmas trees. Oh, mercy.

On the other hand, Abby *had* wanted to give her son a traditional Christmas. What was more traditional than decorating a beautiful old Victorian mansion for the holidays, especially when it was for a good cause?

Still, she was ridiculously underqualified for such a job. Winnie would be better off with someone else to help her. *Anyone* else.

The timer on her watch suddenly went off. "Oh. That's the turkey. It's time to take it out."

"That means everyone will be here soon. I should probably freshen up a bit before my friends get here."

"I think you're lovely the way you are, but I can help you to your room after I take the turkey out. Just give me a moment."

She hurried to lift the giant turkey roaster out of the oven. If she did say so herself, the bird looked beautiful, the skin crispy and golden. It also smelled heavenly. She set it on the counter and tented it with the foil she had already prepared, then returned to help Winnie up.

"I'll try not to wake Christopher."

"It doesn't matter if you do," Abby answered. "He needs to change his shirt and comb his hair, anyway."

With Abby's help, Winnie rose with the walker they had discovered worked better than crutches for her sprained ankle.

"I can spot you."

"Not necessary," Winnie said as she made her slow, painstaking way toward her bedroom. The walker caught on the edge of the throw rug, though, and she started to stumble.

Abby hurried to her side. "I've got you. It might be easier if I help you. Take my arm."

Winnie slipped her arm through Abby's and hobbled toward her bedroom.

"I hate growing old," she muttered.

"You're not old," Christopher said sleepily, appearing at Winnie's other side. Abby hadn't even heard her son wake up. "I think you're perfect."

Winnie chuckled. "Oh, you are a charmer, young man. Do you want to know what I'm most thankful for this year? That you and your mama have come to visit me. I love having new life in my old house."

After Abby and Christopher helped her into her room, the corgis close behind, Abby took her son into their own room so they could change and she could comb his hair.

She couldn't stop thinking about what Winnie had asked her. Holiday House was huge and she had seen only a small portion of it. The task of decorating this massive space for holiday tours seemed so far beyond her abilities that it was almost laughable.

Winnie needed her help, though. It was for a good cause. She could at least give it a try.

She had been looking for new opportunities to stretch herself. She just never thought those opportunities would involve Christmas trees and a huge Victorian mansion.

CHAPTER FOUR

"Everything looks so delicious. I can't believe you did all this today."

Winnie's friend Sofia, a cheerful, stylishly dressed woman with salt-and-pepper hair and warm brown eyes, beamed at Abby from across the heavily laden dining table.

"Winnie called all the shots," Abby assured her. "I only followed directions."

"I've learned it's best in all situations to just do what Winnie tells you," another friend whose name she couldn't remember piped up.

"True enough," the woman's husband said with a laugh. "If I hadn't listened to Winnie, I never would have asked out Teresa. After my divorce, I was done with romance. Winnie kept trying to tell me she knew the perfect woman for me, but I wouldn't listen to her. Guess what? Turned out she was right."

He squeezed the woman's hand with such tenderness Abby's heart seemed to sigh.

She loved seeing people in happy relationships. It gave her hope for the world and hope that maybe she might be able to find that again someday.

Someday. Not yet. She wasn't ready for love again. Sometimes she felt like she was still reeling from losing Kevin. She had thought they would be together forever and was still trying to figure out how to rebuild her life without him.

She had tried to date a few times. Both outings had ended disastrously. The first time, she had been set up by a nurse friend with the woman's brother-in-law, who turned out to have clammy hands and a nervous tic of blinking rapidly during conversation.

The second time, a respiratory therapist at the hospital had asked her out, and they had enjoyed a nice dinner at one of her favorite seafood places. Maybe she had a few too many glasses of wine—she wasn't sure. But when he tried to kiss her at her front door, she had literally been sick to her stomach and had barely made it inside and slammed the door behind her before she'd thrown up.

Not her best moment.

She had been afraid to date again for fear of the same reaction.

Maybe she was destined to spend the rest of her life alone. She could dedicate her life to her son and her career. She had thought about going back to school to obtain her nurse practitioner license. When would she possibly have time to date around studying, working full-time and caring for Christopher on her own?

No. That would be a convenient excuse to put off dating again. Surely she could meet a nice guy in Austin, one who didn't make her physically ill when he touched her.

She wanted love again. More than that, she wanted her son to have a father figure in his life. She wasn't about to date or possibly marry someone only for her son's sake, but if she could find a good, decent man who would be a caring father to Christopher, that would be bonus.

She didn't have to figure that out right now. She would

definitely work on getting them both settled in Austin before she started thinking about dating someone.

She turned her attention back to Winnie's guests and all
the delicious dishes spread out in the middle of the table,
as well as the empty place at the head of the table.

"Do you want to wait for Ethan before we carve the turkey?" she asked Winnie.

"No. He probably got tied up at work. It happens. Let's
go ahead, since everyone else is here. Richard, do you
mind doing the honors?"

"Not at all. Not at all."

That was his name, Abby recalled now. Richard and
Teresa Shannon. The two of them ran the gourmet grocery store in town, Winnie had told Abby when she introduced them.

She liked all of Winnie's guests for dinner. There was
Mariah Raymond, a single mom with gorgeous curly dark
hair and several colorful tattoos. She had a son, Dakota,
who was Christopher's age, but Mariah had told Abby he
was spending the holiday with his father.

"At least I get him for Christmas," she had said, but
Abby hadn't missed the sadness in her eyes as she interacted with Christopher.

She had seen a similar determined cheerfulness on the
features of Emily Tsu, whom Winnie had introduced as
a bakery owner. Emily was around Abby's age and had
brought the most luscious-looking apple crumble pie that
made Abby's and Winnie's pumpkin pie look pathetic in
comparison.

And then there was Father Elijah Shepherd—the perfect name for a man of God, she thought—who turned out
not to be the ancient, shriveled old Episcopal priest she

had been expecting but quite good-looking, with honey-colored hair, blue eyes and an impressive physique beneath his collar.

After five minutes of conversation, she had figured out that he blushed prolifically—and also that Mariah seemed to delight in teasing him to bring out the rosy color.

Others at the table included another married couple, Vicki Kostas and Kathleen Wilson, whom Winnie had introduced as fellow members of the Silver Belles, as well as an older gentleman, Paul Abbot, who had a huge gray bottlebrush mustache and kind blue eyes.

Abby would not have expected it, but she was enjoying herself immensely. Only as she sat surrounded by strangers did she realize how very isolated she had become in the two years since Kevin died.

Yes, she still went to work and she still hung out sometimes with a few close friends, but her social life was almost nonexistent, and she had made very few new friends.

She had missed stimulating conversation.

Though he was the only child present, Christopher seemed to be enjoying himself, as well. He seemed particularly drawn to Rodrigo, the son of Winnie's good friend Sofia. Rodrigo was in his late twenties and had Down syndrome. His speech was a little hard to understand, but that didn't stop Christopher from carrying on a long conversation with him about *Star Wars*.

She was half listening to them talk as Richard Shannon finished carving the turkey.

"Father Shepherd, would you mind saying grace?" Winnie asked.

"I would be happy to," the reverend said. "Would everyone please join hands."

Abby had just reached for Christopher's hand on her left and was about to reach across the table to Teresa Shannon's hand when the front door opened.

Everyone paused, looking expectantly toward the door. A moment later, Ethan walked in, shrugging out of his coat.

He looked gorgeous, she couldn't help noticing. His hair was windswept and he wore a blue dress shirt, loose at the collar. She actually felt a little light-headed.

Oh, how ridiculous. Yes, he was attractive, but he was definitely not the kind of man for her. Not to mention, he still looked at her with suspicion in his eyes, as if he expected her to steal the silverware right off the table when the guests weren't looking.

His grandmother looked delighted to see him. "Ethan, darling. You made it."

Another man followed close behind Ethan, and Abby recognized José Navarro, whom she had met once before at Kevin's funeral. Even if she hadn't met him, she would have known by the resemblance to Sofia that this was her son, especially when he crossed to his mother and kissed her cheek.

"And you brought José. How clever of you!"

Ethan smiled, leaning down to hug his grandmother. "I dragged him away. It took some work, but I finally convinced him Lancaster Hotels wouldn't fall apart if he took an hour away to have some turkey and pumpkin pie. I meant to call so I could warn you but totally forgot."

Sofia Navarro beamed at her son. "Good for you, Ethan. And look, we have just enough place settings since Allison canceled at the last minute."

"Sit down. Sit down," Winnie said. "José, there's a place there across from your brother."

Abby suspected there might be something going on between her notoriously relationship-shy friend and José. She could definitely understand why Lucy would be drawn to the man. He was extraordinarily good-looking, with sculpted features, high cheekbones, his mother's warm dark eyes and incredibly long eyelashes.

"Hi, Ethan. Hi, José." Rodrigo beamed at both of them, his features filled with even more joy to see them.

"Rod. Dude. Happy Thanksgiving." Ethan gave the younger man a long, complicated, obviously well-practiced handshake that had Christopher gawking.

To her dismay, he then took the seat at the end of the table, which happened to be right next to her spot.

"Hi," he said to her. "Happy Thanksgiving."

Abby could feel her face heat, a curse of her red hair. She and Father Shepherd were a matched set when it came to the blushing department.

"And to you."

That was all she could manage.

"Everything looks great," he said.

"I'm sure it tastes delicious. We were just about to say grace so we can see for ourselves," Winnie said tartly. "Everyone, grab the hand of the person next to you."

Oh, snap. That person was now Ethan Lancaster. She didn't want to hold his hand but couldn't figure out a way to decline without causing a scene.

She took Christopher's slightly sticky hand in hers again. After a moment's hesitation, she took Ethan's outstretched fingers. His hand was warm, the fingers big and strong. Abby tried not to shiver at the feel of his skin brushing hers.

Abby did her best to ignore her reaction and focus on

Father Shepherd's blessing. She needed to get control of herself right now. She would be here for two weeks and would no doubt encounter Ethan again during that time. She was here to help Winifred, not make a fool of herself by developing a completely inappropriate crush on the woman's grandson.

She only caught half of Father Shepherd's prayer, but what she did hear seemed very sweet and sincere. Though she shouldn't have been looking, she thought she saw Mariah watching the clergyman under her eyelashes.

After the prayer, everyone began passing around the food.

"You've been busy today," Ethan said, after handing her a heaping dish of stuffing.

"Everyone else brought most of the meal except the turkey and a few of the sides. Oh, and we made a pumpkin pie, but I'm afraid the verdict is still out on that one."

"That's still a lot of work and probably not what you were expecting when you agreed to come up here to help out Winnie after her fall."

That wasn't all Winnie wanted her to do. Did Ethan know about his grandmother's fundraiser tours of the house? He seemed so protective of Winnie, Abby couldn't imagine him being thrilled about them.

"Your grandmother had everything organized today. I was merely the kitchen help, following her directions."

"Don't listen to her," Winnie said from the other end of the table. "She and Christopher did it all. You all would have been eating canned ham if not for her."

"To Abby and Christopher," Mariah said, lifting her wineglass. Everyone at the table toasted her, as well. Christopher didn't seem to know what was going on, but he beamed, anyway.

"To my friends, both old and new," Winnie said. "I'm thankful for each one of you."

"You made a rhyme," Christopher said gleefully.

She grinned at him. "So I did."

For the next few moments, others around the table made various toasts to things they were thankful for that year.

"Okay. Enough of this," Winnie finally said. "This food will be cold if we don't eat."

People tucked into the meal, and conversation became more general around the table.

"How was Winnie last night? Did she sleep all right?" Ethan asked Abby.

She couldn't help but be touched by his concern for his grandmother. "She's obviously in pain and doesn't want to admit it. But I watched to make sure she took a pain pill, and she went to bed early. She said she slept soundly."

"If you were able to make her take any pain medication, I'm impressed."

"I didn't *make* her do anything. I suggested it. She must have needed it or she wouldn't have agreed. I tried to get her to take another one earlier this afternoon, without success. I'll work on her again before bedtime tonight."

"Kudos to you for trying, at least."

She made a face. "If I have to, I'll tell her that if she doesn't take one willingly, I'm going to slip it into her pumpkin pie."

He looked startled. "Would you really do that?"

"No. But Winnie doesn't need to know that."

He chuckled, and she told herself that shiver down

her spine was simply a chill coming in through the huge stained-glass windows in the dining room.

ABBY POWELL SEEMED to have amazing skills at managing his grandmother.

Ethan wasn't sure how she did it, but somehow Abby was able to persuade Winnie she wasn't needed in the kitchen to clean up dinner, that she should instead sit in her favorite chair in the room off the kitchen and visit with her guests.

He waited for Winnie to protest. Instead, she meekly complied. Richard and Teresa Shannon took the hint and helped her to the chair, covering her with a blanket.

Winnie must be in pain or she never would have agreed. She would have been right in the middle of the action as the table was cleared and leftovers divided into containers for each guest to take.

While the Shannons asked Winnie questions about historic holiday celebrations in the house—a conversational gambit destined to distract her as nothing else could—everyone else pitched in to help clean up.

Ethan washed dishes, his traditional role after holiday meals.

At first, Mariah Raymond was helping dry the dishes and trying to flirt with him, as she always did. Her phone rang before she really got warmed up.

"Oh. That's my baby," she exclaimed, dropping her dish towel in the drying rack and reaching for her phone.

As she left to take the call, someone picked up her dish towel. The scent of vanilla clued him in that it was Abby even before he looked up from the dish he was scrubbing to find her standing next to him.

"You should let someone else do that. I believe we can all agree you've done enough today. You ought to be in the other room with Winnie, sitting in the chair next to her with your feet up."

"I can dry," Rodrigo said eagerly. "I do that at home."

"Great. Sounds like a plan," Ethan said.

"Here you go," Abby said, giving José's younger brother her towel. "How about this? You dry and then Ethan can tell both of us where to put things."

"You're assuming I know where things go. It's been a few years since I lived here."

As all three of them worked together, a kind of peace swirled around them. He had always found washing dishes to be a very zen kind of job, for some strange reason.

"Hey, Ethan. Knock-knock."

"Who's there, Rod?"

"Figs."

"Figs who?"

"Figs your doorbell, it's not working."

He groaned, which made Rodrigo bust up laughing.

"I've got one," Abby said. "Knock-knock."

"Who's there?" Rodrigo said quickly.

"Police."

"Police who?"

"Police let me in, it's chilly out here."

He laughed even harder at that one. "Now you, Ethan."

"Wow. It's been a long time since I did a knock-knock joke. Let's see. Knock-knock."

"Who's there?" Rodrigo said.

"Nana."

"Nana who?"

"Nana your business."

Abby and Rodrigo groaned, and then Rodrigo started another round.

All in all, it was the most fun Ethan had ever had doing dishes.

Rodrigo Navarro held a very special place in the hearts of everyone who knew him. He was endlessly loving, filled with kindness and joy toward everyone he met. He was so popular in town that a birthday party in his honor each December—a gingerbread house competition for charity—was one of the highlights of the holiday season.

Being around him always made Ethan feel like a better man than he was. Or at least made him *want* to be a better man than he was.

"There you are, *mijo*."

Sofia joined them when they were nearly finished.

"I'm helping," Rodrigo said proudly.

"He's been wonderful," Abby told Sofia. "I had no idea anyone could dry dishes so quickly."

"And I tell good jokes," Rodrigo said, obviously preening under her attention.

"You sure do."

"Are you about ready to go home?"

"I'm having fun with Eth and my new friend Abby."

"You can come back and visit her another day. But your sisters and your nephews and nieces are coming tonight. They'll be here soon and we don't want them to come home to an empty house, do we?"

"I guess not." Rodrigo carefully hung the towel on the stove and waved to Abby, then held his hand out. Ethan knew what he wanted. He dried his hand so the two of them could once more perform their regular complicated handshake ritual, developed over years of friendship. It seemed to become more elaborate every year.

"You need to go tubing on the new hill," Ethan said. "I hear it's a lot of fun."

Rod's face lit up. "Can we go tomorrow?"

Sofia laughed and shook her head. "You can't tomorrow, remember? We're having another Thanksgiving dinner tomorrow. That's why everyone is coming tonight."

"How about Saturday, then?"

"Maybe not Saturday," Ethan answered. "But soon, I promise. We'll get you there."

"Thanks, Ethan." The handshake apparently wasn't enough because Rodrigo reached out to hug Ethan. He hugged him back.

"Bye, Abby." Rodrigo hugged her, too.

"Bye. It was nice to meet you. I hope I see you again before we go."

"Hey, knock-knock."

"Who's there?" Ethan and Abby said in unison.

"Europe."

"Europe who?" Ethan said.

"No I'm not, you are," Rodrigo said gleefully while Sofia shook her head.

"And on that lovely joke, we will say *adios*."

She ushered her son out of the room, which left Ethan alone with Abby.

Tendrils of auburn hair had escaped her loose bun, curling around her face in the steam of the kitchen. Her green eyes were bright with laughter.

Ethan felt a jolt go through him. He wanted to curl a finger around one of those tendrils and to kiss each one of those light freckles scattered across her nose.

"He's wonderful," she said.

"Yeah," he said gruffly, trying to get himself under control. "One of my favorite people. I wish everybody had a Rodrigo in their world to remind them what's really important in life."

She looked startled, eyes wide, and he regretted saying anything.

"That looks like the last of the dishes. That wasn't so bad."

"Not at all. I guess I'd better check on Winnie and Christopher."

The two of them walked together to the great room, where they found Winnie playing a card game with Elijah Shepherd, and Christopher asleep on the sofa nearby under a blanket.

"Did everyone go home?" They hadn't been in the kitchen that long, had they? Maybe he had lost track of time.

"Yes. The Shannons were the last to go and they left a moment ago, right after Sofia and her boys. That's one of the problems with having Thanksgiving dinner in the evening, I suppose. Afterward, everyone wants to go home and sleep off the tryptophan."

"I should probably go, as well," Elijah said. "I promised I would stop in and visit Charlotte Frye this evening. She's still recovering from her heart valve surgery and didn't feel strong enough to go out."

"Thank you for coming," Winnie said.

"Thank *you* for a delightful evening and a delicious Thanksgiving, all of you. The holidays make me miss my family in Boston, but spending time in these beautiful surroundings with such convivial company took away much of the sting of missing them."

Ethan wasn't sure how he did it, but Eli Shepherd somehow managed to make even the most banal of statements sound like a sermon.

"We love having you, Elijah. You know you're welcome anytime," Winnie said graciously.

She made a funny little signal to Ethan, and he interpreted it to mean she wanted him to play host and show the man out.

"Your grandmother seems to be feeling better after her accident," Eli said as they walked toward the front door.

"I hope so."

"She's a remarkable woman. It's so brave of her to go forward with her plans to open this beautiful house up for tours during the holiday season, despite her injuries."

"Brave." He couldn't think of anything else to say, completely taken off guard. Last he and Winnie had spoken after her accident, he thought she had decided to cancel the whole damn thing, which he had never approved of in the first place.

"It can't have been an easy decision. What a blessing that she has the wonderful Ms. Powell here now to help her get the house ready and carry some of that burden."

Was that the real reason she had wanted Abby to come from Phoenix to Silver Bells, so that Winnie would have someone to help her run the event Ethan had vigorously opposed? He should have suspected as much.

"Yes," he said mechanically. "Isn't that great?"

"He's a nice man, don't you think?" Winnie said when he returned to the sitting room. She had turned the cards into a solitaire deck. "Much warmer than old Reverend Simon. Elijah's sermons are still a little dry, truth be told, but they seem to be getting better every week. It will come, I'm sure."

"No doubt." He sat down across from her, trying not to glare. "I did find his parting words quite interesting. For some reason, Father Shepherd has the crazy idea that you're going ahead with the Christmas at Holiday House tours that I was quite certain you had decided you should cancel after your accident."

His grandmother snorted, slapping another card down. "You mean the event *you* decided I should cancel. I told you I would have to see how quickly I recover."

"Winnie. I admire your determination to help out a good cause, but this isn't the year for you to take on something like this. You know I think the accessible outdoor recreation center is a good cause or I wouldn't have agreed to donate the land to build it. But surely there's another way your Silver Belles can raise the necessary funds. You've got the gingerbread contest. That's always a big event."

"It is. But we can't raise nearly enough with the contest alone. We've already made twice what we do for that event in ticket preorders for the house tour. That's not including the proceeds from the gift shop we're going to set up in the front parlor. This is important, to me and to the other Silver Belles. I can't cancel it now, simply because I wasn't watching where I was going one evening and suffered a little fall."

Her accident was much more serious than a little fall. He frowned. "You can't be everything to everyone, Grandmother. You just can't."

She reached for his hand, her expression softening. "I know that. I only want to help where I can, which is offering Holiday House—your ancestral home—as the venue to help people find a little holiday spirit."

"You can barely walk and you're down to one arm. How

are you possibly going to be able to do all you need to get the house ready?"

She pointed to Abby, who was sitting by the fire, leafing through a magazine. "She's going to help me. Isn't that wonderful?"

Ethan could think of a few other choice words besides *wonderful*. Abby was blushing, he could see that now. He wished he didn't find that so enticing.

"It's going to work out perfectly," Winnie went on. "We made a great team today while we were working on Thanksgiving dinner. I just figured we could do the same thing while getting the house ready. We're already working on making a list. I only have to find a comfortable chair where I can sit and boss her around."

Abby gave a small, strangled sort of laugh but didn't say anything.

He looked between the two of them, not willing to let the matter drop. "I appreciate your work-around solution, Winnie. I do. I'm sure Abby could be a great help. But, as I told you after your accident, I still don't think it's a good idea to open your home and have strangers traipsing through every night during a time when you should be focusing on resting and recovering."

"I'm nearly eighty years old," Winnie said, her voice suddenly stern. "I'm not a child. While I appreciate your concern, the decision is ultimately mine and I've made it. Christmas at Holiday House is going forward, and that's my last word on the subject."

"No matter what I think."

Winnie sighed. "I know you have my best interests at heart, darling. I appreciate that, I really do. I love you and I'm so grateful to have you in my life."

"But?"

"But I need you to accept that I am still perfectly capable of making my own decisions."

"I never said otherwise."

"You want me to move out of the house I have lived in since the day I married your grandfather. To sit in a rocking chair in some assisted living center and waste the rest of my life instead of using this house to benefit a cause I care about."

"I never said I wanted you to waste the rest of your life. I just don't want you overdoing it. There's a big difference between sitting in a rocking chair and running a marathon. You just got out of the hospital, Winnie."

"I spent one night there, only because that young pup of a doctor wanted to cover his ass and make sure I didn't have another injury they hadn't found yet."

That wasn't the entire story, as Winnie well knew. The doctor had wanted to be sure she didn't have internal bleeding.

"Look," Winnie went on, "the event doesn't start for two weeks, and I'm sure I'll be feeling much better by then."

"What if you're not?" he countered.

"I will be. Anyway, I'm only leading some of the tours and talking about the history of the house and Christmases past. Other Silver Belles will be taking care of the entertainment, the food and the hot cocoa. Abby has agreed to help me get the house ready and a few days after we start the tours, Lucy should be home."

He knew without question that his sister would take Winnie's side of this disagreement. "What you're saying is that my opinion doesn't matter. You intend to go ahead with it despite my view that you're making a mistake and will be taxing yourself unnecessarily."

Her features softened and she reached for his hand. "I know you mean well, darling, and are only worried about me. But this is a cause I am passionate about."

"I understand. That still doesn't make me happy about it."

"I know. If it makes you feel any better, I don't expect you to lift a finger to help. Not one single finger. I know what a busy time of year this is for you."

"I'm going to hold you to that."

Winnie glanced at Abby. "Well, almost nothing."

He frowned, not liking the sound of that. "What does that mean?"

"I was hoping you might show Abby the rest of the house. She's only seen a few rooms on this level."

Abby, he couldn't help but notice, looked slightly alarmed at that suggestion.

"I'm sure I'll have the chance tomorrow to wander through on my own," she said quickly.

"Why would you want to do that when you could have someone from the family show you around?" Winnie asked. "Ethan knows all the history of the house and can share things with you that you won't get simply from walking around on your own. You should take advantage of him."

"Excuse me?"

"It shouldn't take you long to walk through the house. Go on. I can keep an eye on young Christopher, here. If he wakes up, I can find a Christmas movie for us on the Netflix."

"You want us to go now?" Ethan asked.

Winnie shrugged. "What better time? You're here, she's

here. If you don't show her tonight, I'll have to do it, and I'm not sure I'll be up to the task tomorrow."

"I just thought Abby might be tired, after a long day of driving yesterday, then spending today in the kitchen preparing Thanksgiving for a bunch of strangers."

Winnie looked stricken. "Oh. I hadn't thought of that. Forgive me, my dear. I should have been more considerate."

The younger woman looked at Winnie and then at Ethan. "I'm fine. I'm up for a tour, if you are. It shouldn't take us that long. I would actually find it quite helpful so that I know where to start first thing tomorrow."

He had to help. What choice did he have? He couldn't refuse a direct order from his injured grandmother.

"All right. I'm game if you are."

"Let me just grab a notebook so I can jot down a few things as we go. There's one in the kitchen I can use."

She hurried away, leaving him to wonder what in the world he had just gotten himself into.

CHAPTER FIVE

WHAT IN ALL that was holy had she gotten herself into?

Abby hurried into the kitchen for the notebook and pen she had been using earlier to make a list with Winnie.

She did not want to spend a moment longer than necessary in the company of Ethan Lancaster. Not when she was fighting this extremely inconvenient attraction to him. She ought simply to have told him she did not need his help and left it at that. She could have explored on her own later tonight after Christopher was in bed or in the morning. She wouldn't have had the full historical context about the house, but she could always get that later from Winnie.

Maybe this was a good thing. Maybe spending a few moments with the man, getting to know him a little better, might help her relax so that she could feel more comfortable with him going forward.

He seemed kind, underneath his somewhat brusque exterior. She had seen the genuine concern in his expression when he had discussed his grandmother's plans to open her house to strangers. On some level, she empathized with him. When her great-aunt had been dying and Abby had been her caregiver, she had been just as protective.

Winnie wasn't dying, though. While the other woman had injuries that might slow her down physically right now, Abby had spent the entire day with her and had come to know a sharp, energetic woman who definitely knew what she wanted.

And right now she wanted Abby to take a tour of the house in the company of Ethan Lancaster, like it or not.

With a deep breath for courage, she returned to the great room.

"Okay. I'm ready," she said. It was a complete lie, but neither of the Lancasters needed to know that.

"We shouldn't be long," she said to Winnie. "I have my cell phone with me. Just call or text if Christopher wakes up or if you need something."

"Got it. Have fun."

She managed not to roll her eyes at that as Ethan led the way up the big, sweeping staircase. "What did you want to see first?"

She followed a few steps behind him. "I have no idea where to start. What would you suggest? I suppose I need to see everything."

The look he aimed at her over his shoulder was almost sympathetic. "You have no idea what's up here, do you?"

That sounded ominous, but maybe she listened to too many true-crime podcasts.

"You make it sound like your grandmother is hiding Frankenstein's monster in a back bedroom."

"She very well could be, for all I know. I'm not certain anyone but Winnie has seen all the rooms up here. I *am* fairly certain she couldn't tell you everything that's up here or where to find it."

That sounded both fascinating and terrifying. "Why don't you start by telling me what you know about the history of the house?"

"That is not a small order." He flipped on a light switch,

illuminating a long hallway with rooms on either side. Christmas music wafted up the stairs from something Winnie must have turned on in the great room.

"All right. Start by telling me when it was built."

"Okay. See that portrait there of the dastardly looking guy with the big beard? That's my third great-grandfather—Winnie's husband's great-grandfather, William Lancaster. He was a silver miner in his youth who staked a claim on a small plot of land and ended up extraordinarily lucky when he discovered one of the richest veins of silver in the area. He was a crafty young man who didn't tell anybody about his discovery. I don't know how he managed to keep it quiet, but over the course of a year he somehow managed to acquire the stakes of everyone else in the area until he owned the entire mountainside. He then turned his claim into one of the most lucrative silver mines in the entire West, the Lucinda."

He tapped another picture of an elegant-looking but unsmiling woman. "William founded the town of Silver Bells, brought his childhood sweetheart out from Boston, not coincidentally also named Lucinda, and built the house for her."

"How romantic," she said, though the woman didn't look particularly appreciative of the gesture.

"I don't know if I would go that far. She hated it here in Colorado, especially the winters. She hated the mine, she hated the weather, she hated the people. Lucinda was a snob, and after a few years she left with their children and insisted on living in Boston, which she considered far more civilized. They stayed married, probably so she could spend his money, but lived apart for most of the year. At her husband's insistence, she agreed to spend summers here with their children, hence the name."

"Holiday House. So the name really has nothing to do with Christmas."

He shook his head. "No, which makes Winnie's obsession with the season rather amusing."

"Okay. The original owners were Lucinda and William. What about subsequent inhabitants?"

"They left the house to their oldest son, Howard. By that time, thirty years after William struck it rich, the mine was played out. Howard did his best to waste what was left of his family's fortune on wine, women and song. The old story. He ended up marrying a woman from his mother's Boston set and rarely came to Colorado, so the house fell in disrepair."

"How sad."

"Some silver barons managed to hang on to their fortunes while some ran through it with frightening speed. The Lancasters were in the second category. By the time my great-grandfather came along, the original miner's grandson, they had very little left. They did, however, have this house and the land. After World War I, Great-grandfather Thomas had the grand idea of turning the mountainside into a ski resort. This house was the first hotel in town. I guess you could call it the first ski lodge."

He pointed to another picture of people in old-fashioned clothing with long skis clustered around what she assumed was an early ski lift and another next to it that showed Holiday House with a fire blazing in the great-room fireplace and people clustered around it looking tired and happy.

"There were thirty guest rooms, and skiers would be taken to the slopes in a horse and sleigh."

"Oh, how charming."

"I'm sure it was for a few years. Except then the Great Depression hit and nobody could afford to go skiing, especially not to come all the way out here for it. The town was dead or dying because all the mines had dried up. And then World War II came, and people had more important things on their mind than winter recreation. At that point, Holiday House was used to house recovering soldiers injured in the war."

He pointed to another picture that showed row after row of cots down in the great room.

"Finally after the war, Thomas, along with his sons Thomas Jr. and Clive, my grandfather and Winnie's husband, reopened the ski resort and used what little was left of their fortune, along with a mortgage on this house, to build an actual lodge closer to the slopes. Things took off from there."

"What a story Holiday House has to tell." The house really was exceptionally lovely. She admired the thick gleaming woodwork around the windows, the elaborately scrolled hardware on the door hinges and knobs. "It sounds as if this place is inextricably tied to your family's history."

"For good and bad. My great-uncle and my grandfather did a great deal to repair the family fortunes. They were the ones who transitioned from owning a ski resort and lodge to focusing almost exclusively on the hotel business. In the sixties, they started buying small hotels in other strategic travel locations around the globe. Clive ran the company until he died while I was in high school."

She heard the sadness in his voice and sensed how much he must have cared for his grandfather.

"You couldn't have been old enough to start running

the company after he died, were you? Did your father take over?"

He made a scoffing sort of sound. "My father? No. There would have been nothing left if Rick had been left in charge of Lancaster Hotels."

It had been a stupid question, she realized in retrospect. She knew enough of the grim details of his family life from what Lucy had told her to guess his father wouldn't have taken much interest in the family business, other than to spend his trust fund as quickly as possible.

"No, my great-uncle Thomas, Clive's brother, ran the company after Clive's death. He was brilliant and expanded the hotel operations exponentially."

He pointed to a picture of two men together that looked like it was from the sixties. One was larger, nattily dressed and more confident looking. The other was younger and looked like a beatnik.

"Is he gone now, as well?" she asked, though she suspected the answer from the stark grief on Ethan's features.

"Yes. He died of a heart attack three years ago and I miss his wisdom every day."

"I'm sorry."

She certainly knew enough about grief to fill several sets of encyclopedias.

"While Thomas had a longtime partner, whom he married as soon as gay marriage became legal here in Colorado, the two of them never had children. He became a mentor of sorts to me and helped groom me to fill his role."

He must have been extraordinarily young to take over as CEO of the company after his great-uncle died. She knew he was only three years older than Lucy, who would be thirty in the spring.

He gave her a rueful look. "And now that I've bored you endlessly with my family history, I suppose I ought to show you the house."

"You didn't bore me at all. I love hearing other people's histories, probably because I don't know much about my own."

He gave a short laugh. "Everyone has a history. We all come from somewhere."

"True. But not everybody is lucky enough to know all those details. I don't know anything about my father's side. I don't even know his name. My mother would never talk about him. And while my great-aunt sometimes shared stories about her childhood growing up poor in Texas, I don't know much beyond her parents, mainly because *she* didn't know. Someday I might have to do some research."

"Is that why you're moving to Austin after the holidays? To find out more about your heritage?"

How did he know she was moving to Austin? Had she told him? Maybe Lucy had mentioned it to him.

"Not really. I haven't given that much thought, though I suppose that might be an unexpected benefit. No. I just needed something new."

She didn't tell him how tired she had grown of living with the memories, of feeling as if she was stagnating in the mire of her pain.

"I decided that if I was going to make a change, I should do it before Christopher starts elementary school. He'll be in kindergarten next year so I knew time was running out."

"Yeah. I get that. I moved around a lot in elementary school and middle school. It wasn't easy. Finally, when I was starting my final year of high school, I told my parents I was done. Lucy and I needed to stay in one place.

We ended up living here with our grandmother during the school year and trading custody with our parents during the summer, which made life much better."

"That couldn't have been easy for you."

"No. There was a healthy amount of drama. I want to think maybe our parents both realized how their constant fighting was hurting us, but I suspect Winnie probably laid down the law and threatened to cut them off if they didn't agree."

At least their grandmother had stepped up to give them something of a stable home.

"Now that I've rambled on, I suppose I ought to show you what you're up against."

She wanted to protest that he hadn't rambled at all, but she knew their time was limited. She would have to help Winnie to bed shortly.

"We can start here." Ethan opened the closest door. "This is one of the many bedrooms in the house and is a good example of what you will encounter throughout the rest of the house."

He flipped on a light and stepped aside so she could look in. She brushed past him, aware as she did of that expensive soap scent she had first noticed the day before, masculine and outdoorsy and delicious.

She forgot all about how good he smelled when she caught a look inside the room.

"Oh, my."

He gave a rough laugh that made her shiver despite herself. "Yes. Exactly."

"Is every room like this?" she asked faintly.

Everywhere she looked were nutcrackers of myriad shapes and sizes and colors. Scores of them. Probably hundreds or even thousands. The furniture in the room was lovely, a standard bedroom set, but every flat surface, along with several areas of the floor, was covered with wooden statues.

"No. This is the only nutcracker room."

"Whew. I guess that's something."

"And next door is the angel room. Picture this room, only with wings. The room after that I believe is one of several crèche rooms. My grandmother loves to collect things. Can you tell?"

She had no answer, overwhelmed with the enormity of the collection. The nutcrackers alone could fill a museum.

"Winnie isn't a hoarder, at least not in the classic sense. Or, who knows, maybe she would be if her house wasn't a vast historic mansion with plenty of room to store her various collections."

She picked up a nutcracker that was about twenty inches tall with a thick hairy mustache and a bushy black beefeater hat. "Are they antiques?"

"Some of them are. I think a few of them are museum quality from the 1700s. But Winnie always says the beauty of her collection is that no one can tell the valuable pieces from those she bought at yard sales and thrift stores. I'm not sure even she knows."

The longer she was here, the more she found it charming. She could imagine some people could spend hours looking at each whimsical creation.

Winnie had talked about putting up Christmas trees in some of the bedrooms. There was an empty space next to the window that would be perfect, and some of the smaller nutcrackers would look charming as ornaments. She jotted a note down and then turned back to Ethan.

"I suppose you had better show me the rest."

His teeth gleamed with his smile. "Prepare yourself."

He led her to the room next door and flipped on the light. This time, Abby was prepared for the sight that greeted them—hundreds of angels, large and small. A few appeared to be suspended in air around the giant four-poster bed. When she looked closer, she saw they were hanging by clear fishing wire. Still more angels graced the top of several antique-looking tables around the room.

Even the paintings on the wall contained angels in various poses.

"When I was a kid, I never wanted to sleep in this room, even if Winnie would have let me. It creeped me out. I don't mean angels. I've got no problem with them, but one or two are enough for me, thanks. An entire flock is a little much for a ten-year-old boy."

"I can imagine," she said, though she had a hard time picturing him as a boy running through these halls.

She had a feeling one problem the Silver Belles would have with their plans for Christmas at Holiday House was the time element. People would want to linger in each room to examine all the treasures contained inside.

"She must have been collecting these things for years."

"Winnie likes to say that if she has the money and spends a good percentage already on charity, why can't she use some of it to buy things that bring her joy?"

"Good point."

"I can't argue. I mean, my father spends plenty on yachts and vacation homes in the Caribbean. Winnie spends maybe twenty dollars a Saturday at yard sales and thrift stores around the area."

The angels definitely made a statement. She was particularly drawn to three cherubs on top of a display case who looked down with varying expressions of interest.

"I don't have words," she said honestly.

He laughed. "Yeah. It's a lot to take in. And we're not done yet."

The next room contained a huge train that ran on a track around a multilevel Christmas village made up of houses, churches, ice-skating ponds. She made a note that she would definitely have to bring Christopher into this room, though she would have to supervise him closely.

The room after that was entirely ringed by shelves that contained at least a hundred Nativity scenes. The crèche room, Ethan had called it.

"These are actually mostly valuable," he explained. "All of Winnie's friends and extended family members know she collects Nativities. As long as I can remember, everyone sends them to her from their travels. My grandfather started it and my great-uncle Thomas and his husband carried on the tradition. I imagine Lucy alone has probably sent her at least a dozen from around the world."

"They're gorgeous, especially all clustered together in here."

"She has a few larger Nativities she likes to set up downstairs. I imagine she will direct you where they go."

"I could spend all day looking at them."

"When we were kids, Lucy and I always loved to look at the Nativities. Our favorite is the one in the coconut shell."

She liked this version of Ethan so much more than the somewhat autocratic, commanding man she had met the day before. She remembered his sweetness with Rodrigo and felt that tug of attraction again.

Back out in the hallway, she scribbled a few more notes down in her book.

"The other bedrooms on this level aren't as kitschy and won't take nearly as much time to go through. Winnie has left many of the original Victorian furnishings from the time the house was used as a summer home by William and Lucinda."

"What I've seen is remarkable. People will want to spend hours looking at everything she has. I wouldn't be surprised if they want to come back again and again."

"Don't think I haven't thought about that. My biggest concern is security. She's basically inviting people to come see what she has so they can come back and rob her."

"She might. But she has a security system, right?"

"When she remembers to use it."

Fear was a topic she had spent two years thinking about in great depth. Her inclination after Kevin died had been to hide away with Christopher where nothing bad could touch them, but she had decided she couldn't deprive her son of all the good and bad that came from embracing life.

"Appropriate caution is necessary in life. Only foolish people go blithely forward without thinking about potential consequences. But over the past few years, I've learned that fear can be paralyzing."

He studied her, his blue eyes searching. She suddenly wished she hadn't said anything. "Because of your husband's death?"

Of course he would know about Kevin. His sister was one of her closest friends. She would have been more surprised if he *hadn't* known.

"Yes. After he was killed, it would have been too easy to hide away in my apartment, but I didn't want that for

Christopher and I knew Kevin wouldn't have wanted it, either."

"Totally understandable. And admirable."

She swallowed, uneasy with the intensity of his expression. "Unless we want Winnie to send a search party after us, we should probably keep going."

"You're right. We have quite a few rooms to go, but the rest shouldn't take as long."

CHAPTER SIX

WALKING THROUGH THESE rarely used parts of the house always left Ethan feeling a little hollow. He wouldn't call it melancholy, exactly, merely a certain sadness that the house wasn't being used to its full potential.

He couldn't have said what purpose the house would better serve. A reception hall, perhaps, or maybe even a cozy bed-and-breakfast.

This time, seeing it through Abby's eyes seemed different. She had a genuine appreciation for every detail that he usually overlooked. She spent a great deal of time admiring the woodwork, especially the intricate carvings around the doors and windows. The tile work around the fireplace mantels in several of the bedrooms sent her into ecstasy. He thought she was going to cry when he took her to the bedroom on the third floor that contained a slipper tub right in the bedroom.

"This place is incredible," she said after they had briefly toured all the rooms on the second and third floors. "I could spend a lifetime wandering through it, and I would still find new and wonderful things to discover."

He had to smile at her enthusiasm. Abby Powell didn't seem to hold anything back. Her eyes were a bright green, glowing with light and life, her smile radiant.

He could have spent the remainder of the evening enjoying her company.

He did not want to be so drawn to her. What was the point? He certainly couldn't start anything with the woman. She was a sweet, vulnerable widow.

He remembered Brooke's last words to him. *Something is broken inside you. I hope you truly fall in love someday, but I'm not sure you're capable of it.*

Over the past year of self-reflection, he had come to admit the truth of her words. He had never loved a woman with the kind of fierce passion his grandparents had had for each other or that he had seen in other happy relationships. As Brooke had said, he wasn't sure he could—which meant soft women like Abby Powell were off-limits.

He would have to do his best to ignore this growing attraction to his grandmother's temporary nurse. He should probably try to avoid more situations where he was forced to spend extended time alone with her. That would be a good start.

He looked away from those bright green eyes to the period lighting that lined the hallway.

"Winifred has been a dedicated caretaker of the Lancaster family legacy, even though she married into it instead of being born into it."

"I can totally understand why she loves it so much. If this were my house I don't believe I would ever want to leave."

Guilt pinched at him and he sighed. "I understand how much Winnie loves Holiday House. This place represents so much more than only somewhere to live. It's history, it's family, it's our heritage. And in large part, I think it represents my grandfather, whom she loved with all her heart."

"That's sweet," Abby said softly.

"Winnie is part of this house and it's part of her now.

I understand that, believe me. Just as I accept that, eventually, Lucy and I will have to figure out what to do with the house when she's gone."

Winnie had been telling them for years that she was leaving Holiday House to the two of them, not to her own son, who would only sell it to the first buyer he could find with enough cash.

Ethan had no idea what he and Lucy were supposed to do with it after Winnie was gone. He didn't want to think about that day so he pushed the question out of his head, as he had been doing for years now.

"Now that you've seen the rest of the house, I'm sure you will agree it's too much for a woman approaching eighty years old to manage on her own."

Abby ran a finger along the polished wood chair rail along the wall. "Her current injuries aside, Winnie still seems pretty spry to me. She also told me she has a good cleaning service that keeps things dust-free."

"For now."

"As long as she is still capable of managing things, I guess I feel like she's the one who should decide what she's going to do with the house."

Her words echoed Lucy's—and Winnie's, for that matter. Apparently, he was the lone voice of reason.

"Winnie will stubbornly insist she's perfectly fine and handling things until she wears herself out. She's already broken her wrist. It's a miracle she didn't break a hip or her back when she fell. I worry that's what's next."

He knew how devastating a more serious injury would be for Winnie. Something else he didn't want to think about.

"I understand your concern. It's hard for someone her

age to come back from a major orthopedic injury like you're talking about. But why worry about something that hasn't happened yet and probably won't? That's another lesson I've learned over the past few years. Endless worry about tomorrow only steals joy from today."

Lovely *and* wise. An intoxicating combination.

Abby glanced at her watch. "We've been at this nearly an hour. I can't believe it's so late. I should probably go check on Christopher."

He suspected Christopher and Winnie were probably both sound asleep in the great room together.

"If you can give me a few more minutes, I have one last thing. I should probably show you where Winnie keeps all the Christmas decorations?"

"You mean there's even more than we've seen so far?"

The astonishment in her voice made him smile. "We've seen the highlights. I only meant ribbons, lights, ornaments, that kind of thing. But, yes, I understand that it's a lot to take in. Don't worry about the rest. You can explore on your own when you get the chance."

She hesitated. "We're here. I guess you should probably show me anything else you think I might need to know."

"This shouldn't take long."

He opened a door at the end of the hall to reveal another staircase.

"Yet another level?"

"The attic."

He flipped on the light and ascended the stairs toward the vast space that ran the length of the house. It was filled with trunks, cardboard boxes, ornament containers, wreaths and at least a dozen pre-lit artificial trees.

She gaped at the assorted items. "Oh, my."

"I agree. It's a lot to take in."

Abby looked back at the stairs behind him. "Surely she doesn't carry this all up and down by herself?"

"Well, I haven't showed it to you yet, but there's an elevator that goes to all the floors." He pointed to what looked like a large built-in closet in one corner. "My grandfather had it installed a few years before he died."

Some of her tension seemed to trickle away. "I can see where an elevator will be a lifesaver!"

"Winnie also never decorates alone. Seems like she always has a friend to help her. I've pitched in to fetch and carry where I can in previous years. If I'm not available—which seems to be the case usually of late—I will loan her a few workers from one of the hotels in town for an afternoon to carry things down. I usually ask the staff who would like to volunteer on their day off and then I pay their salaries. They also know Winnie will give them a big tip."

"That sounds like a brilliant solution. Too bad you've already said you're not going to help this year," she said pointedly.

"You're going to throw that back in my face?" he said.

She laughed. "You *did* say it."

"I suppose I could probably find one or two people to pinch-hit for an afternoon so you don't have to carry everything down by yourself. Even with an elevator, that's many trips up and down."

"You can work that out with Winnie, but it's probably not necessary. I told her I would do it."

He had to admire her willingness to jump in and help, even as he could see the prospect overwhelmed her. "You're still okay with all this? It's probably not too late to change your mind about helping her. She can find someone else."

"Are you kidding?" Her laugh sounded vaguely hysterical. "I've changed my mind back and forth a hundred times since the moment we walked into the nutcracker room. This job is entirely too much for me. I don't know how I let Winnie talk me into it. She needs a professional decorator, not a nurse who could barely decide where to hang pictures on the wall of my apartment."

"I'm sure you'll do fine."

"I have no idea what I'm doing," she said. "I'm not sure why I ever agreed to help her. For that matter, how did I let Lucy talk me into coming to Silver Bells in the first place?"

Her honesty was refreshing, even if he could hear the edge of panic to her words. "Few people can withstand my sister when she has her mind set on something."

"I know. Believe me. I can't tell you the number of times she dragged me off to some party or other when I had every intention of sitting down to study for my anatomy class."

He had a hard time picturing her as a young nursing student, rooming with his wild, wandering sister.

"Three guesses where Lucy learned her powers of persuasion."

"Winnie. Winnie. And Winnie."

"Exactly."

He could still see the edge of panic in her eyes and was driven to comfort her, for reasons he couldn't have explained.

"Don't worry. My grandmother will be there to help you every step of the way. If you can stick an IV needle into a wriggling, crying pediatric patient, you can certainly hang some Christmas lights on a tree."

She gave a shaky smile. "The two things are not at all analogous, but thank you for the vote of confidence."

He smiled and she gazed at his mouth, an odd, almost arrested expression on her features.

Ethan felt suddenly breathless. "Have you seen what you need to up here?"

"I… Yes. I think so. We had better go back down to Winnie and Chris."

"Elevator or stairs?"

"Stairs are fine. That way we can turn off lights as we go."

He nodded and led the way to the attic stairway. "Watch your step up here. There are a couple of tricky floorboards."

"If there's anything that could trip me, I'll definitely find it."

The words were no sooner out of her mouth than she stumbled on a small box that had fallen off a stack.

He wasn't aware of moving, but somehow he must have instinctively lunged to catch her. She gave a little gasp as she settled into his arms, soft and curvy and smelling like pumpkin pie spice.

He gazed down at her, struck again by the fierce urge to press his mouth to those freckles scattered across her nose. She looked up at him, eyes wide and that strange, intense expression on her lovely features again.

He couldn't seem to look away and he held her entirely too long. He should have simply set her back on her feet and released her, but he couldn't seem to make his muscles cooperate.

Color climbed her cheeks, as deliciously pink as the wild roses that grew around the house.

"I told you I was clumsy." She gave a small, embarrassed-sounding laugh. "Thank you for saving me from a hard conk on the head."

Was it his imagination or did she sound breathless, her voice huskier than it had been earlier?

He finally came to his senses enough to help her to her feet and release her. To his chagrin, he had to clear his voice before he trusted himself to speak.

"You're welcome. You can't be too careful up here."

"I'll keep that in mind when I come up again. Should we go back down?"

He didn't want to. He wanted to press her against the wall and kiss her until neither of them could think straight.

The impulse came out of nowhere, kicking him in the gut like a wild horse. What was *wrong* with him?

"Probably a good idea," he said instead, gesturing toward the stairs.

"I'll be more careful this time," she said with a self-conscious smile.

He then headed back down the stairs.

"So your Thanksgiving was nice?" Lucy gazed at her laptop, open on the tiny kitchen table of her apartment in the Old City of Chiang Mai. Winnie's face beamed out at her, lined and weathered and wonderful, her hair a cotton-candy-pink cloud around her face.

"Oh, it was wonderful," her grandmother answered softly. "Abby is such a treasure. She was a champion, pitching right in to throw together dinner at the last minute."

"I'm so glad. I knew she would be the perfect one to help you until I can get home to Silver Bells."

"Weren't we both lucky that she was available?"

"Definitely," Lucy replied. Beside Winnie, she could see Christopher snuggled on the sofa, a blanket pulled over him, his dark curly hair sticking out.

"We missed you, of course. How was your day?"

"It's not Thanksgiving here, so it was simply another school day, though I did try to explain the holiday to them. I'm not sure they quite grasped the concept of the Pilgrims and turkey and all."

"This has been a good job for you, hasn't it? You seem to love your students."

She did and she very much enjoyed Chiang Mai. While Bangkok was the capital of Thailand, Chiang Mai was the historic capital, filled with temples and flea markets, ancient architecture and warm, generous people.

She didn't want to tell Winnie yet that while she loved her students, she was beginning to feel a restless itch between her shoulder blades, as if something was missing.

"Where is Abby?" she said instead. "I see Christopher sleeping there but not his mother."

Winnie waved her unbroken hand in a vague gesture. "I asked Ethan to give her a tour of the house, since I am not able to get around well with this stupid ankle."

She hated seeing Winnie like this, unable to do all the things she would like.

Right now, her grandmother looked old and tired, without her natural exuberance. Lucy didn't want to admit it, even to herself.

Winnie frowned a little. "Come to think of it, they have been gone awhile. Maybe they found something more interesting to do than look at my nutcrackers."

That innocent expression of her grandmother's didn't fool Lucy for a moment. She narrowed her gaze. "Winifred Elizabeth Lancaster. What are you up to?"

"Who, me?"

"Don't get any ideas about Abby and Ethan," she warned.

"Would I do that?" Winnie's eyes twinkled.

"In a heartbeat."

Winnie looked around, as if to make sure the two people in question weren't close enough to overhear. "You have to admit, they would make a lovely couple. Your brother needs a little softness in his life. Someone like Abby would be perfect for him. Much better than that Brooke Fielding ever would have been."

Lucy could not disagree with that. She hadn't loved her brother's ex-fiancée. They had shared a friendly enough relationship and Brooke had been nice to Lucy. If Ethan had married her, Lucy would have tried hard to love Brooke like a sister. But Lucy had never been certain the other woman was right for Ethan. She had always had the vague impression that Brooke looked down on her for her eclectic fashion sense and for her career and life choices.

She had also noticed that whenever they were out in public, Brooke always looked around the restaurant or venue to see who might be looking and would become much more noticeably affectionate to Ethan if anyone paid them any attention.

That was probably petty of her, she admitted. She couldn't help it. Despite Ethan saying the breakup had been a mutual decision, Lucy strongly suspected otherwise.

None of that mattered now. Brooke was happily married and had a huge social media following with her athlete husband.

"Abby might not be available," Lucy warned. "Her heart was shattered when she lost Kevin. I don't know if she's ready to jump into something else. It's only been two years. Plus, geography is an issue. She's moving to Texas next month. Don't meddle, Grandma."

"I didn't meddle," Winnie protested. "I only asked them both to help me with something. Together. That's not meddling."

Her grandmother quickly changed the topic before Lucy could point out that was exactly what meddling meant.

"By the way, we had a particular friend of yours over for Thanksgiving. Sofia and Rodrigo were here, of course. I already told you they were coming. But then José joined us unexpectedly. It was so nice to see him. He looks good."

It was a very good thing Lucy wasn't prone to blushing, unlike Abigail, or she would be red as a beet right now.

Two weeks. She would see him in two weeks. She was so torn. She missed him terribly but had no idea if they could pick up any remnants of their friendship after what had happened that last night in Thailand.

"How nice."

"Rodrigo can't wait for you to come home. He told me to be sure you're home in time for the gingerbread competition."

"Of course. I wouldn't miss it," she said. "I love that guy."

She meant Rodrigo, of course. Who else?

"It's hard not to love him, isn't it?"

"He was the best prom date I could ever ask for. We had a great time that night."

After Rodrigo asked her to his senior prom, some of the girls at school had made fun of her. A few had even told her she should say no. Why would she want to go with someone from the special education classrooms to what many considered the most important dance of a girl's high school career?

Lucy refused and dropped those girls as friends. She

would never regret it. Rodrigo had been sweet and kind to her and so very excited to go to the dance with their peers.

"He has a new job at Lancaster Silver Bells. Did you know? He was excited to tell me all about it. He's been busing tables at the restaurant at the resort but is starting a new job working with the bell desk, delivering luggage to guests and working in bag storage."

"That's terrific. I bet he's wonderful at it. You can't have a bad day when you are around Rodrigo."

"That's what I always say. And he has a girlfriend. Another girl who goes to the same job-training program he does. Cindy. She's very sweet. He told me she lets him hold her hand."

"Oh, that makes my heart happy."

"Right? They're a sweet couple."

On the video call, Winnie's expression was suddenly nonchalant. "Sofia tells me he and Cindy double-dated with José and the woman he is dating."

Her insides seemed to freeze. "Wait. What? José is dating someone?"

Winnie shrugged. "It's not serious, from what I understand, but they have dated a few times and Sofia has high hopes. A mother can only dream. Just like a grandmother, right?"

He was dating? That was impossible! Just a few months ago he had claimed to be in love with *her*, and now he was dating someone else?

Okay, she had been pretty clear that they were looking for different things from a relationship and that she wouldn't change her mind.

But she had never expected him to start dating someone else the minute he returned to Silver Bells.

Her stomach felt twisted into knots, as if she had eaten something bad at the Chiang Mai night market.

"Is it...someone I know?"

"Oh, I doubt it," Winnie said blithely. "Quinn Bellamy has only been in town six months or so. She works in public relations for Lancaster corporate and she's very pretty. And nice, too. Originally, I was thinking she might be good for Ethan, but I guess José made a move first."

"Did he?"

Her stomach again twisted. Maybe she *did* eat something that didn't agree with her.

She certainly wasn't jealous. That would imply she had feelings for him, which was impossible.

"No matter," Winnie said cheerfully. "I think Abby makes a much better fit for your brother than Quinn ever would."

She pressed a hand to her stomach, trying to force her attention back to the present instead of that last night between them when José had kissed her with such aching tenderness.

Obviously, he hadn't been in love with her. She had been right to push him away. Look how quickly he turned to another woman.

"You know I adore you, Winnie, but I have to strongly advise you not to get any ideas about Abby and Ethan. Seriously. Just don't. She was devastated after her husband was killed. The last thing she needs right now as she's about to start a new life is to be tangled up with something that will only lead to heartbreak."

"Who's to say your brother will break her heart?" Winnie countered. "Maybe he'll find she's the perfect woman for him. And vice versa."

She adored Abby and couldn't think of another woman who would be better for her brother. But she also knew Ethan. He was raised amid the same chaos she was. They shared many of the same scars.

She considered it proof that he had never had a relationship that lasted longer than a few months, except for Brooke.

"Leave it alone, Winnie. Please. Abby is doing us both a huge favor by coming out to help you. I would hate to repay her by setting her up for a broken heart. That would make me a lousy friend."

"What would make you a lousy friend? Hi, Lucy."

She and Winnie both gasped when Abby walked into the room, followed closely by Ethan. How much had they overheard?

"I was saying it would make me a lousy friend if I brought home *malong tod*, which is fried insects, for the annual Silver Belles white elephant exchange," she improvised promptly.

"Please don't."

"Hi, sis. Happy Thanksgiving." Ethan leaned over Winnie so that he could be in the frame. As Lucy saw him and Abby together, she wondered if Winnie might be onto something.

She wasn't sure how she sensed it across thousands of miles, but there was a certain vibe between them.

Was it possible? While she would love the idea of her best friend and her brother being together, she just couldn't get over her fear that Abby would end up shattered if things went wrong.

Oh, she hoped Winnie didn't cause trouble for Abby.

"How did you like the house?" she asked.

"It's an amazing building," Abby said. "With about eight thousand rooms that need to be decorated."

Lucy winced, not missing the pointed look Abby sent her. She should have expected her grandmother would enlist Abby's help, but Winnie's accident had made her forget all about the upcoming house tours.

"Oh, my."

"And you know how talented I am at decorating. I mean, my dorm room at ASU was fabulous, right?"

Lucy had to laugh. "By the time we left school and you married Kevin, you had a few more skills, didn't you? I dragged you to enough flea markets and thrift shops. Some of my genius must have rubbed off."

Before Abby could answer, Christopher awoke, probably disturbed by the new voices.

"Hi, Mommy," he said sleepily. Lucy watched as Abby became the consummate mother, hugging her son and smoothing down his hair.

The picture wasn't completely clear because of the crappy internet in her apartment, but she thought she saw Ethan watching the two of them with an odd look.

They talked about inconsequential things for a few more moments, until she saw Winnie yawn.

"I should go so you can rest. I'm glad you had a good day."

"Goodbye, sweetheart. See you soon," Winnie said.

As soon as Lucy ended the call and closed her laptop, she stared at the walls of her apartment—nicely decorated, she had to admit.

He was dating someone.

Only a few months after telling her he loved her, José had decided she meant what she said and was moving on.

Some of her excitement in returning home had dissipated like dew on the grass under the morning sun.

She wasn't even sure she wanted to go home now, if she would have to face José dating some faceless woman. What kind of name was *Quinn* anyway?

She started to flip open her laptop to search for the woman online but made herself close it again. It wasn't any of her business. She had made her position clear and couldn't blame José for believing her and moving on.

This only proved her own philosophy. Love wasn't real. It was a construct that turned otherwise rational people into something she never wanted to become.

CHAPTER SEVEN

IF ABBY THOUGHT coming to Silver Bells would be a nice, relaxing holiday break, she was destined for a rude awakening.

Over the next week and a half, she worked harder than she remembered in her life, even during the tough years when she first started as a nurse, when she was working fifty hours a week to support herself and Kevin, who had been deep into medical school.

That time in her life had been tough, yes, but she wouldn't have traded it for anything. She and Kevin had been focused on the same goal, excited about their future. She believed their marriage had been stronger because of the hardships they had faced together.

"What's next?"

Abby pushed away the echo of loss and forced a smile for Mariah Raymond, who had brought her son, Dakota, over to play with Christopher. The two boys were happily laying out a wooden train set Winnie had found in a closet, one she told them cheerfully she had bought for Ethan when he was the boys' age.

Abby stepped back to look at the vintage-ski-lodge-themed Christmas tree she and Mariah were working on in one of the second-floor bedrooms.

"That looks great to me. I don't know what I would have done without you and the other Silver Belles. Honestly.

Every time I think we can't possibly get this place ready, someone else shows up to help."

The women—and a few men—in Winnie's circle had rallied around the project. Abby strongly suspected that her help wasn't really necessary. If she hadn't been there to coordinate things, Winnie still would have been fine. Sofia Navarro likely would have taken charge and organized teams to take care of every item on Winnie's to-do list.

Since Thanksgiving, Abby and the other Silver Belles had put up and decorated more than a dozen Christmas trees in the various rooms of the house. This one was almost the last.

The Silver Belles had picked specific decorations for each tree. After talking it over, Winnie had decided to do an underlying theme of Christmas Through the Years for the house tours. The music and the tours themselves would focus on the different ways the holidays had been celebrated at the house throughout its existence, from frontier days to now.

Of the trees they had decorated, one of her favorites was done in 1950s style, with old 45 records as ornaments and a huge pink-and-black poodle skirt around the base of the tree. Another was an old-fashioned cowboy tree, decorated with gingham ribbon, strings of popcorn and homespun ornaments.

Of course, the angel room had an angel-themed tree, and the nutcracker tree would definitely be another crowd-pleaser.

This was the last tree she had to decorate, except for the giant twenty-foot-tall tree in the great room.

She was going to have to find someone else to help her

with that one, but she knew Mariah had to leave for work shortly.

"You've been wonderful," she said now to the woman she considered a good friend after the past several days. "Thank you for your help."

"I only wish I could come more often. My work schedule right now is killer. I'm working so much overtime. I hope things relax a little when we actually do the tours on Friday."

"Who watches Dakota for you?"

"He goes to a good preschool three days a week while I work the day retail job, and then his dad usually takes him on the weekends so I can do my bartending gig."

"When do you find time to paint?" Winnie spoke up from her easy chair where she had alternated between offering them advice and doing sudoku puzzles.

"I try to paint after he goes to bed or sometimes early in the morning." Mariah shrugged. "When you're an artist, you find time whenever you can to create."

What a struggle that must be, trying to juggle her creative endeavors around the jobs that put food in her son's mouth.

Abby was deeply grateful that of all her worries, money really wasn't one. As a nurse, she earned a decent wage and Kevin had held a healthy life-insurance policy. Added to that, the hospital had paid her a settlement after his death, which she had tucked away for Christopher's college expenses.

She wasn't Lancaster-family wealthy, but she had enough for her needs and a little extra.

"I would love to see some of your art," she said. "Where are you showing it?"

She didn't have anywhere to hang art right now, but that would change once she and Christopher were settled in Austin.

"The Silver Rose gallery in town. It's off of Center Street downtown. I've had a show there for about a month now."

"I'll take a look."

"Well, I hope you like it."

"She will," Winnie piped up confidently. Did the woman know her that well already, or was she merely that certain of the artwork's appeal?

"What about you? Do you paint or sculpt or do anything creative like that when you're not saving lives at the hospital?"

Since she had come to Colorado, she was increasingly determined to pick up a few more hobbies once she settled in Texas.

"I'm afraid not. I recently started knitting, but I'm not very good at it," she said.

"Do you sing? We can always use more strong voices in the Belles."

"Not me," she said quickly. "Sorry. Winnie has already tried to recruit me. I love music but much the same way I love art. I can't draw or paint but can still appreciate beautiful art without actually creating it."

"What about skiing, cross-country or otherwise?" Winnie asked.

The very idea terrified her. She really needed to get over her fear of heights.

"I'm afraid not. I've spent my entire life in warmer climates where snow is rare. It makes it a little tough to become an expert at winter sports."

"Well, that's not an issue here. We have plenty of snow," Mariah said. "You should take advantage of it while you're here to learn. Skiing is really fun."

If she was so afraid of climbing the ladder to put the ornaments on a twenty-foot tree, how could she have the courage to strap little sticks to her feet and zoom down an icy mountainside?

"That might be another one of the skills I leave to others. Like singing and artwork."

"You never know what you're going to love unless you try things," Mariah said. "That's what I tell Dakota. You can't say you aren't good at something until you have at least given it a chance."

"Good advice," Winnie said.

It was, Abby had to admit. That still didn't make her want to rush out and buy a lift pass.

"I'm actually pretty proud of myself for following my own advice this year. A guy I was dating wanted to take me canyoneering and I was scared to death."

"What's canyoneering?" Winnie asked.

"It's kind of like rock climbing except you're going the opposite direction, down a rock or canyon."

It sounded like the stuff of Abby's nightmares, but she didn't want to interrupt Mariah's point by saying so.

"My point is, I was afraid to do it, but after this guy took me out one day, I fell in love with the sport. The guy and I didn't click, but that's another story. The point is, I tried something new, I loved it and now I have a new hobby. I can't wait until the snow melts so I can go again."

"No, thank you. I'll leave that kind of thing to you younger girls," Winnie said. "But I would agree that you should at least let Christopher try skiing. If you introduce children when they're young to a lifetime sport like skiing, they pick it up more easily and are more likely to continue it on when they're older."

"I couldn't agree more," Mariah said.

"That's the whole reason we're doing Christmas at Holiday House," Winnie said. "So that everyone can have the opportunity to enjoy our beautiful surroundings and the recreational opportunities here."

"My brother uses a wheelchair after he lost the use of his legs in a motorcycle accident and I know he misses skiing," Mariah said. "I can't wait for him to have the chance to do it again."

Her heavily lashed eyes went soft when she spoke of her brother, which Abby found touching. Mariah might put out a hard front to the world, but in only a short time Abby had discovered the woman had a sensitive center. It made her even more interested in seeing her artwork.

"Your brother lives close?"

Mariah nodded. "He built a house up the canyon and works remotely in computers, developing programs for some company in Silicon Valley. He doesn't get out nearly as often as he should. I'm hoping the new accessible ski program will change that."

It was a good reminder about why they were going to all this trouble. The work might be hard and exhausting and completely out of her element, but it helped to remember they were working toward a good cause.

"THAT WAS A really fun day," Christopher said that night after he had bathed and they were cuddled into a comfortable chair by the fireplace in the sitting room attached to the bedroom they were sharing.

"I'm glad you had fun. Dakota seems like a nice kid."

"I asked him if he could play again later this week but he said he's going to his dad's house." Christopher looked troubled. "Why don't his mom and dad live together?"

She brushed his curly dark hair away from his olive features, this sweet-natured son who was the perfect cross between her and Kevin and who seemed like a miracle to her every single day. "We've talked about this before, remember? Families come in lots of different shapes and sizes. Sometimes kids have a mom and dad who live together, sometimes they live with only their moms or only their dads. Sometimes they have two dads or two moms. Sometimes they trade off between them. And sometimes, like I did, they live with their mom and their great-aunt. As long as they have someone to love them—someone who loves them and takes care of them and keeps them safe— that's the most important thing."

"And in our family, we have a mom and a boy."

"That's right. Aren't we lucky to have each other?"

He hugged her, and Abby cuddled him close while she read him a tender, charming story about a mouse trying to find his way home on Christmas Eve.

Her childhood hadn't been perfect, she thought as she tucked him into his bed. Her mother had been ill so often and Aunt Elizabeth hadn't always had the strength to keep up with an active child.

But she had always known she was loved.

"I miss Daddy," Christopher said as she was kissing him good-night. "I wish he was still here."

The words came out of nowhere, just about knocking her to her knees.

She gave Christopher an extra hug. "We know he's here in our hearts. But you're right. I miss him, too, honey."

Christopher eased away, already moving on to something else. "So when can Dakota come and play?"

"I don't know. I'll have to talk to his mom about their schedule, but I promise we'll set something up another day before we leave for Austin."

"Do we have to go to Texas? I like it here."

Where had *that* come from? "I think you'll like it there, too. We already have an apartment, remember? And it has that fun park next door with the splash pad and the pickleball courts."

"Oh, yeah. That was fun when we went there." He cuddled Mr. Jingles for a moment longer before Abby lifted the cat and set him on the floor. "Will I find friends there?"

She didn't want to tell her son she had been wondering the same thing about herself.

"I guarantee it. Who wouldn't want to be friends with a great kid like you?"

He smiled sleepily at that and hugged her. "I love you, Mommy."

"Love you, too, sweetheart." She kissed the top of his head one last time and then turned off the light in the bedroom, ushered out the cat and grabbed the baby monitor she still used to keep an eye on things when she was working in another area of this vast house.

When she walked into the kitchen, she was shocked to find Winnie there wearing a fuzzy pink robe over the nightgown Abby had helped the woman change into an hour ago. Abby thought when she settled her into her bed with a bowl of popcorn and the remote that Winnie would be out for the night.

"What's going on? Did you need a snack? You should have called or texted me. I could have brought it to you so you didn't have to miss your program."

Winnie shook her head. "Ethan texted me a few minutes ago asking if he could drop by to check on me. I recorded my show. I'll watch it later."

Why did he have to come visit Winnie so late, after his grandmother was already tucked in for the night? She frowned, annoyed for a moment before she realized that wasn't fair. Ethan called and texted frequently to check on his grandmother, but Abby knew he had been out of town dealing with a crisis at another of the Lancaster properties.

She hadn't seen him since Thanksgiving, since that moment when she had been almost certain he wanted to kiss her.

She had to have imagined that look she thought she had seen in his eyes up in the attic. He wasn't interested in her and she *certainly* wasn't interested in him.

Still, butterflies jumped around in her stomach when she realized he would be there shortly.

Oh, she was ridiculous.

"What are *you* doing out here?" Winnie asked in return. "After the busy day you had, I should have thought you would be sound asleep by now, dreaming about tinsel and popcorn strings."

Abby held up her water bottle before refilling it from the filtered pitcher in the refrigerator. "That big tree out there in the great room is haunting me. My Moby Dick. I keep thinking that with a few hours of hard work, I can finish decorating it and get that very large monkey off my back."

Winnie winced, her wrinkled features twisted with

guilt. "I'm so sorry, my dear. I never meant for you to work yourself to the bone. You have already done so much."

Abby shook her head. "You have nothing to apologize for. I haven't minded any of it, especially meeting your friends. I've enjoyed having a project. You know I like staying busy, and I've had great fun decorating your house for the holidays."

Winnie reached a hand out and Abby squeezed her age-spotted fingers.

"You have been amazing. I don't know what we would have done without you."

"You know it's been a team effort. All of the Silver Belles have pitched in."

"But you have done the lion's share. And you're not even part of the choir! After this, we will have to make you an unofficial member."

"Official or unofficial, I still can't sing."

Winnie made a dismissive gesture. "Do you want to know a secret? Half the people in the group can't carry a tune in a bucket. Somehow we make up for it. I've always said that in our case, enthusiasm trumps talent any day."

Abby wasn't entirely sure she bought that, but then she had never actually heard the Silver Belles.

"I can't believe we only have three days before the official first night of the tours," Winnie went on. "I can't tell if I'm more excited or more nervous."

Abby knew her emotions definitely fell in the nervous category. She had never done anything like this and likely never would again.

It had been an experience she wouldn't trade, though. Before she could tell Winnie that, she heard the front door open, obviously by someone familiar with the code since she knew she had locked it.

A moment later, Ethan poked his head in.

"Hi. I followed the light and found you both here."

Abby felt momentarily stupid. How had she forgotten how good-looking he was, with that dark windswept hair and his deep blue eyes?

"Hi," she managed, in what she hoped wasn't a squeak.

"Hello, darling," Winnie said, lifting her face for Ethan's kiss on the cheek.

"I'm sorry again to drop in so late. I've been in San Francisco until this afternoon. We managed the crisis and all is fine."

"Oh, good," Winnie said. "Regardless, you know I'm always glad to see you, day or night."

"You are looking good. How are you feeling tonight?"

"Good. I haven't needed the dumb walker all day. The ribs still hurt and having the wrist in a cast is a pain in the patootie, but I'm trying not to let it stop me."

"No doubt."

Ethan shifted his attention to Abby. "I see you've survived being Winnie's lackey."

"Oh, hush," his grandmother said. "Abby is marvelous. She has made amazing progress since Thanksgiving. The house looks more beautiful than I've ever seen it. You should have her give you a tour while you're here."

For an instant, he looked alarmed at the suggestion and she wondered if he was remembering the last time they had walked through the house together, when Ethan had almost kissed her on the attic stairs.

She could feel herself blush and hoped he and Winnie

didn't notice. Escape was probably her wisest course of action in this situation.

She cleared her throat. "I'll leave you two to visit. I have, um, things to do." She gestured vaguely toward the open doorway of the kitchen.

"Ethan can help you," Winnie said suddenly.

She froze in the act of scraping back her chair. "That's totally not necessary. I've got everything under control."

"Don't be silly," Winnie admonished. "I know how nervous you've been about climbing up the ladder, with your fear of heights. You've been putting it off all week. Ethan is the perfect person to help. He's tall, for one thing. Also, unlike you, he doesn't suffer from acrophobia. He could help you decorate the higher branches of the tree while you do the lower. That way you wouldn't have to climb the ladder at all."

"He came to visit with you, not to decorate that beastly tree."

"He came to check on me, which he did," Winnie corrected. "I'm fine, as you can clearly see."

"Oh, yes. I can see clearly all right," Ethan said, his tone dry.

What did he mean by that? Abby wondered.

Winnie gave a yawn that looked obviously fake. "The truth is, I'm beat. I thought I could stay up a little later to visit with you, but I can hardly keep my eyes open. I'm so sorry. I think the best thing for me would be to trot back to my bedroom and let you young people burn the midnight oil without me. You don't mind helping, do you, darling?"

"Ethan has been traveling," Abby said a little desperately. "I'm sure decorating a Christmas tree is the last thing he wants to do right now."

He looked at her and then back at his grandmother. "I don't mind at all," he said. "It shouldn't take us long."

Even five minutes in his company was too long right now when she had the beginnings of a completely ludicrous crush on the man.

"Shall I help you back to bed?" Abby asked Winnie.

"Oh, no. I'm fine. I'm ready, I only have to take off this robe. Look how smart I am. I didn't bother to tie it, so I wouldn't have to struggle to untie it with one hand."

"You're a genius," Ethan said in that same dry tone that only made his grandmother laugh.

"Don't I know it. Now go take care of your Christmas tree. Ethan, darling, I'll see you later."

She hurried out of the room, leaving the two of them alone for the first time since Thanksgiving.

Abby fought down her butterflies and wrangled them into a corner. "You really don't have to stay. She'll never know if you drive away and escape into the night."

"If you're naive enough to believe that, you obviously don't know my grandmother. She knows everything."

Did Winnie guess that Abby was attracted to her grandson? Oh, she hoped not. She had tried not to let any reaction show whenever his name was mentioned. Maybe she hadn't been as good at concealment as she had hoped.

"You made it clear you don't want to help with anything to do with Christmas at Holiday House. I'm sure Winnie would understand if you went home. You've no doubt had a busy day of work and travel."

He frowned. "If I leave now, you would have to decorate the entire tree alone. I gather a ladder is involved. And also that you don't like heights."

"Both things are true. But I will manage."

"Have you always been afraid of heights?"

"No," she admitted. "They never used to bother me until about a few years ago when I treated a teenage girl who was helping her dad hang Christmas lights. She fell off the roof and broke her spine, leaving her paralyzed. For some reason, that triggered something in me. I was her nurse for three weeks and came to really care about her. She had been a dancer, on track to become a professional, and in a second everything changed. Now, every time I climb a ladder or stand on an overlook, I see Sami's face and start to panic."

Sympathy flitted across his features. "Oh, no. I'm sorry. That must be tough."

"I have to get over it. I know I never will if I don't face my fear."

"You don't have to face all your fears tonight, you know," Ethan said softly. "I want to help."

She couldn't figure out a way to refuse. It was his family home, after all.

"All right," she finally said. "If we hurry, it shouldn't take long."

She only hoped she could keep it together that long and not do something insanely stupid like give in to her attraction for the man.

CHAPTER EIGHT

WHEN HE WALKED into the great room of Holiday House, Ethan gained a small idea of how much work Abby and the other Silver Belles had been busy doing around the house.

The intricately carved mantel was festooned with fresh evergreen branches, ribbons and glossy red ornaments. Fairy lights twinkled among the green.

A garland of evergreen boughs and more ribbons twisted up the stairs.

A fire glowed in the fireplace, which Winnie had converted a few years earlier to the cleaner-burning gas. This time of year, he missed the snap and pop of a real fire, but this one was much more practical, without the mess and inconvenience of hauling logs and trying to keep it lit.

A huge tree stood in the corner, bare of ornaments. No wonder Abby hadn't finished that one, he thought. The job looked like it would take days.

Even without the tree decorations, the room looked festive and cheerful.

Ethan always associated good memories with Holiday House at Christmastime, probably because those holidays spent away from his grandparents were usually tense and contentious.

He didn't have many great memories of the season as his parents were usually at their most punitive and vitriolic as they fought over visitation during the holidays.

If his dad had custody that year, his mother would plan a special vacation anyway, then complain when Rick wouldn't let Ethan and Lucy go. When they did spend the holidays with their father, it was usually in the company of Rick's latest girlfriend or the occasional wife, who weren't always thrilled about having to enjoy Christmas with two children who wanted to be somewhere else.

He remembered two good Christmases from his youth, both of them spent here with Winnie when his parents couldn't agree on the custody arrangements that year.

Those were the years that taught him Christmas could be about joy and love, a time of peace, reflection, hope.

He found it funny that just standing in the great room right now could bring back many of those same feelings. The tension of travel inconveniences and long meetings seemed to melt away from his shoulders. He wanted to close his eyes and breathe into the peace.

"It looks great in here. Where did you find so much greenery?"

He knew he shouldn't be so fascinated by the way her eyes lit up, sparkling like the fairy lights. "The pine trees outside. Christopher and I had loads of fun wandering the grounds and clipping a branch here and there where they wouldn't be noticed."

"Winnie has plenty of trees. I'm sure you probably can't even tell anything is missing."

"That was the idea. I promise, we didn't want any glaring bald spots on the trees. She had some fake wired garlands she's used in the past but they had seen better days, with bald patches and needles falling out. We decided a special year at Holiday House required actual greenery."

"I saw a few lights on the porch when I drove up. Are you decorating the grounds at all?"

"Winnie already had a plan for the outside. She hired a local garden company to take care of that part. They're supposed to be here all day tomorrow with a crew, and then they'll take it all down again after the holidays. And, yes, I agree that's cutting it too close since the event is in three days. But they were overbooked. They couldn't get here any earlier."

"I'm sure it will be fine."

"I wish I had your confidence," she said. "It's going to seem so strange if we don't have anything more out there than a wreath on the front door."

"The house is the real draw. You can put a simple candle in every window and let the lines of the house shine through."

Her eyes widened. "You're absolutely right. Christmas at Holiday House is about the house and the simple beauty of the season, isn't it? We don't need lasers or synchronized light shows. Thank you for the reminder."

"You're welcome." He wanted to glow under her praise and had to yank himself back to the issue at hand.

"Now. What are we up against here?"

She seemed to collect herself and headed toward the tree and the ladder propped against the wall.

"Winnie wants to use the same ornaments and garland on this tree she's used for the past few years. That's what's in all these boxes. As she suggested, if you want to handle the higher branches, I can work down here."

Ethan had a better idea. He wanted to wrap his arms around Abby, tug her down to the rug in front of the fire and spend the night kissing her while the fire flickered and the tree lights sparkled.

Instead, he rolled up his sleeves, literally, grateful he had changed out of his work suit into something more casual, jeans and an oxford.

"Sounds like a plan."

"We should probably start with the star and then the garland."

While he set up the ladder, she dug through boxes until she found a huge gold foil star he remembered always being on the top of this big tree. She handed him that and also a spool of wide, sparkly gold ribbon.

"Are you sure you can climb the ladder with both of those? If not, start with the star and then come back for the garland."

"I can carry them both." He tucked the garland spool under his arm and gripped the star, then began to ascend the ladder.

"Be careful," she said a little breathlessly. Was she worried for him or for the fragile star?

"The star has a clip that should attach it to the top branch, right there on the back."

While she watched, he fastened it, adjusting it until it appeared right to him.

"Is that straight?"

She stood away from the tree a little and tilted her head. "Perfect. Good job."

He had only placed a star on a Christmas tree, he hadn't ascended Mount Everest. Still, he felt a ridiculous sense of accomplishment.

"I think we need a little Christmas music, don't you?"

She looked surprised but ordered Winnie's smart speakers that he had set up for her a few years earlier to play a holiday jazz station, and soon a soft, mellow version of "Silent Night" played through the room, adding to the festive mood.

"Okay, what's next? I have no idea how to hang a garland."

She looked up at him with an astonished look. "Have you never decorated a Christmas tree before?"

He scanned his memory banks but came up empty. "I can't say I have. Sorry."

"Ever?"

"That's not precisely true. I've hung a few ornaments on this one when Winnie persuaded me to help her, but I've never done the setup from the beginning, at least as far as I can remember. I might have helped Winnie once or twice when I was a kid and Lucy and I were staying here, but if I did, I don't remember."

"What about with your parents when you were growing up?"

"My parents always had housekeeping staff to take care of the holiday decorations. After I left for school and my career, I've never bothered with a tree."

"All you do for a garland is start at the star and wind it around. Yes. Just like that. Maybe not so tightly. Perfect. Just keep going like that until it gets low enough that I can reach."

He moved lower on the ladder as the garland twisted lower. The lower he went, the wider the tree and the more difficult it became for him to reach the spool as he unrolled it on the far side of the tree, but he managed with some creative tosses and even more skillful catches.

"Why didn't you ever want your own tree?" Abby asked

from below as she waited for him to work his way down the tree.

"Since I've been back in Silver Bells, I'm usually working during the holidays. Also, I never really felt the need. The Lancaster corporate offices are connected to our main hotel in town, the Lancaster Silver Bells, and it's always lavishly decorated for the holidays. My own condo is just next door to the corporate offices in another building we own, which the staff decorates well. And when I'm not at work or at my condo, I am often here with Winnie and can simply enjoy her decorations. It doesn't make sense to put up my own."

"I get it. Plenty of people don't have Christmas trees. If I didn't have Christopher, I probably wouldn't have bothered to put up a tree last year."

She gave a little laugh. "It's ironic, isn't it? I didn't want to go to all the bother of putting up a Christmas tree in my apartment since we are moving right after the holidays. Yet here I am. Since I've been here, I think I have decorated at least a dozen Christmas trees now. I consider myself something of an expert."

He zeroed in on her earlier words as he took another step down on the ladder with the garland. "So why didn't you want to put up a tree in Phoenix?"

She busied herself with fluffing ribbons he assumed would go on the tree when he was done. "It may seem hard to believe right now, considering I've been doing nothing but decorating for a week, but I'm not a big fan of Christmas. It's so much stress and angst, you know? Especially when you don't have the perfect family situation."

"Few people do, right?" He had so many ex-stepparents and stepsiblings, he wasn't sure he could remember all their names.

"I was just talking about that with Christopher tonight. What does *traditional family* even mean anymore?"

"A valid question."

"I had a very loving family, just a little nontraditional, I guess." She hesitated, met his gaze and then looked away. "My mom was a former drug addict who had lingering health issues throughout my life. HIV, hepatitis. A whole messy chart. She died when I was twelve, but I was fortunate enough to have a great-aunt who raised me after that."

"That's good." He found it an interesting coincidence that they both had been so impacted by older female relatives.

"Yes. Except she was diagnosed with cancer when I was fifteen, unfortunately. Colon. By the time they found it, it had spread everywhere. She died when I was seventeen."

Oh, no. So then she had no one. Poor Abby. He slowly wound the garland down until he was almost to floor level. "Did you go into foster care?"

She shook her head. "I became an emancipated adult at that point for my final year of high school. My mom and Aunt Elizabeth had left me a little money. Not a huge amount but enough to cover my rent and tuition to nursing school."

"That took grit," he said, unable to keep the admiration out of his voice.

He could see color rise on her cheeks. "You do what you have to do. I met my husband halfway through nursing school in Alabama and moved out to Phoenix to be closer to him while he was in medical school. That's where I met Lucy."

"So you always knew you wanted to be a nurse?"

She laughed. "Oh, no. I never wanted to be a nurse. I wanted to be a ballerina. Unfortunately, I have ankle problems, so that wasn't in the cards for me."

"A ballerina. Wow! Were you good?"

"To my preadolescent brain, I was brilliant. To everyone else, probably not."

Her wry self-reflection made him smile. He was fiercely drawn to her, even though he knew it wasn't smart.

"I was good at caring for sick people. Between my mother and my aunt, I had plenty of experience. Somewhere in there, I realized I found much more satisfaction in helping other people than anything else I had done. It made sense to pursue a career in it."

He knew many people who would have whined and complained about the cards they had been dealt if they had been in Abby's situation, orphaned, alone. Instead, she had turned her pain outward to help others.

He twisted the garland around a branch and fluffed it out a little.

"That's perfect. You're very good at this."

He made a face. "Please don't say that too loudly. I don't want Winnie to commandeer me into helping her next year."

"Your secret is safe with me," she said with a smile.

He gazed down at her, feeling an odd tug in his chest he didn't recognize.

She was the first to look away. "Okay. I can reach the garland from here and do the lower branches."

He bent down to hand her the spool of ribbon. As she reached up to take it from him, the alluring scent of her swirled around him, mingling with the evergreen garlands in the room: vanilla, almond, cinnamon. Luscious.

He wanted to kiss her. Ethan closed his eyes and willed away the urge.

"What about you?" she asked as she moved away. "Why don't you like the holidays?"

"Who says I don't like the holidays? I'm here decorating for holiday-palooza, aren't I?"

"Only because your grandmother conned you into it."

He laughed. "You've been here for more than a week and probably know how good Winnie is at convincing people to do what she wants. I seem to be overly susceptible."

Her smile lit up the room. "Only because you love her so much," she said softly.

His hands were actually shaking from fighting the urge to pull her into his arms. That had never happened before. Ever.

He cleared his throat. "Okay. My part of the garland is done. What's next?"

"Ornaments. Hundreds of them. Let's start by putting the giant balls on, which take up a lot of real estate on the tree. We can fill in the holes with all the other ornaments after that."

"Fine. Point me to the giant balls."

He couldn't say that without discovering a twelve-year-old boy still lived inside him who found that sentence hilarious.

She pointed him to several large boxes. "Take one box up and then I can hand you more as you need them. We need to space them out as much as possible so we have enough for the whole tree."

Fortunately, the giant balls were light and he was able

to carry two boxes in one hand as he ascended the ladder again. He set one on the top of the ladder and held the other box while he hung the huge glossy red and gold baubles on the tree.

There was an odd sense of satisfaction in the work, he thought after hanging the balls and then going down the ladder for more ornaments.

He would never have expected it. Maybe this was why people enjoyed decorating the house so much for the holidays, this sense of adding something new, something beautiful. The Christmas music and the flickering firelight contributed to his mood as did the lovely woman working below him.

"I am not disliking this is much as I expected I would," he said.

Abby gave him a startled look.

"Don't get me wrong. I would still probably rather be plucking out my eyebrows, but the result is nice."

"It looks good, doesn't it? I'm glad I didn't have to pick the decorations out, I only had to put them up."

He wanted to ask her a hundred questions. Why were she and Christopher starting over in a new town where they knew no one? How was she handling the death of her husband, two years after? How did she continue to be so cheerful after she had endured a string of terrible losses?

Ethan didn't want to ruin the moment by bringing darkness into it. He was enjoying himself too much.

He even found himself humming along to some of the familiar songs.

He could only hope his grandmother didn't wander out to find them or she would probably fall again, in shock this time to find him showing a little holiday spirit.

ABBY HAD SPENT more than a week decorating Holiday House for the season. She had strung countless ornaments on countless boughs, twisted together pine branches, tied ribbons, created ornaments.

She should be tired of it by now, but something about this huge tree in Winnie's great room was different. Or perhaps her enjoyment of the moment had more to do with her companion. She found a soft, bewitching sort of peace in Ethan's company, which she found both unexpected and odd.

Something seemed to have changed between them and she wasn't quite sure what.

He wasn't enthusiastic about his grandmother's plans to open her house to strangers. Ethan had made his position abundantly clear. Yet he was still willing to step up and help Abby decorate the big tree, simply because she was too afraid of heights to tackle the job on her own.

"Your son is sleeping, I would guess."

"Yes. He put in a big play day with Dakota Raymond. I'm keeping track of him with the baby monitor."

"Smart."

"It's not really necessary. He turned five last month and is old enough to know how to come looking for me if he wakes up, but I'm a bit of an overprotective mother, I guess."

"Not overprotective at all. No need to traumatize the kid by having him wake up and not know where his mom is."

She gave him a sharp look, unable to help it. He didn't look at her, though she couldn't tell whether he was avoiding her gaze or simply busy hanging ornaments.

She knew enough about his childhood to know there was something autobiographical in that statement. Lucy hadn't wanted to talk much about her life growing up, but she had said enough that Abby understood their complicated history.

Lucy had processed that pain by frequently saying she wasn't interested in the complications of romantic love. Had Ethan taken the same attitude? No. He had been engaged, she remembered, but it hadn't worked out.

She wanted to ask him about it but sensed Ethan wouldn't welcome her curiosity.

"I think that's everything," she said after she hung the last ornament from the final box, except for a few broken bulbs that hadn't survived the year.

"I'm out here, too." He held up an empty box.

"I think that means we're done."

"Well? What do you think?"

She stepped away to take a better look at the entire massive Christmas tree, which had been pretty enough with only the white lights. Now, with the star and garland and the ornaments, it quite literally took her breath away.

"Oh, Ethan," she exclaimed softly. "It's beautiful."

He climbed down the ladder. "Any bare spots?"

"Not that I can tell. You did a wonderful job. Almost like a pro."

"Turn the main lights down so I can see the full effect, would you?"

She crossed to the wall and flipped off the main chandelier in the room so that only the tree and a lamp in one corner illuminated them. The lights on the tree reflected off the shiny ornaments, magnifying their glow.

"It's lovely. Don't you think so?"

"Absolutely."

His voice sounded oddly intense. When she looked over,

she met his gaze and discovered he was not looking at the tree at all, but at her.

She felt warm everywhere and those butterflies returned to flit around inside her.

He could *not* be attracted to her. The idea was laughable. She was bedraggled and dusty, her hair falling out of her messy bun. Any trace of makeup she had put on that morning, only mascara and a quick brush of lipstick, had likely worn off hours ago.

Still, she couldn't deny that expression in his eyes, hot and hungry, or her answering reaction. She fiercely worked to fight it down.

"Thank you for your help," she said into the silence. "I honestly would not have been able to tackle this job without you. There's a chance Winnie could have found a Silver Belle to help, but if not we would have ended up with a half-decorated tree, completely bare above about seven feet."

"I enjoyed it. But, again, please keep that between us."

"Well, if you enjoyed that, I have plenty of other decorating jobs you could help with. Tomorrow evening after the grounds are decorated, we're hanging more greenery around the windows outside."

He frowned a little, as if doing some mental calculations. "I could maybe swing by after work again tomorrow. I have a meeting in the afternoon but could come after that."

She didn't know what to say, touched that he would be willing to come again despite his opposition to the fundraiser.

"You don't have to do that. I was only teasing you. A

couple of the Silver Belles are bringing their husbands tomorrow. We should have enough people to finish the job."

"Well, if anything changes, let me know."

"Thank you."

That heady moment of mutual attraction seemed to have passed. Or maybe she had imagined the whole thing. She was relieved, Abby told herself, as they spent a few moments picking up the empty boxes and loading them into the elevator.

"I can take them up tomorrow," she told him. "Christopher loves to push the button on the elevator and help me stack the empty boxes where we can find them again after Christmas."

Except she wouldn't be here after Christmas, she reminded herself, feeling a little pang. Someone else would have to take all the decorations down for Winnie. Maybe Ethan would send a crew from his hotel to earn more overtime by helping out.

"Oh, look," she said. "It's snowing!"

She hurried to the window so she could look out at the sight that still enchanted her every time.

He followed her to stand next to her, gazing out at the giant snowflakes that fluttered softly to the ground. "This is the Rockies. Snow isn't exactly a rarity around here."

"I grew up in Alabama and have been in Arizona for the past ten years. Snow still feels magical to me."

"Almost makes you have a little Christmas spirit, doesn't it?"

"Almost. Not quite."

He laughed, a low, husky sound that had her toes tingling again.

"You're a fraud, Abigail Powell. You said you didn't

want to put up a tree but I think you're secretly into all this holiday decorating. The snow, the ornaments, the lights. All of it."

She nudged him with her shoulder. "I am not the one who just admitted he enjoyed decorating his grandmother's Christmas tree."

He smiled down at her for a moment that seemed to stretch out between them, soft and seductive.

His gaze locked with hers and his smile slowly slid away. The music on the speaker shifted to something slow and entirely too sultry to be on a Christmas playlist.

She opened her mouth to make some kind of a meaningless comment. Before she could, he leaned down and brushed his mouth against hers, just as she had been imagining him doing since that day up in the attic.

She froze for a moment, the memory of the last time a man had tried to kiss her flashing across her mind.

She waited for that first hint of nausea, the overwhelming urge to rush away and be sick.

It didn't come. At all. She wasn't sick in the slightest. Far from it. She wanted him to keep kissing her for the rest of the night.

When her fear that she would make a fool of herself again began to recede, she was so elated she kissed him back.

Oh, she enjoyed kissing. And Ethan was exceptional at it. His mouth danced over hers and his arms wrapped around her, making her feel safe and warm and protected while the snow fell softly outside.

They kissed for far longer than they should have, until her thoughts were whirling and she was beginning to feel the delicious flutterings of desire, feelings she thought were long dead.

She didn't want him to stop, but after several moments Ethan pulled away, his expression torn between desire and confusion.

"Sorry," he said, his voice low and rough. "That kind of came out of nowhere. One moment we were talking about snow and the next I knew I had to kiss you. I hope you don't think I'm the kind of guy who steals kisses every time he decorates a Christmas tree."

If he did, she imagined women across Silver Bells would be inviting him over to help them trim the tree.

"You don't have to apologize. Really. I'm, um, actually glad you kissed me."

"Glad?"

"Yes. I didn't throw up." As soon as she heard her own words, she couldn't believe she had just blurted out those words. She might as *well* have been sick. Oh, she was an idiot.

As she might have expected, he drew away farther, blinking a little. "Always the reaction I'm hoping for when I kiss a woman."

Abby's face felt hot. She should just stop talking now. That would be the sensible thing to do, but she felt like she had to at least try to explain such an odd statement.

"Since Kevin died, I've been afraid I would never be able to endure another man's touch. That probably sounds stupid to you."

His astonished expression seemed to ease a little. "Not at all. It sounds as if you loved your husband very much."

It seemed odd to be talking about her late husband five

minutes after she and Ethan had just been exploring each other's mouths, but she didn't know how else to explain.

"Kevin was a wonderful man. Once I fell for him, I never looked at anyone else."

He raked a hand through his hair. "Now I feel even more like a jerk who took advantage of you in a weak moment. I shouldn't have kissed you like that. I'm sorry."

She met his gaze and held it. "You weren't a jerk, Ethan. Far from it. I'm glad you kissed me. Just as I said. Kevin has been gone for two years. I miss him and part of me will always love him. He gave me Christopher, my greatest joy."

She folded her hands in front of her. "As much as I loved him, I'm not prepared to wrap my heart in tissue paper like one of Winnie's fragile ornaments and tuck it away on a shelf somewhere for the rest of my life. I'm ready to move on. That's one of the reasons I've decided to relocate to Austin."

"To move on?"

"I've been on two dates since Kevin died. Both of them were with perfectly nice men. The first one I wouldn't let kiss me, though he wanted to. Just the idea of it made me feel sick. The second man I dated, I decided to let him kiss me good-night so I could see what would happen. It wasn't pretty. As soon as he kissed me, I seriously had to throw up. Like, right that minute. I ended up literally shoving him out the door and barely made it to the bathroom in time."

Was she really telling him this? If there was anything guaranteed to make sure he didn't try kissing her again, this story would certainly do it.

"I was convinced something was wrong with my psyche and I probably would have to go through some heavy-duty therapy or something." She smiled. "Thanks to you, now

I don't think so. I'm happy to report I didn't feel a hint of nausea when you kissed me. In fact, I very much enjoyed it. So thank you."

"You're...welcome?"

He still looked extremely uncomfortable with the entire situation. She felt a pang of regret that she had just given him ample reason not to ever kiss her again.

"I should...probably go," he said, gesturing to the door.

She wanted him to kiss her again but knew that wasn't likely to happen again. Just the fact that she wanted him to still felt like a victory.

"Right. Well, good night. Thank you again for helping out with the Christmas tree. Winnie will love it."

"That's the important thing," he said with a lopsided smile.

She *was* glad he had kissed her, she thought as he grabbed his coat, wished her good-night and walked out the door. Ethan wasn't the man for her, she knew that. But at least she had learned she was capable of feeling desire again.

The only downside was that she suspected she would be aching for more now every time she saw him.

CHAPTER NINE

"The big tree looks marvelous, darling. Thank you so much for helping Abigail last night, especially after you had been traveling. I can't tell you how much it means to me that you were willing to help, despite your personal feelings about the fundraiser we're throwing."

Ethan fought the urge to roll his eyes. He said one thing about worrying for his grandmother's safety and everybody made him out to be some kind of ill-tempered ogre, stomping around in protest of the Silver Belles and their efforts to raise money for a good cause.

"You are a hard woman to say no to," he told his grandmother into the speakerphone. Outside the windows of his corner office, it was snowing again. He had a mental image of Abby's sheer joy in the snowfall the night before. And then he remembered what came a few moments later, the heat and delicious taste of her, and had to turn away from his office window.

"I'm sorry I bailed after you came all that way to visit me last night. I was so tired from everything we've been doing to get ready. Still, I feel terribly guilty I didn't try to stay up to help you decorate the tree. Were you there long?"

About fifteen minutes longer than he should have been. If he had been smart and left as soon as they'd finished decorating the tree, he would not have made a fool of himself by kissing Abby.

The memory of their kiss had haunted him all night long. If he closed his eyes, he could still feel her soft skin, taste the sweetness of her mouth, feel that strange tug and pull in his chest.

He could legitimately say he had never before had a woman thank him for not making her nauseous with his kiss.

He had to hope to heaven it never happened again.

"I left around ten. It wasn't terribly late."

"Well, I'm grateful. When my arm is out of this stupid cast, I promise to make you some of that banana bread you love."

"You don't owe me banana bread," he said, though the idea of it made his mouth water, and he realized for the first time that he had skipped breakfast. "I was glad I was there so Abby didn't have to climb the ladder on her own."

"She does have a thing about heights. Mind you, that hasn't stopped her from climbing up and down while she's been decorating, but I know that big ladder you have to use for the great room tree had been making her nervous. She had been putting off the job for days. Thanks to you, it's done now."

"Glad I could help," he said again.

What would Winnie say if she knew he had kissed her nurse until neither of them could think straight?

"That actually reminds me," Winnie said. "I wonder if I could ask another favor of you."

For some reason, he was seized by sudden trepidation. "Tell me you don't have any more twenty-foot trees you need me to decorate."

She chuckled. "No. One is plenty. But this favor does involve Abigail."

Yes. He was definitely right to be nervous. "Oh?"

"Well, Abby and Christopher, actually."

"What?"

"She's been so wonderful since she's been here. What a treasure. But I'm afraid I've been working her so hard. She never takes a rest. I was thinking she and Christopher might enjoy a chance to play in the snow a little. I wondered if you could arrange for them to try out your new tubing hill at the ski resort."

That much at least he could handle with minimal effort on his part. He let out the breath he had been holding. "Sure. That's no problem. I can leave passes at the sales office for them."

"Thank you, my dear. That would be nice, but I was actually hoping you might be able to take them yourself. Christopher has never been sledding or tubing before. He told me so. I suspect Abby hasn't, either. They could use someone to show them the ropes."

"Um, there's not much skill involved when you go to the tubing hill. You take the magic carpet up the hill, grab a tube and slide down. That's about it."

"Abby's afraid of heights, remember? I'm not sure I could convince her to take Christopher on her own if she didn't know someone else could take him if she chickened out."

"Why not wait for Lucy to get home?" he countered.

Winnie's disappointment came through loud and clear in her overlong pause. "I guess that would work. She'll be here early next week. Christopher has waited this long. He can wait a little longer. Thanks, anyway."

Oh, she was so good at manipulating him. He wished he could be a little tougher and withstand her. Without blinking an eye, Ethan could negotiate with everyone from rival executives to international labor union leaders. His grandmother was totally in a class of her own.

He might try to withstand her machinations if he didn't actually think it would be fun to take Christopher on the tubing hill.

He had been meaning to make time to try it out since the season started. He was a little embarrassed he hadn't been able to manage it yet. This would provide the perfect excuse.

He didn't want to encourage Winnie—if he gave an inch, who knows what she would ask of him next?—but he still found himself nodding. "Sure. I can take them. When did you have in mind?"

"How about tonight?" she asked brightly. "Tomorrow everyone from the Silver Belles is coming over to do a run-through before our first tours on Friday. This would be the best chance. The only chance, really. Is your schedule free?"

"Mostly. I can rearrange a few things."

"Great. Why don't you come for dinner first around six and then the three of you can leave after that. Thank you, darling. I'll see you then."

She hung up before he could argue. So not only had she managed to persuade him to take Abby and Christopher sledding, she had also somehow thrown his attendance at dinner into the mix without giving him a chance to tell her whether that worked for him or not.

He shook his head, wondering what his grandmother might be up to. She sounded positively gleeful, which raised about a hundred caution flags in his head.

Winnie was known for being high-handed but this was

a new level, even for her. Had she somehow gotten wind of his kiss with Abby? He wouldn't put it past her. Winnie seemed to know everything.

If she continued with this kind of thing, he would simply have to sit her down and tell her what she wanted was impossible and that she should turn her matchmaking efforts elsewhere.

He wasn't in the market for another relationship. Not now and probably not ever. He had learned his lesson well.

Oh, he couldn't say his heart had been irreparably damaged by the end of his engagement to Brooke.

Or damaged at all, really, if he were honest.

That had been her entire reason for giving him back the ring. He didn't love her like she loved him, and she had come to accept that he never would.

He had tried to protest that he wouldn't have asked her to marry him if he didn't care about her. He had believed that at the time.

One year out, he could certainly see her point.

If he had loved her, he surely would have been shattered when she walked away.

Mostly, he had just been annoyed at the inconvenience of the whole thing and the questions people still sometimes asked him about her.

He missed some things about his relationship with Brooke. Having someone to talk to at the end of each day had been wonderful, and Brooke had been funny and creative and a great hostess when he needed her. He wanted to think he had given her what she needed, too. He had been attentive and loyal, trying to show her daily how much he enjoyed having her in his life.

He had cared about her. He wouldn't have asked her to

marry him if he hadn't. In the past twelve months of reflection, he had come to realize she had been right. He had
cared for her more like a valued business associate who
held a cherished position in his life, not with the kind of
passionate, all-consuming love she needed.

Was he even capable of that kind of love or had his parents' endless romantic drama ruined that for him? That
was the question he had been asking himself since his engagement ended.

His sister had made it clear since she was about ten or
eleven that she wasn't ever going to fall in love. Love was
a joke and only made otherwise rational people behave in
humiliating and demeaning ways. So far she had kept to
that vow.

Ethan wouldn't go that far. He wanted a partner, someone he could share his life with and be a partner to in turn.
He had seen enough happily married couples to know it
was possible, and he yearned for that kind of connection.

He had to wonder if maybe he was missing something
in him, either because of nature or nurture, that made
him incapable of that.

Abby had it. She had glowed when she talked about
how much she loved her late husband. Hearing her had
left him feeling a little envious. Not because he was
jealous of Kevin Powell and what they had shared but
because Ethan had wondered if he would ever love anyone like that.

He shook his head. Winnie had to get any ideas about
him and Abby out of her head right now.

When she had known a love like that, why would Abigail Powell settle for a man simply because he didn't make
her feel sick to her stomach when they kissed?

"THAT'S THE WAY. Just keep pressing down with the cookie cutter. Yes, like that."

"Can we do a dump truck cookie?"

Abby smiled at her son, who loved all things mechanical right now, especially dump trucks. "They're not very Christmassy. I'm also not sure if Winnie has a dump truck cookie cutter. We might have to stick with ornaments and angels for now."

"Okay. Can we find a dump truck cookie cutter sometime?"

"I'll keep my eyes open," she promised.

He was cutting out a row of circles to be decorated as ornaments when Winnie hobbled into the kitchen. While she was getting around so much better than she had when Abby first arrived at Holiday House, she still moved at times like a woman who was nearly eighty years old. Which she was.

"It smells delicious in here. You're making cookies?"

"I thought I would make some for dress rehearsal tomorrow."

"You're so thoughtful. Thank you, my dear. You really do think of everything, don't you? That's exactly what I came to talk to you about. I think you need a break from everything, so I've arranged a little outing for you and Christopher."

"An outing? What kind of outing?"

Winnie looked evasive, which made Abby suddenly feel nervous.

"Oh, just a fun chance to play in the snow for a few hours. I've just hung up with Ethan. He's coming for dinner tonight and then would like to take you and Christopher to the new tubing hill at the resort."

"What's tubing?" Christopher asked.

"It's like sledding, only you sit on an inner tube that has a plastic bottom," Winnie explained.

Christopher's face lit up. "That sounds fun!"

"It can be. The resort has been working on a tubing hill for a few years now. I've heard it's a big hit."

Abby remembered Rodrigo mentioning it at Thanksgiving, which seemed a lifetime ago.

Her nerves seemed to jangle. Ethan. Tubing hill. An evening spent in his company. How could she do it without making an even bigger fool of herself around the man?

She closed her eyes for an instant, remembering his mouth on hers, warm and hard, his arms holding her close, the heat that had swirled around them.

She swallowed, pushing away the memory firmly. "I can't possibly go tonight."

"Why not?"

"You do remember that you have two hundred guests showing up here in two days, right? And a hundred things still to do before then."

"What do you still have to do?"

Abby went through her mental list, which, she had to admit, had shrunk down to a few remaining details. "Plenty of things," she said.

"Everything looks great to me. You've been amazingly efficient. The house is decorated, the landscaping crew did an excellent job outside, others are taking care of the refreshments. What else do you have to do?"

She would think of something. Anything.

"Think about it, darling. You deserve a night out. If not

for your sake, what about for Christopher, who has been such a good boy to help us."

"I want to go tubing," Christopher said, his eyes pleading.

Oh, my word. How was she supposed to withstand *both* of them?

"Would it help if I told you that you won't have to worry about a thing? You won't even need passes as you'll be going with Ethan. He will be there the whole time to watch out for both you and Christopher, if you decide you don't want to go on the tubing hill."

Winifred was difficult to say no to. The woman was relentless.

"I told you I would wash all the Holiday House serving platters so Emily can use them for the refreshments," she suddenly remembered.

"Nonsense. I can take care of that. Sofia and a few others who are singing a number together asked if they could come over tonight to practice with the piano. They can help me with the serving trays."

She tried to think of some other excuse but ran out.

"You have been working so hard this past week. Honestly, I don't know what we would have done without you. That's why I want you to go have a little fun with Christopher. He's a little boy who has never gone sledding, even though right now you're smack-dab in the middle of the Rocky Mountains. You can fix that tonight."

"We don't have snowsuits or boots or anything."

"I've already thought of that. Mariah is bringing over some of Dakota's extra winter gear for Christopher, and she has some of her own things that you can use."

"You've already talked to her?"

Winnie shrugged, plopping down into her favorite

kitchen chair. "You can't blame me. I was only trying to anticipate all the excuses you might throw at me."

Oh, yes. Winnie had manipulation down to an art form. She couldn't even really be mad since the woman was only trying to do something nice for her and for Christopher.

"I have a chicken noodle soup in the freezer that's one of Ethan's favorites. I'm going to cook that for dinner, so you won't have to fret about a thing on that front, either."

She really *had* thought of everything. Abby didn't know what to say. While she would love the chance to have some fun with Christopher, who really had been a dear through this whole process, why did Ethan have to be part of the equation? Couldn't they go tubing on their own?

How could she tell Winnie that she wasn't sure she was ready to spend an evening in his company? That, in fact, Abby would be perfectly happy avoiding the man for the rest of her life?

Every time she thought of their evening together, she wanted to cringe. That kiss had been delicious, yes. She still couldn't think about it without her knees feeling a little weak.

While the kiss had been dreamy, what came after could only be described as the stuff of nightmares. Had she truly told him about being physically ill after her last date?

Every time she thought about it, she wanted to dig a snow burrow out in the garden and climb inside for the rest of the winter.

She could only imagine what he must think of her.

Still, apparently he wasn't completely repulsed, or he wouldn't have agreed to take them tubing in the snow.

"I really want to go, Mommy. I like Ethan. Can we? Please?"

How could she say no? Christopher had been such a sweetheart, happy to entertain himself with coloring books or trains or his tablet while she was so busy decorating the house.

He would love the chance to create memories in the snow. How could she deprive him of this opportunity, even if it meant swallowing her embarrassment and facing Ethan once more?

She could do it. She only had to remember that Ethan meant nothing to her. Yes, they had kissed once and it had been spectacular, but it certainly wasn't going to happen again. In a short time, she would be going home to Phoenix and then on to her new life in Austin, and the man would only be a memory.

"Please, Mommy?" Christopher pressed one more time when she didn't answer.

"Listen to the boy," Winnie advised.

She simply didn't have the strength to withstand the combined entreaties of her son and his septuagenarian accomplice. Who did?

"Fine. We will go. It sounds like fun. That means we have to hurry and finish these cookies. You had better get stamping."

"I can help," Winnie said. "Decorating sugar cookies is one of my favorite things. Should we put some Christmas music on?"

"Yes. I want to hear 'Rudolph the Red-Nosed Reindeer,'" Christopher said.

"I think that can be arranged," Winnie said, grinning at him before ordering her home speaker to play the Gene Autry version, and soon they were all laughing and singing along.

"HEY, I'M TAKING Rod and a couple of his buddies to The Pie House for pizza and to watch the game tonight, since my mom has some kind of choir practice thing. You interested?"

If only José has asked him an hour ago, when his calendar for the evening had been completely free. Pizza and the game would be a lot less awkward than trying to figure out how to talk to Abby again after their kiss the night before.

"Sounds great but I can't. Sorry. I have plans."

José raised an interested eyebrow. "Hot date?"

Ethan stacked papers on his desk, avoiding his friend's gaze. "The exact opposite, actually. I'm trying out the new tubing hill with my grandmother's houseguest and her son. Sure you wouldn't rather take Rod and his friends with us to do that, instead?"

He wasn't sure why he asked other than that he wouldn't mind a little buffer between him and Abby.

"Ordinarily, yeah, since the tubing hill is now one of Rod's new favorite things, but we just did it a couple nights ago with my sister and her kids. We've got a real hit on our hands. Everybody had fun. Christopher should have a great time."

"I hope so. That would make one of us."

José gave him an interested look. "I get why *you* would rather be skiing down a black diamond slope instead of taking an inner tube down the slow lane. What about Abby? Why wouldn't she have fun tubing with you and her son?"

As much as he suddenly wanted to confide in José, how could he possibly tell anyone about that disaster of a kiss?

"Abby seems great," José said as Ethan struggled for an answer. "I met her before when I went with Lucy to her husband's funeral, but that was a tragic situation. I never really had a chance to talk to her one-on-one much except since she's been here in Silver Bells. I liked her a lot when I was there for Thanksgiving. I also went over one night last week with just my mom and Rod when Sofia took tamales over for dinner. We all stayed and ate together and had a great time."

Why hadn't anybody invited Ethan over for tamales? He felt a little left out, until he remembered he had been out of town.

"Rod is pretty taken with her and I always consider him an excellent judge of character," José went on. "Plus, my mother said Abby has single-handedly saved the Silver Belles fundraiser at Holiday House. In fact, Sofia has been talking about her so much, I get the distinct impression she wants me to ask her out."

Would Abby be able to kiss José without feeling sick? Ethan didn't want to know the answer to that. In fact, thinking about the two of them together made *Ethan* feel vaguely ill.

"What about Lucy?"

José seemed to freeze, his features going stiff. "What about her?"

Why had he said that? His sister was the one taboo topic of conversation between him and José. He knew they were friends, too, that they hung out overseas. He knew they had met up in Thailand a few months earlier when José took a rare-for-him-these-days trip for Lancaster Hotels to a new property.

He suspected something had happened there, judging by José's dark mood when he returned and Lucy's careful avoidance of the topic. Just as well. He didn't want to know.

He picked his words carefully, wishing he hadn't opened his big mouth. If there was something between José and Lucy, neither of them wanted to talk about it.

"Nothing. Only that she's coming home this weekend and I know you guys usually hang out when she's home. I guess I just assumed you would again this year. Am I wrong?"

"Yes. You're wrong," José snapped. "Contrary to popular opinion, I am not stuck in limbo, waiting for your sister to come home from whichever exotic destination has caught her fancy currently. I have a life. It's a damn good one."

Ethan wasn't quite sure how to respond. He had obviously touched a nerve. What was that about?

"Sorry, man. I shouldn't have said anything." He paused, then decided to broach the subject they never talked about.

"I guess over the past few years, I've sort of hoped you and Lucy might get together. You would be good for her."

José's fist clenched around the door frame, and for an instant Ethan saw stark, desolate pain in his eyes.

"Not happening, bro. Lucy has made up her mind that she doesn't want anything serious. Not with me, not with anyone."

Sometimes Ethan wanted to punch his parents in the throat for what their constant romantic drama had done to his sister.

"I'm sorry," he said, the words completely inadequate.

José shrugged. "It's my problem. A woman who doesn't want anything serious would probably be fine for some guys. They would see it as a dream come true. I'm not one of those guys. I want forever."

José was in love with Lucy. The truth stared at Ethan

through bleak, dark eyes. His best friend was in love with his baby sister, who had sworn for years that she would never let herself be vulnerable enough to love anyone.

His chest ached all over again. José was one of the best people he knew. Caring, funny, hardworking. Brilliant at his job and passionate about his family. Look at the career sacrifices he had made so that he could come home and help his mother with his differently abled brother.

That Lucy was blinded by the scars of their past to what was right in front of her made Ethan infinitely sad for his sister and what she might be missing out on.

José looked embarrassed and seemed to collect himself. "I didn't mean to dump all that on you, man. Lucy is her own person, right? She's always done her own thing. I get that. I'm doing my best to accept what she wants and move on, you know?"

José deserved the best possible future. He deserved someone sweet and kind and open to love.

Someone like Abby Powell.

Though it again made him a little nauseous, he forced a smile. "I get it," he said. "Listen, I could take Rodrigo and his friends for pizza, if you wanted to take Abby and Christopher tubing tonight. I would be fine with that."

It was a blatant lie, but what else could he say? "She seems like a great person and I'm sure the two of you would really hit it off, if you spent a little more time together."

José appeared to consider the offer but finally shook his head. "Abby seems great, but she's also Lucy's best friend. I couldn't do that. Anyway, Rod is counting on me. Thanks, though. Have a good time."

"Another time, then. Enjoy your evening."

José still looked miserable, but he nodded and headed out of Ethan's office.

CHAPTER TEN

As DINNERS WENT, she had to say it was one of the more awkward of her life.

Throughout the meal—a delicious chicken noodle soup and freshly baked bread a neighbor had brought over—she was painfully aware of Ethan. He talked to all of them, but she knew he had to be remembering the scene that had played out in the next room the night before.

Their kiss and the humiliating aftermath seemed to play through her head like an internet video stuck on repeat.

She ended up stirring her spoon around the noodles in her soup instead of actually eating any.

"Do you believe in Santa Claus?" The question from Christopher to Ethan finally yanked her out of her thoughts, stopping the video replay in her head.

Ethan glanced at her, his expression obviously seeking guidance. She could only give an almost invisible shrug, not quite sure how to respond.

"Why would you ask that?"

"My friend Jake at our old apartment is six years old, one year older than me, and he said his big sister told him Santa wasn't real. I said he was too. Jake said I was a baby and I told him if he said Santa wasn't real, Santa wouldn't come give him presents."

"That sounds about right," Ethan said. "What did, er, Jake say?"

"He said the moms and dads give presents on Christmas and I said, well, I don't have a dad only a mom and he said I would probably only get half the presents, then."

Christopher took a bite out of his bread, obviously having no idea how his words broke his mother's heart. That Jake. She had never much liked him anyway and wasn't sorry they were moving away.

Unfortunately, no matter where they went, there would be other Jakes with other big sisters. Kids only too willing to destroy a little boy's illusions. She wanted to wrap her five-year-old's heart in Bubble Wrap to keep him safe from thoughtless, unkind children.

Before she could answer, Ethan spoke up. "If you talk to Jake again, you tell him for me that Santa doesn't work that way. And anyway, the number of presents a kid gets doesn't matter much. Santa looks at how he acts toward other people all year round to decide whether he deserves any presents at all."

It was apparently the right answer for Christopher, as well. He beamed at Ethan as if *he* were Santa Claus. "I will. That's just what I'll tell him."

She didn't want Ethan to have to solve any more of her son's existential crises. "Christopher, if you're finished eating, take your plate into the kitchen and then go find the boots and snow pants Dakota lent you."

"Okay." He happily took his plate and carried it into the kitchen.

"Sorry about that," she murmured to Ethan. "The existence of the real Santa Claus seems to be the question of the week. We went to see a mall Santa downtown yesterday at lunchtime and it seemed to spark all kinds of questions."

"He basically asked me the same thing earlier today," Winnie admitted. "I told him to ask his mother."

"He brought it up when we were making cookies and I kind of brushed him off by distracting him. I guess I had better have a talk with him."

"He's only five. It's okay for him to believe a little longer," Ethan said.

"When kids want to believe, it doesn't matter what any neighbors say," Winnie said. "My older brother believed until he was twelve, until I finally had to advise our mother that she had to tell him the truth because he was starting to get into fights at school over it. I think I was eight or nine myself."

Abby smiled as she cleared Winnie's bowl for her. She reached for Ethan's bowl.

"You don't have to clean up after me," he said. It was probably the most direct thing he had said to her all evening, and for some reason she could feel herself blush.

"Were you done?"

"Yes. But you still don't have to do that."

"I don't mind," she answered as she carried everything over to the sink. She should be putting on her own winter gear. Was she trying to avoid going for as long as possible?

A moment later, her son returned to the kitchen.

"I'm all ready," he said gleefully. She heard a snicker of laughter, quickly quashed, from Winnie and turned around from the sink to find that Christopher had the pants on backward and his boots on the wrong feet.

Maybe she should have been supervising him a little better instead of angsting over spending the evening with Ethan.

"Good job, bud. You might be more comfortable if we

reposition things a little. Come on. You can help me get ready."

She took him back to their bedroom.

"I like Ethan. He's nice," Christopher informed her as she was helping him out of his boots so they could twist the bib pants around.

"He seems to be," she agreed. Not to mention a great kisser.

"Do you like him, too?"

Too much. Far more than she should. She forced a smile. "Sure. He's Winnie's grandson, so of course he's nice."

"I love Winnie. And I love her dogs. I wish we could live here all the time."

"But then we wouldn't be able to move into our new apartment in Texas, and you wouldn't be able to start at the new school we looked at already."

"I guess."

She tried to ignore the little pinch in her heart as she finished helping him into his snow clothes, then put on her own borrowed snow pants and boots. When they were sufficiently bundled, she returned to the kitchen.

"You two look like you're ready to hit the slopes," Winnie said cheerfully. "You should be warm all night."

"Are you sure you'll be all right on your own?" Abby asked.

Winnie didn't exactly roll her eyes, but her expression said the same thing. "I'll be alone for all of thirty minutes before a half dozen of the Silver Belles drop by to practice their number. I've lived here alone for almost sixty years. I think I could manage not to burn the house down in thirty minutes."

"What about falling down the stairs?" Ethan asked pointedly.

Winnie sighed. "I'll sit in my comfortable chair in the great room and read a book until everybody gets here. Will that make you happy?"

"As long as you don't get a paper cut."

She laughed and shooed him away. "Don't worry about me for a minute. Go on and have a great time."

"Are you guys ready?" Ethan asked.

"When you are," Abby answered.

"All right. Let's go play in the snow."

A SHORT TIME later, Abby stood with her stomach in knots, looking at the enclosed moving sidewalk that carried both people and inner tubes up the tubing hill at the ski resort.

Everyone here seemed to be having a great time. People laughed and shrieked with excitement as they sailed down the hill.

All she could think about were the ER visits that might result from those few minutes of fun.

"If you're not into this, I can take Christopher up the hill and you can wait for him down here."

Her own fear frustrated her so much. She found it so odd that she had never been bothered by heights until around the time Kevin died, which made no logical sense. He hadn't fallen any great distance. He had been shot by a mentally unstable patient in a random assault on what had otherwise been a routine night in the ER.

She had been at work that night at the children's hospital, tending to Sami. Maybe somehow her subconscious juxtaposed those two things—Kevin's attack and the girl she had been caring for when she found out about it.

The two things had to be related. She should probably ask the grief counselor she had seen for the first year after his death.

None of that helped her right now when her son was waiting for her to take him tubing.

"Seriously. I don't mind," Ethan said.

She shook her head, swallowing hard. She could do this. "I can't simply dump my child on you."

"I'm happy to take him. You can watch us the whole time from down here. They've even got a covered seating area there by the fire pit, where you can keep toasty and warm."

Was this her future? Always afraid to take risks for fear of some nebulous consequence?

She gazed at Christopher, who was just about jumping out of his snowsuit with excitement for the coming adventure. She wouldn't disappoint him. Not about something as silly as tubing down a small mountain.

She released a breath and forced a smile. "Let's do this."

Ethan wasn't fooled by her attempt at cheerfulness. "Are you sure?"

She really wasn't sure of anything, other than that her palms were sweaty inside her gloves and her knees would have been knocking together if she wasn't wearing so many layers.

She wouldn't let this fear rob her or her son of the memories they might build together. The past two years had been about finding the requisite courage to tackle the next thing. Going back to work. Christopher's first birthday without his dad. Facing their wedding anniversary on her own.

This was a small thing. And anyway, it helped to know Ethan was there.

"Let's go," she said, hoping he didn't hear the quaver in her voice. "This will be fun."

"Yay!" Christopher did a little shuffling dance around her and she had to laugh. *This* was why she could tackle her fear. She didn't want to raise a timid child who never wanted to try new things. The only way to ensure that was to show him by example that she wasn't afraid.

Ethan led the way to the attendant at the bottom of the lift, a young man with blond dreadlocks and a goatee. "Hi, Mr. Lancaster," the guy said, with a sort of awed reverence in his voice.

"Evening, Luke," he answered with a smile. Abby could tell the kid hadn't expected the big boss to know his name. "This is our first time. From what I understand, we can choose the speed of both our tube and the run we pick at the top, right?"

"Correct. The faster tubes are the yellow ones. Blue ones are slightly slower."

"Three blue tubes, then. Thanks."

"Coming right up."

The kid went to a pile of tubes and came back with three blue ones. "You know what to do from here?"

"Walk us through it, why don't you," Ethan suggested.

"Sure thing. See that big tube right there with all the lights on it? There's a moving sidewalk inside it that will take you up the hill."

"Like a magic carpet?" Christopher asked.

Abby had to smile. Right now the Disney movie with the magic carpet was his absolute favorite.

"Just like that, bud," the guy said with a grin. "We even

call it the magic carpet. Except you're all standing on the same magic carpet and it's only going to one place, the top of the hill. Hold your tubes on the lift in front of you. Once you get to the top, you just step off and my pal Becky will be there to direct you to the run you want, which all depends on how fast you want to go."

"Slow," Ethan said at the same moment Christopher said "Super fast."

"You can work that out at the top. That's all you need to know. You can go down as many times as you want. Especially when you're with the boss who owns the whole mountain, right?" he said with a grin toward Ethan.

She supposed that did carry a few privileges.

"All right," Ethan said. "Thanks for your help, Luke. Say hi to your mom for me."

"I'll do that," he said, still sounding a little awed.

"Do you know all your employees' names?" Abby asked as they headed toward the large tunnel illuminated by red and green neon lights.

"I should. But not even close," he said. "Luke's mom has worked at the front desk at the main Lancaster Silver Bells hotel in town since before I was a kid. Jolene is kind of a fixture."

"That's nice," Abby said, her nerves jumping again as they approached the tunnel.

Ethan gave her a careful look. Could he see her fear written on her face?

"How about this, Christopher," he said. "I'll hold your tube and take it up for you while you hold your mom's hand."

"Okay," her sweet son said happily, holding out his mitten for her. She grasped it tightly. Holding her tube in front of her with the other hand, as Luke had instructed, she stepped onto the moving sidewalk, which made a gradual ascent up the side of the mountain.

Once they reached the top, they were met by another attendant in the same official ski-resort jacket.

It was much easier to focus on her than on how far they had to tube down.

"Hi, Mr. Lancaster." The young woman at the top of the lift was obviously expecting them, probably warned by her cohort below through the two-way radios they carried. "How fun to see you up here!"

"Hi, Becky," he said courteously. "How have you enjoyed working up here on the tubing hill?"

"It rocks." She beamed, her long braids beneath her beanie swinging. "Seriously. Everybody's having so much fun. You and Mr. Navarro were so smart to put this in."

"It was all José's idea," Ethan said.

Despite her nerves, she had to admire the way he gave credit to Sofia's son. She had worked for too many bosses who snatched up any praise for themselves when it was being handed out.

"We're first-timers. Luke tells us we can choose our run speed."

"Yeah. Some are definitely faster than others. What's your pleasure?"

"Slow for us, at least for now," Ethan said before Christopher could add his speed demon vote. She wanted to kiss him.

"We'll see how we feel after the first run."

"Totally cool," Becky said.

"This is my first time sledding or tubing or anything," Christopher informed her.

"You got this, little dude. You're going to have so much fun. Your slower runs are all on the left, faster in the middle and fastest of all are on the right."

Ethan led the way to the left section of runs, just as another group of riders went down with yells of excitement.

For a slow run, that still seemed entirely too fast to Abby.

Some of her nervousness must have shown on her features. "Are you still okay?" Ethan asked her. "You can walk down, if that would make you feel better."

She couldn't imagine the humiliation of having all these families and children watch her walk down the hill.

"I'm fine. Totally fine. Let's do this."

His features were illuminated in the bright night-skiing lights along the hill. The admiring look in his eyes made her feel like he had just lit a cozy little fire inside her.

"Okay, whenever you're ready, it's your turn," Becky told them.

"What do I do?" Christopher asked.

"Just sit down on the inner tube with your feet up. That's the way. I'll give you a little push when you're ready."

"I want a *big* push," Christopher said.

Becky grinned at him. "You got it, kiddo. One big push coming up."

"I'll go first so I can be at the bottom first," Ethan said. "Abby and Christopher, you can come down at the same time."

She didn't have time to dwell on her stress. Everything happened in such a blur. Ethan took off down the hill and before she knew it, Becky was giving first Christopher a push then Abby.

Her fear of heights lingered for only the first few seconds, and then she was too busy having fun to remember to be scared. The wind whipped her hair beneath her beanie, stealing her own cries.

She felt young again, a girl racing down a hill with her arms out as fast as she could go.

Somehow she managed to stay on her tube as it slowed down where the hill leveled out. Black plastic grids in the snow helped the tubes come to a stop.

Before she could stand, a hand reached down to pull her up. Ethan. Christopher already stood next to him. Well, Christopher jumped next to him, anyway.

"That was the most fun thing I ever did in my whole entire life," her son exclaimed. His voice radiated excitement and his eyes sparkled with happiness. "Didn't you think it was so fun? Can we go again?"

She had survived it and had even enjoyed herself. In that glorious moment or two of soaring down the mountain, all her anxiety had disappeared like melting icicles.

"What do you think?" Ethan asked, watching her carefully.

She thought she couldn't deprive her son of something he loved so much.

"I think we need to go again," she answered.

They headed for the lift, Christopher in the lead. "You really feel okay?" Ethan asked her as they headed again toward the moving sidewalk that carried riders up the hill. "You did great, but I'm sure it wasn't easy on you."

"I'm actually fine. As long as I focus on what's right in front of me and don't worry too much about what might be far below, I seem to be handling it."

"You're doing great, but if you need to take a breather,

I can do a few runs with Ethan and you can stay at the bottom."

"Thank you. I appreciate that. So far I'm okay, but I'll let you know."

His smile left her breathless, and she was quite sure the elevation up here had nothing to do with it.

ABBY POWELL CERTAINLY had pluck.

After the first few runs down the tubing hill on the slow route, Abby had agreed to go on the medium-fast route that Becky had pointed out, and now she was letting Christopher talk her into taking the fastest run.

"I hope I catch air on this one!" Christopher said.

"What do you know about catching air?" she asked, cheeks pink from the cold.

"I went with Marta and Joey to the skate park when she was tending me once. Marta and me just watched. Joey said how fun it was to catch air with his skateboard. It looked cool."

Abby was going to have her hands full with Christopher when he grew up a bit. Ethan tugged the pom-pom on the boy's beanie. "I don't think we'll be doing any ollies or alley-oops in inner tubes. But since you like this so much, you really should try skiing or snowboarding while you're here."

"He's only five," Abby protested. "Maybe he should wait until he's a little older."

"How old were you when you started skiing?" Christopher asked.

"My granddad Clive took me when I was around your age. By the time I was in middle school, I was a snowboarder all the way. I moved around a lot when I was young, but no matter where I was, every winter I tried to come back here as much as possible so I could board with my buddies like José and a few others in town. Then I finished out high school here in Silver Bells, living with my grandmother. I still enjoy boarding but I've gone back to skis the past few years, I guess just to mix things up."

"Do you come up here to the mountain often?" Abby asked.

"Not as often as I should. I used to try to make a few runs after work a couple nights a week, but so far this season I've been so busy I've only gone once since we opened before Thanksgiving."

It was a shame, really. Clive would have been disappointed in him. His grandfather used to go just about every Saturday of the ski season.

"What about you?" he asked Abby. "Want to give it a try?"

She snorted a little. "I can barely handle a tubing hill. How would I take a ski lift?"

He wished he could figure out some way to help her overcome her fear of heights.

"You've done fine tonight. Better than fine. If I'm not mistaken, I think you've even enjoyed it a little."

"I have," she admitted. "It still takes me effort to face the hill each time, but the moment I start down, I'm glad I did it."

She was facing her fears, one tubing run at a time. He had to admire her courage.

"You really should try skiing, at least once. It's the same rush as tubing, only magnified."

She didn't look convinced, but they had reached the top of the moving sidewalk lift and had to step off.

"We're going on the fastest one this time," Christopher informed Becky at the top.

"Good for you! Hang on and have fun."

The run was fast and fun. Christopher shrieked the whole way with excitement and even Abby let out a cry, though Ethan couldn't tell whether it was terror or enjoyment.

"That was the best. Can we go again?"

If Christopher had his way, Ethan suspected he would want to tube all night. Abby was beginning to droop, though. He could see it in the fine lines of exhaustion around her mouth.

Poor thing. He knew she had been working hard for days, helping his grandmother.

"Last run," she said.

"Aww. I want to keep going."

"It's already past your bedtime. One more time up and down again and then home. We have another big day tomorrow."

Christopher was clearly not happy at having to end for the night. Still, he didn't whine or fret, which Ethan admired.

"Can we go down the fast one again?" Christopher asked.

Abby gave an almost imperceptible sigh, clearly not looking forward to it.

"How about I take Christopher and you can sit this one out by the fire."

She seized on the suggestion with gratitude in her eyes that made him feel about as tall as the ski lift towers.

"I'll do that."

"Watch me, though. Okay, Mommy?"

"You got it, bud. I'll watch the whole time."

On the way up, Christopher slipped his mitten into Ethan's hand and chattered away about his friends back home and his cat Mr. Jingles and a time he went to Disneyland with his mom and they rode every ride.

Ethan was aware of a weird tenderness in his throat, an overwhelming humbleness that this sweet boy trusted him to keep him safe.

He wanted a family.

Was it possible he could be a parent and not completely screw it up like his own father had? He had no idea, he only knew that he longed to build a warm, supportive family unit, the kind he had never had.

He would remember this night always. The cold night air, the red and green lights of the tubing hill, and especially the joy he had felt sharing this with Abby and her son.

"I never had so much fun," Christopher said happily as he settled into the back seat. "Will we have snow in Texas, Mommy?"

"Um, not much, I'm afraid. But we can always visit a place with snow again."

"Can we come back here and go tubing again?"

"Maybe," she answered in that noncommittal way parents had.

Christopher seemed content enough with that. He looked out the window at the falling snow and the Christmas lights they passed as Ethan drove back to Holiday House.

"That kid has no fear. You should have seen him on that final run. He wasn't nervous for a minute."

"I wish I were five again and had no concept about all the scary things in the world."

"He's a terrific kid. You're doing a great job with him."

"Thanks," she said with a startled look.

"It can't be easy, on your own."

"It's not. Being a single mom is much harder than I ever imagined. I wish I could tell my own mom thank you for all the sacrifices she made on my behalf."

He glanced in the rearview mirror and saw that Christopher's eyes were closed, his face nestled against the leather upholstery.

"Looks like he's asleep," Ethan said in a low voice. "That was fast."

She turned around to look at her son, her features soft with a tenderness that made something ache inside him.

"He's always been a kid who plays hard and sleeps hard."

Maybe that was Ethan's problem, why his sleep was often troubled. Maybe he wasn't playing hard enough these days.

"I don't mean to nag, but you really should think about taking Christopher skiing while you're still in Colorado. The resort has an amazing beginner hill and some stellar instructors. I think he would really love it."

She sighed. "I know he would. He loves any kind of active adventure things. His father was the same way. My own natural instinct is to curl up with a good book on a snowy day, but since his father isn't here anymore, I guess part of my job as his mom is to step outside my comfort zone when I have to."

"Exactly what you did tonight when you took him on the tubing hill. I was impressed by your courage."

She sent him a quick look and then looked away. He

could see color climb her cheeks but wasn't sure if she was blushing or if it was a reflection of the streetlights.

"Why don't you let me take him skiing?" Ethan suggested.

As soon as the words were out, he couldn't quite believe what he had said. He couldn't find time to take *himself* skiing these days. Why was he offering to take a five-year-old?

He wasn't quite sure he knew the answer to that, only that he had enjoyed spending time with Abby and Christopher tonight more than he had anything in a long time.

"You wouldn't have to go," he went on. "You could stay in the lodge and watch the whole time."

"That's very…kind of you."

She seemed as confused by Ethan's offer as he was. Something told him Abby didn't like accepting help unless she didn't have any other choice.

That was one more thing they had in common.

"I would enjoy it," he said truthfully. "Anyway, it never hurts to work on fostering a love of skiing in the younger generation. I'm creating new customers, one by one. Makes all the business sense in the world."

Her laughter tingled down his spine and made him want to stop the car and pull her into his arms.

"I'll think about it. I should tell you that I don't know how much longer we'll be in town. Once Lucy comes to town next week, Winnie won't really need my help. But if we are still here and we are able to coordinate something that works with your schedule, I'll consider it."

She was leaving before the holidays? He had assumed she and her son would stay through Christmas.

He didn't want them to go.

Ethan reached Holiday House while he was still process-ing that information and the tumult of emotions it stirred in him.

He pulled through the gates, trying not to think about it.

"Thank you again for taking time out of your busy schedule for us. Tell me the truth. Your grandmother conned you into it, didn't she?"

"I don't know if I would use the word *con*. More like strongly persuaded."

She winced. "I'm sorry. Christopher begged me this morning to take him sledding. He probably would have been content with taking a cardboard box to a park some-where, but Winnie obviously had other ideas."

"You did me a favor. I've been meaning to check out the new tubing hill but never seemed to find the time. It was much more fun giving it a test run with you and Christo-pher along than it would have been on my own."

He parked in front of the house, but Abby made no move to open her door and climb out. Perhaps, like him, she didn't want the night to end.

"I've been meaning to talk to you about last night," she said after a moment.

"Last night?" he asked warily.

"When we…kissed. Thank you for not making me feel like a total idiot. Every time I think about the things I said to you, I want to curl up and pull a pillow over my head."

Ah. That kiss.

Apparently she couldn't forget it, either.

"You have no reason to be embarrassed. I'm the one who kissed you without warning. Which, by the way, is something I never do. I am not sure what came over me."

He studied her in the moonlight. This time the color

on her cheeks was definitely a blush. "I found your honesty refreshing."

She gave a small laugh. "Honesty is one thing. Blatant oversharing is something else entirely."

He smiled. In that moment, he wanted to tug her across the space between them and kiss her fiercely. Even with her son in the back seat and with Winnie inside, possibly peering out the window at them, he wanted to kiss her.

He even leaned forward a little, driven by a soft tenderness mingled with a need he couldn't control. She looked up at him, eyes wide, and he almost thought she leaned forward, too.

He caught his breath but just before their mouths connected, Christopher woke up.

"Are we home now?" he asked sleepily.

Abby sat back in her seat, shock and dismay on her features. "Um. We've just arrived."

"I fell asleep." A gust of wind suddenly blew down from the mountains and rattled the car. "What's that?" Christopher asked, his tone fearful.

Abby seemed to gather her composure. When she turned to face her son, he saw none of the confusion from seconds earlier, only a serene, calm parent.

"Just the wind. Nothing to worry about, sweetheart."

"It won't blow me away, will it?"

For all his bravado on the tubing hill, Christopher sounded genuinely nervous. Just another reminder, Ethan thought, that everyone was a complex mix of courage and fear, pluck and panic.

"No. That might have happened to little tiny Piglet in the *Winnie-the-Pooh* book, but you're five years old and too big for a wind to blow away."

"Except a tornado," he pointed out.

"Fortunately we don't have too many of those around here, especially in December," Ethan said. "Why don't we get you two inside?"

He opened the rear door and helped Christopher out of his booster seat, then lifted the seat out.

"That wind is pretty fierce all of a sudden. I heard we were supposed to have windy conditions over the next few days."

"I hope they're gone by Friday for our first night," she said anxiously.

They all rushed into the house as another gust of cold wind blew through, icy and somehow forbidding.

The house offered shelter and safety against the weather, as it had offered it to him as a child.

He half expected his grandmother to be waiting for them, but she was nowhere in evidence.

He set down the booster seat on a bench in the entryway.

"Thank you again for a wonderful time. Christopher, what do you say to Ethan?"

Christopher beamed up at him, and Ethan was aware of a curious knot in his chest again.

"Thanks for taking me tubing. Can we go again sometime?"

"I'll see what I can do," he promised.

The boy flashed him a smile, which slid away quickly. He danced in place in his boots, giving his mother a worried look. "Mom, I gotta go to the bathroom. Really bad."

"Oh, dear," Abby exclaimed. "We'd better hurry."

She helped him out of his many winter layers. As soon as he was down to long underwear, Christopher bolted down the hall toward their room.

"Whew. Hope he made it in time." Ethan had to smile.

Abby shook her head, folding up her son's snow pants. "Lesson learned. The intricate logistics of getting in and out of winter gear is rough on a kid when nature calls."

He smiled back at her, struck by the amusement in her green eyes and the wisps of red hair slipping from her beanie.

He wanted to tug her close, take off that beanie, dip his hands in her hair and kiss her.

He released a heavy breath, catching himself just in time before he could act on the impulse.

"Good luck with everything. The show, I mean."

"Thank you, but I don't have much to do with it once the house is ready."

"Sounds like you've done plenty to make Christmas at Holiday House a reality."

"You know, I feel as invested in the fundraiser as if I organized the whole thing myself from the beginning instead of coming in only a few weeks ago."

"You should feel invested. You've made it possible. The house looks great. Better than I've ever seen it. The lights outside as we drove up were beautiful and our giant tree is magnificent, if I do say so myself."

She smiled. "You've got a new career in the works, if you ever get tired of running a hotel."

"I could say the same, if saving lives ever gets old."

"How about in the future we both stick to what we're good at?" she suggested.

He laughed, again fighting the urge to kiss her. He was glad he hadn't given in when Christopher came back, drying his hands on his shirt.

"I made it," he announced. "And I sang 'Jingle Bells' while I washed my hands."

"Good for you." She shifted her smile to her son, and Ethan was aware of that knot in his chest again.

"I should go," he said. "Have a good night."

"Thank you." To his astonishment, Christopher followed up his words by throwing his arms around Ethan's waist.

He froze for a second before hugging the boy back. "Thank you for going with me."

"You're welcome," Chris said.

When the boy stepped away, Ethan wondered how he should say good-night to Abby. She solved his dilemma by leaning up and kissing him on the cheek. The scent of her, vanilla and cinnamon, stirred his senses.

"Thank you from me, as well. It was a night I know neither of us will ever forget."

"Nor will I," he said, his heart pounding far more than it should from a simple kiss on the cheek as he let himself out the door and headed out into the cold.

ABBY WATCHED ETHAN go, heat burning deep inside her.

She had been quite certain he wanted to kiss her again. And she had wanted him to, despite knowing Winnie was somewhere in the house and that Christopher likely would come barging in at any moment.

She meant her words to him. She would never forget the evening. He had been so sweet. He had seen her fear of heights and had done everything he could to help her manage it.

The man was an enigma. Brusque one moment, kind the next. Her feelings for him were becoming as tangled as Christmas lights.

He had been so patient with Christopher all night. It was obvious her son adored him for it. Christopher seemed to have found a kindred spirit. Both of them had seemed to relish the adrenaline kick of soaring down the mountain at high speed.

She could fall for him without much effort at all.

Abby frowned. No. She wouldn't let herself. This was a simple attraction. That's all. He was the first man to spark that ache inside her since Kevin died.

She had her immediate future mapped out, and none of it included a detour where she fell for a completely inappropriate man and ended up mired in heartache and disappointment.

She had to keep her focus on her ultimate goal. After this fun interval at Holiday House was over and after Christmas had passed, she and Christopher would be starting an exciting new phase of their lives. She couldn't risk that by falling for Ethan, a man who wasn't at all available for love.

"This is a disaster! Why did this have to happen today of all days? What are we going to do?"

Winnie's wail echoed everything racing through Abby's mind two days later as she stood on the porch beside the older woman, looking out at the carnage of her yard.

Two trees had been completely uprooted and were lying on their sides in a tangle of broken limbs and Christmas lights.

In addition to knocking over two trees, heavy winds in the night had also knocked down several branches from other trees.

Ethan had said they didn't have tornados here and she had never heard of any in the wintertime anyway, but the scene looked like the carnage from a small cyclone.

"We have to cancel." Winnie looked heartbroken. "I don't see any other choice."

"There has to be another option. We've worked so hard to get ready for Christmas at Holiday House."

"What other option? It's a disaster out there. Forget about the damage itself, safety is a bigger concern. At this point, we can't get people safely from the front gate to the house with all those fallen limbs in the way. I had better call the rest of the Belles and cancel the opening night until we can get a crew out here to clean things up."

Abby wanted to cry in frustration. All those many hours of work. All ruined in a windstorm. Ethan had warned her high winds were forecast for the area. Throughout the day before, there had been occasional gusts but nothing too terrible. She thought they had escaped the worst of it until she and Winnie had awakened to the power going out around four in the morning and a heavy crash outside, followed shortly by another one. Christopher had slept through it, but she and Winnie had huddled by the gas fireplace in the great room and fretted until the sun came up enough that they could see the damage.

It was far worse than she had feared. All the hard work the lighting crew had done earlier in the week was for nothing. Strings of lights hung everywhere, drooping off the porch and dangling from the few undamaged trees.

How could they possibly clean this up in time for the tours to begin in only a few short hours?

They had to try, didn't they?

She held out a hand. "Wait. Don't do anything yet. We can figure this out."

"How?"

"I don't know," she admitted, her voice shaking. Tears burned, and she wanted to sit down right there on the front porch and cry out her disappointment.

At the moment the tears threatened to spill over, she felt Winnie's arm around her shoulders. "It will be okay. We'll just cancel tonight and hopefully clean this up for tomorrow."

Abby rested her head on Winnie's shoulder, drawing on the woman's strength.

"Okay. Where do we start?"

"I'll call the same crew that put up the lights and see if they can—" Winnie broke off before finishing the sentence, staring down the driveway.

Abby followed her gaze in time to see the gates swing open and a man walk through, up the driveway toward them.

Ethan.

Abby could feel her heart begin to pound. How had he known they needed him so badly?

He made his way around the fallen limbs and uprooted trees.

"My boy. Look at this mess." Now it was Winnie's turn to sound emotional, and in a moment her grandson wrapped his arms around her.

"José called me first thing and said he'd heard this neighborhood was hit hard by wind last night. He was worried about things over here. He wasn't exaggerating, was he?"

"It's a nightmare. We're going to have to cancel the entire event."

"Or maybe not. Let me make a call. I can get the grounds crew from the hotel here within the hour. We can fix this."

"It's such a mess," Abby wailed. "And it was so lovely before."

"Everything is ruined."

"I can't guarantee it will look like it did before, but we can at least clear away the debris from the driveway so your visitors can park and reach the front door."

Winnie looked stunned. "You would do that, even though you were against this fundraiser from the beginning?"

"This is important to you, so it's important to me," he said simply.

Oh. How was she supposed to resist a man like this, who could be so overwhelmingly sweet to his grandmother?

"Give me a minute to make some calls."

While Abby fixed bacon and her famous whole-wheat pancakes, Ethan sat at the kitchen table drinking coffee and making call after call.

By the time he finally closed his cell phone and took a moment to eat a couple of pancakes, she was in awe of his negotiation skills.

"These are delicious," he said with an appreciative smile. "Wish I had time for about a dozen more but the first crew is going to be here any minute."

A honk sounded from outside and Ethan slid away from the table. "That should be them."

She and Winnie both went with him to the door and watched a utility vehicle pull through the gate. The doors opened and several men and a couple of women climbed out in all-weather coveralls.

On the surface they might have looked rough, but as far as Abby was concerned, they were angels.

"Thanks for breakfast," Ethan said, throwing on his own work gloves. He kissed his grandmother on the cheek, then surprised Abby by kissing her, too.

When he hurried off the porch to join his crew with handshakes and smiles, she watched him for a minute, then turned to find Winnie watching her with a particular gleam in her eye.

"What?"

"Nothing," the older woman said, her pink hair a fuzzy cloud around her head. "Nothing at all. We should probably go in out of the cold, that's all. With all that noise out there, that boy of yours is going to be waking up. I'm surprised he's not already up looking for you."

She spared one more look at Ethan, who appeared to be taking complete charge of the crew. He might be a polished executive by day but it was obvious he had no problem getting his hands dirty.

She shivered a little, thinking of those hands on her the other night, then hurried inside to make a few more pancakes for Christopher and get ready for the long day ahead.

She was so busy taking care of last-minute details for the evening ahead that she didn't have a chance to talk to Ethan until a few hours later, when she bumped into him in the kitchen, grabbing another cup of coffee.

Dirt smeared his cheek, and sawdust from the chainsaw was sprinkled over his jacket. Her hands itched to brush it away, but she managed to refrain.

He had taken his beanie off, and his hair was plastered to his head.

She found she liked this side of him as much as she

liked the man who could look so gorgeous in bespoke Italian suits.

"How's it going out there?"

"We're making slow progress. It's a shame about the two pine trees she lost, but I had worried about their integrity as far back as last summer. They were a bit too pampered and never put down deep enough roots. There are a couple others that lost significant limbs. The good news is, none of them caused any damage to the house or the other structures on the property."

"Oh, good."

"It's a miracle actually. I don't know quite how. As I drove here and saw some of the other damage in town, I was afraid I would show up and find the roof collapsed."

"What a relief."

"We're going to try to string the lights as best we can, but it probably won't look as good as it was originally. I've talked to the original company that hung them, and they're going to come out Monday to rearrange everything. I'm afraid that's the best I can do."

"It's wonderful. Thank you so much, Ethan. Seriously."

He smiled down at her and Abby felt breathless all over again.

"We should be out of here in a few hours. That should give you plenty of time before the first guests start arriving."

She wanted to hug him, right there in the kitchen, but Mariah Raymond walked in before she gave in to the crazy impulse.

The other woman's gaze lit up when she caught sight of Ethan. "Mr. Lancaster. I didn't know you were here."

Abby was startled at the sudden burst of possessiveness she felt toward Ethan. Where had *that* come from?

Ethan gave Mariah a polite smile. "My crew is cleaning up the wind damage outside."

"I saw them when I pulled up. I didn't realize they were from Lancaster Hotels. That is so wonderful of you."

Mariah was *definitely* giving him a flirtatious look. Abby drew in a breath, annoyed at herself. Mariah was her friend. What did it matter to her if Mariah was interested in Ethan or vice versa? One heated kiss didn't mean Abby had some sort of claim on him.

She would be leaving Silver Bells soon anyway, possibly as early as next week, depending on when Lucy could make it home, which was still up in the air.

Really, when she thought of it, the two of them would be good for each other. They would make a lovely couple. Ethan was so good with children. She thought of his gentleness and kindness with Christopher when they went tubing. He would be great for Dakota.

Somehow the rationalization didn't make her feel any better.

The two of them talked a few moments more, then Ethan set down his coffee mug and reached for his work gloves. "I'll see you both later."

"Will you be here tonight for the first night of our fundraiser?" Mariah asked.

Abby expected him to say no. She would have assumed Ethan wanted to stay as faraway as possible from his grandmother and her friends.

Instead, as he had been doing since she arrived in Silver Bells, Ethan once more surprised her. "I wouldn't miss it," he said promptly. "After all the hard work everyone has put into making it a success, I'm sure the night will be wonderful."

Mariah smiled broadly. "Great. I'll look forward to seeing you twice in one day."

He gave her a distant sort of smile, waved to both of them and headed out the door.

Mariah watched after him, then shook her head. "Well, that was interesting."

"What was?" Abby asked absently.

"That man. I might as well be invisible to him. I keep trying to get Ethan to notice me, but I might as well be one of those Christmas trees scattered all over the house." She raised an artfully shaped eyebrow. "You, on the other hand, get a completely different reaction out of him."

Abby felt her face heat. "You're crazy."

Mariah gave her an amused look. "Am I? I don't think so. I thought I noticed a certain vibe between you on Thanksgiving, and it was more obvious today. Is something going on between you two?"

Abby willed herself not to blush, trying to push away the memory of that heated kiss. "Nothing. We're friends. That's all."

They were, she realized. She never would have guessed that day she had arrived at Holiday House that she would become friends with Ethan, but she genuinely liked him.

And, okay, she was fiercely attracted to him, but that was an entirely separate issue.

"Lucky you," Mariah said with a teasing smile. "Half the women in town would love to be friends with Ethan Lancaster. Friends with benefits, anyway."

Abby rolled her eyes and tried not to think about how much she truly missed benefits.

CHAPTER ELEVEN

HE DIDN'T KNOW what standards the Silver Belles were using to judge how well Christmas at Holiday House was going, but from Ethan's point of view the evening was a smashing success.

Later that night, he was sitting at a table in the great room with a middle-aged couple he had learned were from Nebraska and were staying at the Lancaster Silver Bells hotel.

Bill and Nancy Maughan were sipping hot cocoa out of Winnie's elegant Christmas-themed china, listening to the choir perform their final number, a beautiful rendition of "Silent Night." Nancy had tears in her eyes as she listened and even Bill looked touched, though he wasn't crying.

Around them, the great room was filled with others who lingered over their cocoa and cookies to listen to the music.

He hadn't really been able to catch the vision of what Winnie wanted to do until this evening. Apparently, the ticket holders were divided into small groups of twenty or so, with staggered arrivals. Winnie led his particular tour group, but he had seen different Silver Belles leading others.

Visitors were given some of the history of the house, including things Ethan hadn't known. The tours discussed Christmases through the years since the house had been built and how various historical events had shaped the celebrations.

All along the way, other members of the Silver Belles performed Christmas songs that were popular during those significant moments in history.

He had to admit, he was impressed. Everyone seemed to enjoy the tours immensely, and those in his group lingered in each room to examine the contents and talk about Winnie's collection.

His grandmother was definitely in her element. She seemed to love talking about the house and the people who had lived here. She glowed as he hadn't seen her do since probably his grandfather died.

The evening was an intimate, unexpected delight, and he couldn't wait to tell Winnie and Abby how much he had enjoyed it.

The number came to a tender close, and the choir was met with thunderous applause from those in the great room.

"Oh, that was so marvelous," Nancy Maughan said. "I'm so glad we were able to get tickets. I grew up in Silver Bells and used to dream about coming to a Christmas party here. It always looked so elegant and festive to me when I was a child, like something out of a movie set. I can't believe we actually had the chance."

Ethan had no idea if Winnie and her friends could continue on with this much energy and enthusiasm as everyone had shown tonight. If they could, he had no doubt Christmas at Holiday House would become the most talked about seasonal event in this region of Colorado.

The house sparkled. Everywhere one looked, beautiful holiday touches added to the mood of warmth and welcome in the house. Abby had truly outdone herself.

He looked around to tell her so but couldn't spot her in the crowd. She must have slipped away during the singing.

On a hunch, he rose himself and carried his cup and plate into the kitchen. He wasn't surprised when he found Abby washing dishes there, Christopher standing on a stool and helping her by drying. The sight warmed something deep inside.

He stood for a moment, watching the two of them interact. She was laughing at something Christopher had said while a strand of wavy auburn hair slipped free from the updo she wore.

The sight made him ache, aware of a flurry of emotions inside that he didn't know how to process.

Christopher was the first one to spot him. The boy must have seen Ethan out of the corner of his gaze. He almost dropped the cup he was holding but managed to catch it in time before setting it in the drainer, hopping down and rushing to hug him.

"Ethan! Hi!"

"Hey, bud." He hugged him back, warmed by the fond reception. Abby gave him a quick smile but turned back to the sink.

He wanted to hug her, too.

"How did you like the hot cocoa?" Christopher asked eagerly. "I helped put the snowflake marshmallows in. I had to wear a glove and everything."

"It was fantastic. I particularly enjoyed the snowflake marshmallows. I can honestly say it was the best hot cocoa I have had in forever."

He didn't add that it was also the *only* hot cocoa he'd had in forever.

"Did you like the cookies? I did. I ate four."

Abby made a strangled sound.

"They were delicious. What kind were your favorite?"

"Snickerdoodles," the boy said promptly. "I love them the most."

"I totally agree," he said, which earned him a broad smile.

"We made snickerdoodles once. I helped roll the dough into balls before we dipped them into cinnamon sugar. I had to wash my hands about a billion minutes until they were clean enough to do the cookies."

"A billion minutes. That's a lot."

"Yeah. My mom always makes me wash my hands a lot because she's a nurse. She says lots of germs live on boys' hands."

"Sounds like good advice." Ethan's gaze met Abby's. She gave him a rueful look, and he thought he saw color climb her cheeks.

"Did you enjoy the first ever Christmas at Holiday House?" she asked.

"I did. I didn't know what to expect, but I found it a thoroughly enjoyable evening. Do you know, I've been coming to Holiday House my entire life and thought I knew everything about the history of the place and the people who lived here. I couldn't have been more wrong. I had no idea the caretaker's wife during my great-great-grandfather's time had all four of her children on the kitchen table. I'm not sure I ever want to eat here again."

When Abby Powell laughed, she looked as bright and vibrant as the star on top of that giant Christmas tree in the great room, and it took all his self-control not to kiss her right there in front of her son.

"Now that you've experienced it yourself, tell me the

truth. Do you think the evening was worth the cost of the ticket?"

"Definitely. It was basically the cost of a movie ticket and a bowl of popcorn. And for that, they received a delightful evening filled with music, history and holiday cheer."

"Good point. I know Sofia and the others were worried about that part. I'll pass along what you said."

He really had to stop staring at her. Ethan forced his attention away, toward the sudsy water in the sink.

"Can I help in here? I don't mind washing or drying."

"You can dry," Christopher said quickly, handing over his dish towel so quickly Ethan barely caught it before the boy rushed away and headed toward the kitchen table, where it looked like he had been building something with Legos.

Abby shook her head in exasperation. "You don't have to, really. I'm almost done. I can dry what's left."

"I don't mind."

"But your shirt will get wet."

"It will dry. I'm not worried." Ethan stepped over to the sink and reached for the dishes in the rinse water.

The two of them worked together in a companionable silence for a few moments. The scene felt strangely familiar. It took Ethan a moment to remember they had done this only a few weeks earlier, on Thanksgiving.

Had she and Christopher really only been in his life since then? He felt as if he had known them forever. When he tried to remember his world before they were in it, he had a hard time making the pieces fit together.

The scent of her mingled with the lemony smell from the soap. It was clean, honest, intoxicating. He wanted to draw it deep into his lungs and try to remember this moment forever.

"The grounds looked so wonderful. Thank you so much for stepping in today with your crew. You must have given up half a day at work, but I don't know what we would have done if you hadn't. You truly saved the day."

"My pleasure," he said gruffly. He meant the words. He had enjoyed the morning of working with his hands more than he had anything in a long time. It was sometimes easy to forget the simple satisfaction of encountering a problem and solving it through sheer hard work.

"It meant the world to your grandmother, as well. She had to fight tears today every time she talked about it."

"It was one small thing I could do."

"You know it wasn't small to her. It made all the difference."

He would have cleared away a hundred trees to earn that look in Abby's eyes.

He cleared his throat. "Have you given more thought to letting me take Christopher and you skiing?"

She laughed as she rinsed the final dish in the sink. "I had a nightmare last night about falling out of a ski gondola. So yes, you could say I've given it more thought. Or at least my subconscious has."

"Do you really think I would let you fall?"

Her gaze met his and the moment seemed to stretch out between them, heavy with things unsaid.

He needed to kiss her. He could no longer deny the hunger. It would only take a shift of his body, an angle of his head. He started to move and saw her eyes flicker with heat. Her lips parted. An instant before his mouth would have connected with hers, the door opened and Emily Tsu, who owned a bakery in town, bustled in, carrying a tray.

She stopped in the doorway as if she sensed she had been interrupting something.

"Um. Sorry. I just need to refill the shortbread. Apparently, that's a popular choice tonight."

"They go well with cocoa, I guess," Abby said in a voice that sounded slightly strangled.

"Right. I'll have to make sure I bring more of those for tomorrow." Emily gestured to the sink. "You're not supposed to be washing dishes. That's my job. It's part of the whole caterer gig."

"I don't mind washing a few dishes. You've had a long day on your feet already."

Emily blew her a kiss. "You are a doll. Thank you."

She refilled the plate with more shortbread cookies from one of her bakery boxes on the counter and then hurried back out of the kitchen.

Ethan tried not to be annoyed at the interruption. It was probably for the best. Anyone could have walked in on him kissing Abby.

"She's been so good," Abby said. "All the Silver Belles have. This event means so much to them. They are so excited about being able to help build the adaptive ski lodge at the resort."

"It will be a big asset to the community."

Abby gave him a sidelong look. "Winnie finally told me your family has donated the land for a lodge. What a kind gesture."

He shrugged, embarrassed, as always, to talk about the philanthropic activities of his family's business. "It's a small thing we can do for a good cause."

"Not small at all, from what I understand," she said softly.

"Hey, Ethan, come see my mountain," Christopher commanded.

Grateful for the diversion, he dried the final saucer and slipped it into the cabinet, then headed over to the table.

"That looks great," he said.

Christopher had jumbled together Legos from a box that had probably been Ethan's to create a multicolored mountain.

"That's a person on a sled." Christopher pointed to a mini figure on an improvised blue sled. "It's not very good."

"I think you did an excellent job."

"I wanted to make a tubing hill, but couldn't find any round bricks for the tubes so I made it a sled."

"Good substitution."

"He's had a lot of fun with what Winnie says are your old toys. Thank you for letting him use them."

"I am glad someone can find a use for them. I spent a lot of enjoyable hours building sets."

Christopher yawned suddenly, and Abby set down the cloth she was using to wipe down the table.

"We need to get you to bed. It's an hour past your bedtime."

"But I don't want to go to bed," Christopher informed her in a matter-of-fact tone. "Can't I stay up until the people go home?"

"This was the last tour for the night, honey. But guess what? They'll happen again tomorrow. We get to do it all over again."

"Can I have four more cookies tomorrow?"

She smiled and shook her head. "With all these cookies every night, we're both going to be as big as a barn. We won't be able to fit into our car to drive back to Arizona."

Ethan didn't like the reminder that they would be leaving soon and neither did Christopher, at least judging by his sudden scowl.

Abby ignored her son's expression. "Come on. Time for a bath and then bed."

Christopher cocked his head, looking crafty suddenly. "Can Ethan read me my story?"

"Me?"

The boy nodded. "We're reading all the Christmas stories. Winnie told me some of them were yours and my friend Lucy's."

"That's right. Lucy is my sister."

"I like all your stories. You can even pick what we read."

Abby didn't look thrilled at that idea. "Honey, Ethan has been here all evening after working all day out in Winnie's yard after the storm. I bet he would like to go home today. Maybe he can read to you another night."

"I don't mind," Ethan said quickly.

"Yay! I'll get into my pajamas fast." He raced off in a blur.

Abby sighed. "You really don't have to read to him. He will understand if you change your mind and decide to go home."

"Why are you so convinced I don't want to do things? First drying the dishes, now reading to Christopher. You might be surprised at the many things I can accomplish in a day."

"I wouldn't be surprised at all. But most of those likely don't include indulging a boy you hardly know. You're the CEO of Lancaster Hotels. No doubt you pay people to tell other people to tell *other* people to do things like dry the dishes."

Did she hold his job against him? He couldn't tell by her tone. "I learned early that I can't ask anybody who works for me to do something I'm not willing to do myself. I've worked in all areas of the hotel, including spending a few days in housekeeping. It makes good business sense. I ask everyone in management to be familiar with everyone else's job. How can I expect them to know how to manage people if they don't know what benefit those people provide to the company?"

"That sounds like a smart business model. I wish more hospital administrators could work with patients for a day so they could remember our job isn't about counting tongue depressors but about helping people heal."

He would like to see her in action. Judging by the care she took of Winnie, he could only surmise that Abby Powell was a dedicated, passionate nurse.

Before he could say so, Christopher barreled back into the kitchen holding a stack of books. "I washed my face and brushed my teeth and I'm all ready for a story now."

Ethan tousled his hair, looking forward to the next few minutes more than he had anything else all day.

"Great. Lead the way."

Abby stood in the doorway of Christopher's bedroom, listening to Ethan reading in an animated voice one of their own books, one of Christopher's favorites, about a reindeer named Snowball who ended up saving Christmas.

Who would have guessed that a busy, important executive like Ethan could be so patient with a little boy who was well on his way to developing hero worship for him?

She thought of her impression of Ethan the first time they had met—of an arrogant, hard man who wanted to put his grandmother into assisted living for his own convenience.

First impressions rarely showed the entire picture, which seemed to be an important life lesson she needed to learn over and over again.

During the past few weeks, she had discovered that Ethan was a man of strength and character who cared about his family, his business, his community.

She was fiercely drawn to him, though she knew it was foolish and she was bound to get her heart broken.

"'Christmas bells rang out through the night, pure and sweet. In the reindeer barn beneath the brightest star, Snowball stretched out in the hay and finally closed his eyes and let the bells sing him to sleep, knowing he had helped the world find peace.'"

"The end," Christopher said sleepily.

"The end," Ethan agreed, closing the book. "That's a great story."

"It's my favorite. I like all the Snowball books. And the movie. Maybe you could read me another one tomorrow."

Ethan clearly didn't know how to answer that suggestion, so Abby stepped in.

"Ethan doesn't live here, remember? He lives in his own house. He's only visiting his grandmother tonight for the holiday celebration."

"You said we were doing it again tomorrow. So why can't Ethan come back and read to me again?"

"We'll see," she said, which was the standard parental cop-out when she didn't have the energy for another argument. For now, it worked with her five-year-old son, but she suspected the efficacy would diminish over time.

"It's time for lights out now. Good night, sweetheart. I love you to the moon and back."

"I love you to Pluto and back," he retorted, as he had been doing since learning that the planets were much farther away than the moon and that Pluto was the farthest planet in the solar system.

She smiled and kissed his forehead, feeling that familiar marvel in her heart that this little miracle was hers.

"Can Jingles sleep with me?" he asked hopefully, the same question he had asked just about every night since he'd learned to talk.

"No." She gave the same answer she always did. "You know he likes to wander at night. He'll wake you up."

She scooped up the cat, gave her son another kiss on the forehead and then turned off his light. "I'll see you in the morning."

Christopher nodded sleepily, his eyes already closing.

"How does he go out so fast?" Ethan asked, wonder in his voice after they walked out into the small sitting room connected to their bedroom.

"One of life's biggest mysteries," she answered. "I wish I had that gift. His father used to be the same way. When Kevin was a resident, he could sleep anywhere, anytime."

"I've heard medical residencies can be rough."

"I can confirm that. It didn't help that I became pregnant right after Kevin started his. We were so lucky Christopher was a good baby."

That had been such a joyful time, she remembered now, their life overflowing with possibilities.

She missed many things about her husband, but she grieved most knowing he would never have the chance to watch Christopher grow into a kind, curious, incredible little human.

"Thank you for reading to him," she said now to Ethan. "You've made quite an impression. I've never seen him take to someone so fast."

"I enjoyed it," Ethan said. "He's a great kid. He obviously has a good mother."

She couldn't have said exactly why, maybe because her emotions were already on edge from the long, tumultuous day, but his words seemed to trigger tears.

Most days, she didn't feel like a good mother. She felt frazzled, tired, anxious, impatient. She worried she couldn't provide everything her son needed to grow into the sort of admirable man his father had been.

"Thanks," she managed, praying he didn't see the tear that had slipped out before she could prevent it.

No such luck. His gaze sharpened and he angled his head down. "Are you crying?"

She lifted her chin. "No. I must have gotten glitter in my eyes. That stuff is everywhere this time of year, have you noticed?"

He hesitated for a moment, then pulled her into his arms. Abby froze, knowing she shouldn't be here, that letting him any closer would only result in more pain down the line, but his arms were warm and provided as much peace and comfort as Snowball the reindeer found in his bed of hay.

Oh, how she needed peace and comfort right now. She sagged against him, a little sob escaping. His arms tightened around her and she rested her cheek on his broad chest, listening to his heartbeat and drawing strength from him.

She had no idea how long they stood there in her little sitting room, listening to the distant sounds of the Silver Belles singing on the other side of the house as they performed their show one last time to the final group of the night.

She only knew it was a pure, lovely moment she would never forget.

Finally, she knew she had to extricate herself from his arms or she would want to stay there forever.

She lifted her head. "Sorry. It's been a long day. I guess I was more tired than I thought. Thank you for the shoulder."

"Anytime," he said, his voice gruff again. For some reason, that made her want to cry all over again.

She and Christopher would be leaving soon, returning to Phoenix to pack up the rest of their lives. The time they had spent in Silver Bells was like the bridge in a musical score between the two different periods of her life.

She would dearly miss all the friends she had made during her time here. Mariah, Sofia, Emily Tsu. And especially Winnie.

Ethan studied her carefully. "If I kissed you again, would you be able to hold on to your snickerdoodles?"

She met his gaze, unable to look away. "I can't make any promises," she whispered.

"I guess I'll have to take my chances."

When his mouth met hers, she released a sigh that seemed to come from her toes. She had wanted this all day. All week, really, since he kissed her the first time beneath Winnie's giant Christmas tree.

She was falling for him and realized as his mouth danced over hers that it was far too late to do anything about it.

His hands tightened around her, and he somehow managed to settle them both on the sofa. It was one thing to kiss Ethan when they were both standing up. It was something else when he was half-reclined on her sofa, taking all her weight.

Oh, she had missed this heat surging through her, the delicious ache for more and more.

His hands were under her sweater, his mouth nuzzling her neck when she suddenly thought she heard a knock at her door.

"Abs? You still awake?"

She jerked away, scrambling to find her footing. The two of them stared at each other for a long, astonished second before she hurried to the door, pulling her sweater back into place as she went and hoping she didn't look as aroused as she felt right now.

She cleared her throat so she could speak without a sexy rasp as she reached for the door and pulled it open.

Though it clearly had been Lucy's voice she heard, Abby still couldn't quite believe she was standing in the doorway, hand up as if ready to knock again.

"Lucy! What a surprise! I thought you weren't going to be able to make it back for a few more days!"

Her friend beamed at her. "Surprise! I was able to talk another teacher into taking my last few days before the break, changed my flight and twenty-four hours later, here I am."

She looked over Abby's shoulder and shock flickered in her blue eyes, so much like her brother's.

"Ethan! What are you doing here?"

Lucy *really* didn't need to know the answer to that question right now. Abby looked down, feeling her face heat with a furious blush that could probably be seen from several blocks away.

"He was, um, just leaving. Weren't you?"

"Right," he answered, his voice strangled.

"Ethan was kind enough to read a story to Christopher tonight. The one about Snowball the reindeer. It's his favorite. Well, one of his favorites. It seems like his favorite story changes every night, depending on his mood. He's discovered all your old Christmas stories and is really enjoying the Jan Brett books, especially the ones with trolls."

She was babbling, she realized, feeling like a troll herself. She clamped her mouth shut and stepped forward to hug her friend instead, hoping Lucy couldn't smell Ethan's scent on her.

"It's so good to see you."

"And you. And bonus, my big brother. It's like a two-for-one sale of my two favorite people. Hey, you."

She held her arms out and Ethan gave her a brief embrace. "I'm glad you're home, sis. Next time give us all a little warning. I could have sent a car to pick you up from the airport."

"I rented a car so I would have some wheels while I'm in town."

"I could have loaned you a car, too, but okay. How was your flight?"

She shrugged, exhaustion pulling down the corners of her mouth. "I tend to forget how long it takes to get home from anywhere in Asia. I'm always so glad to step off an airplane. It's so good to be home."

"How long are you staying?" Ethan asked.

"I don't have to be back until January third. How's Winnie? She was busy talking to her friends and didn't notice me. I didn't want to ruin her big night."

"Abby can probably answer better than I can."

The only problem was, Abby didn't have any functioning brain cells right about now. She forced a smile and tried to gather her thoughts. "She's, um, good. The bruised ribs have healed almost all the way, and she no longer has to use a mobility help like the walker or even a cane. The cast has to stay on the wrist for another month, but the doctor says she's healing better than he expected."

"Oh, I'm so glad to hear that." Lucy hugged her again. "Thank you for coming to our rescue. I owe you!"

"I was happy to help Winnie, though you could have warned me that I might end up decorating this entire place while I was here."

Lucy gave her an apologetic look. "I'm sorry about that. I honestly thought Winnie would cancel the event."

"Then you don't know our grandmother as well as you think you do," Ethan said.

"It wasn't as terrible as I feared," Abby said. "I actually enjoyed most of it. Yes, decorating a Victorian mansion was totally out of my comfort zone, but in the end, things worked out."

"For what it's worth, the house looks better than I've ever seen it, at least the bits I saw as I walked through on my way here."

Abby smiled. "I can't take credit for that. The house is beautiful even without Christmas decorations, and the other Silver Belles helped immensely. Plus, Ethan had an entire crew from the hotel come out this morning to rescue us after a windstorm knocked down two trees and blew branches, broken Christmas lights and debris across the grounds."

The morning seemed a lifetime ago, though she couldn't shake the image of him out working with his crew, sweaty and masculine.

Lucy gave her brother a look of surprise. "Good for you. Way to step up."

"We're Lancasters and we help each other." He glanced at the clock. "I should probably run. It's late. I'm glad you're back safe."

He hugged his sister one more time, longer this time, then turned to Abby with an expression she couldn't quite decipher. "Thank you again for letting me read to Christopher. I enjoyed it very much. I'm not sure of my schedule over the next few nights, but tell him I'll try to drop by again soon."

"I'll tell him. He'll be excited." She forced a smile, not quite sure how to say good-night to a man who had been kissing her intimately just a few moments earlier.

He solved the awkwardness by leaning in and kissing her cheek. She allowed herself the indulgence of inhaling the deliciously expensive scent of him, leather and pine and male, before she stepped away.

"Get some rest," he said over his shoulder to his sister. "You look haggard."

Lucy stuck out her tongue at him. "Thank you for those kind words, but you're right. I *feel* haggard. I'll probably sleep for a week."

"We'll catch up when you've rested."

"I'll count on it."

Ethan gave Abby one more unreadable look, then slipped out the door.

When he was gone, Abby turned to her friend.

"I can't believe you came home early. It's so good to have you here."

"It's wonderful to see you, too," Lucy said, trying to hide a huge yawn.

"Ethan's right. You need to rest. Your usual bedroom

is open and ready for you. Also, Winnie made sure it's in one of the off-limits areas of the house for the tours, so you shouldn't have strangers traipsing through."

"Always a bonus," Lucy said with a smile.

"Can I help you carry your luggage up?"

"Nope. I only brought a backpack since Winnie lets me keep clothes and things here year-round. I'm just going to pop out to say good-night to her, and then I'll head up to bed."

"All right. Good night."

After Lucy left, Abby sank onto the sofa. The same one where she and Ethan had been entwined.

That kiss.

She licked her lips, still tasting him there. She should have stopped it. What good would come from indulging in something she knew would never go anywhere?

She was leaving shortly. Maybe even sooner than she thought. Now that Lucy was here, Winnie didn't really need Abby's help. There was no reason she couldn't load up her little SUV, scoop up her boy and her cat and flee into the night.

Christopher loved it here. He loved Winnie. He loved the corgis, the mountains, the snow.

She didn't want to go, either. These past few weeks had been the most enjoyable holiday season she had ever known. She would just have to be careful to make sure when they did leave, neither she nor Christopher left part of their hearts behind.

LUCY AWOKE TO delicious smells seeping through her door that was open a crack and one of her grandmother's corgis crushing her feet.

"Hello to you, too," she said. Her voice sounded raspy from disuse, and she cleared away the sleep as she automatically reached for her cell phone.

It was one in the afternoon. She hadn't quite slept through the clock but close enough.

She sat up, annoyed with herself. She hadn't meant to sleep so long. She'd learned through long experience that it was better to keep to a regular schedule and simply power through the exhaustion for a few days to acclimatize herself to a different time zone. Sleeping until early afternoon definitely wouldn't help her adjust to the rhythms of life here in Silver Bells.

Oh, well. One day of sleeping in wouldn't hurt anything.

"How did you get in here?" she asked the dog, who just looked back at her with a quizzical look. She must not have latched her door tightly after collapsing on her bed the night before.

"Also, which one are you?"

Again, the dog wasn't forthcoming with answers so Lucy lifted the tag and read the answer. "Nick. I should have known. Your sisters are too well behaved to climb into bed with someone they barely know."

The dog just did a circle at the foot of the bed and re-settled himself to a more comfortable position, then closed his eyes.

Lucy looked around her room, with its comforting familiarity.

Winnie had decorated this room when Lucy was a little girl, designating it strictly for Lucy's use when she came to stay. The walls originally were lavender, the bedspread a soft green.

When she was a teenager and Winnie had somehow

managed to persuade Lucy's parents to let her and Ethan come here to finish high school, Lucy and Winnie had redecorated it. They had painted the walls a deeper purple and Winnie had somebody install an egg-shaped swing.

It had been her favorite place on earth.

Winnie had been her touchstone, the anchor that had always brought her back to Silver Bells.

Lucy would have been lost without her grandparents.

She thought of Clive—bushy browed, bald head, mustache and the kindest smile in the world. She allowed herself a moment to miss him fiercely, then decided it was time to get up and go see how her grandmother was doing.

She stretched and was about to push the blankets away when the door opened a crack and an adorable face peeked through. "Hi, Aunt Lucy! I wanted to wake you up but Mom said I couldn't. You've been sleeping *forever*. I checked on you before and you didn't even make a sound."

Ah. Christopher must have opened the door a crack, allowing Nick to wriggle his way in.

"Hey, you. If it isn't my favorite boy in the whole world. Come give me a hug."

Christopher jumped on the bed and wrapped his arms around her. Lucy hugged him, feeling something wild and restless seem to settle inside her.

"You missed breakfast. And now it's lunchtime."

"I know. And now I'm hungry enough to eat a boy." She nuzzled her face in his neck, much to his giggly delight.

Oh, she loved this kid. She hadn't seen him in more than a year, and then only had a few days to spend in Phoenix hanging out with Abby. She tried to stay connected with video calls—yay for technology—but it wasn't the same as smelling the sweet little-boy scent of him.

"Can I sit in your swing?" Christopher asked.

"Please do."

He hopped off the bed, Nick close on his heels, and climbed into the swing. He was busy trying to make it move when the door opened another crack and Winnie appeared in the doorway. "You're really here. Oh, darling. I woke up this morning wondering if I'd imagined it in my old age. It's so marvelous to see you."

Winnie sat on the edge of the bed and hugged her, surrounding her in a cloud of Aqua Net hair spray and White Shoulders perfume, and Lucy felt as if she was finally home.

"How are you feeling?" she asked her grandmother when Winnie pulled away. "You seem to be getting around okay."

"No cane anymore. I'm not sorry to see that go, I'll tell you that. Don't you worry about me for a minute. I'm fine."

Lucy wasn't entirely certain she believed that, but she didn't want to argue with her grandmother in front of Christopher.

"I'm sorry I couldn't come right home after you were hurt. I should have figured out a way."

Winnie waved off her concern and settled in the easy chair next to the bed. "We managed, didn't we, Chris?"

"Yep," the boy said, still trying to make the swing move more.

"I'm just glad you sent me Abby and Christopher. I don't know what I would have done without them."

"Where is Abby?"

"We were running low on just about everything so she made a quick run to the store."

"I'm supposed to watch over Winnie," Christopher said, a pride in his voice that made Lucy smile.

"And what a wonderful job you've been doing, too," Winnie said, winking at Lucy.

"You have to be starving. Get dressed and I'll make you a grilled cheese sandwich."

She rolled her eyes at her grandmother. "How about I get dressed and make *you* a grilled cheese sandwich?"

"I don't care who makes it. I just want a grilled cheese sandwich," Christopher said.

Winnie chuckled. "You already had lunch, young man. I was there when your mom made you a PB&J."

"I can't help it if I'm still hungry."

Lucy had to smile. "All right. Let me jump in the shower, then it will be grilled cheese all around. Give me a minute."

The pulsing heat of the shower felt so good on her travel-weary body that she wanted to spend an hour there. She hurried things along, reluctant to leave Christopher waiting too long for his sandwich.

When she emerged from her bedroom a short time later and walked into the huge, comfortable kitchen, she found Winnie and Christopher at the kitchen table, engaged in a fierce game of slapjack.

She left them to it while she gathered the ingredients for sandwiches. She also found some crisp apples in the refrigerator that she sliced up for them.

She had just slid the sandwiches onto three plates when she heard the front door open.

"Winnie? Mama said you needed more folding chairs for tonight. She said we should go ahead and put them in the great room."

José.

Everything inside her seemed to melt like cheese on a hot burner at his voice, low and rich and beautiful.

"The great room is fine," her grandmother called back. "We're in the kitchen. Come back and say hi."

She had only a moment to steel herself before José walked into the kitchen, followed closely by his brother, Rodrigo.

She was aware they weren't alone. She could hear Christopher's chattering, her grandmother's greeting. Everything else seemed to fade away and she was once more on a Thai beach, in his arms.

A series of emotions seemed to cross his features rapidly when he saw her, until he seemed to gather himself. "Oh. Lucy. I didn't know you were back."

She smiled weakly, unable to breathe for a moment at seeing him again.

Oh, this was so stupid.

They had been friends forever. She adored his family. Rodrigo. She loved spending time with him. They laughed more together than she did with anybody else she knew.

Why did he have to go and ruin everything by throwing around words like *love* and *commitment*?

Ordinarily, she would have jumped into his arms and hugged him hard, as Christopher had done to her a short time earlier.

Now everything was so *wrong* between them, and she didn't know the first thing to say to him.

She hated this.

She should have stayed in Thailand. Or maybe she should have traveled somewhere even farther away. Nepal, maybe. Or Madagascar.

Rodrigo must have just noticed her. He let out a cry of joy.

"Lucy! Hi, Lucy!" he exclaimed, his face lighting up like the sun.

This, she could navigate.

"Hey, Rodrigo." She hugged him hard, feeling renewed hope for the goodness of the world at his open, honest affection.

"I missed you so much," he declared.

"Same goes. How's the Ping-Pong champion of Silver Bells doing these days?"

He laughed heartily. "Good. I've been practicing. Want to play me?"

"Of course, even though I know you're going to kick my butt, as always."

"Maybe we can play later. José is taking me bowling right now after we leave the chairs here. Want to come?"

She flashed a look at José, who was looking anywhere in the room but at her.

"I can't today, but thanks for the invitation. Maybe another day while I'm still in town."

"Okay."

Even when she had been away a year, she and Rodrigo seemed to pick up where they left off. He loved her unconditionally, just as he loved all the other people in his world, and she always felt like the luckiest girl on the planet.

"Guess what?" he informed her with a gleeful look. "José has a date tonight."

To her chagrin, she could feel her jaw sag. "Does he?"

"With a lady," Rodrigo confided.

"Wow."

She didn't know what to say beyond that.

"Is it that nice Quinn Bellamy again?" Winnie asked. "I sure like her."

RaeAnne Thayne 217

"She's nice and she's pretty. But not as pretty as you," Rodrigo said loyally to Lucy.

She finally risked a glance at José and could see by the hardness of his jaw and the firm set of his mouth that he wasn't thrilled with the direction his brother had taken the conversation.

"I've got one more load of chairs to bring in," he said. "I'll just put them with the rest."

"That's fine," Winnie said. "Lucy, why don't you help him while I give Rodrigo one of his favorite sugar cookies."

She narrowed her gaze at her grandmother but didn't feel she had any kind of choice in the matter, especially since her grilled cheese sandwich now looked as appetizing as a plate of dancing shrimp from the night market in Chiang Mai.

She walked outside with José into the clear, beautiful December afternoon toward his pickup truck.

"So. Quinn. I guess I don't know her. How long have you been dating?"

"We've gone out only two or three times. I'm not sure you could exactly classify that as dating."

"More than once is dating. Have you slept with her?"

"None of your damn business." He pulled two folding chairs from the bed of the pickup, set them against the tire of the truck and reached in for two more, all without looking at her.

"Really? I would have said you kind of made it my business when you came to Thailand and messed up everything."

He faced her finally, and the intensity of his expression made her catch her breath. "I told you I have feelings for you. That I've had feelings for you forever. And you basically told me to go to hell. Who messed up what again?"

She had handled that encounter so badly. If she could do it all over again, would she have done anything differently? She honestly didn't know. She only knew she hated this distance between them and the terrible fear that she could never regain what they had lost.

"I didn't tell you to go to hell."

"Not in so many words. We want different things, you said. You don't believe in love, you said. Why can't we just have a steamy affair and call it good, you said."

Had she really said those words? He made her sound hard, unfeeling. Awful. She wasn't. Was she? She had only been trying to process a moment that had shocked her to her core.

"Give me a break. You sprung all of that on me out of nowhere without warning and I didn't know how to respond."

"Come on, Lucy. You're not blind. You had to see I have feelings for you. Either you ignored it or you didn't want to see. Everybody else in the damn world seemed to guess except you."

She grabbed a chair and held it in front of her as if it were a shield against his words.

He looked at her, looked at the chair, then sighed. "If I had given you days to prepare, would your response have been different? For instance, if I told you that I'm still in love with you and nothing has changed, what would you say?"

I would say then maybe you shouldn't be dating another woman.

She couldn't say those words, and felt small and ugly for even thinking them.

"From my perspective, love ruins everything. Our friendship is a perfect example. We've always had fun together and now everything is different."

She didn't know what else to say and felt ridiculously like she was going to cry. Wouldn't that be a nightmare?

"You have always been a dear friend to me," she finally said. "One of my favorite people on the planet. Every time I see you, I'm happy. We like the same kinds of food, the same music, the same activities. We are attracted to each other. Why can't we just sleep together and let that be enough?"

"You know why. Because it wouldn't be enough for me."

"How do you know? Maybe we would be lousy together."

He raised an eyebrow. "We wouldn't be," he said with an absolute certainty that made her toes curl.

"So it's your way or nothing. You're willing to ruin a good friendship because I'm not willing to play romantic games."

"It's not about playing games. It's about being willing to put your heart on the line. About allowing yourself to be vulnerable to somebody else. You have never done that. You want to be the one in control, the person who holds all the cards. I've seen the way you operate, Lucy. The moment anybody tries to get close to you, you run away without looking back. I would rather not put myself through that."

His words gutted her, left her feeling attacked and hurting. He said he loved her. How could he when he seemed to respect her so little?

She couldn't face him now so she picked up the three

chairs, as many as she could carry, and did exactly what he accused her of doing. She walked away.

Rodrigo was waiting for them in the foyer, a worried look on his face. "I heard yelling. Are you guys mad at each other?"

"Yes," she answered at the same time José said the opposite.

"Which is it?"

"We're just having a disagreement. It's no big deal," she lied.

José said nothing, only gave her a hard look as he walked past her to set the chairs in the great room.

"We better go," he said to his brother. "Those bowling pins won't knock themselves down."

Rodrigo apparently found that hilarious. He guffawed, knocking his shoulder against José's.

She watched the two of them together, touched by the generous affection between them. One of the things she admired most about José was his commitment to his family. He was a wonderful, loving brother and son.

Why did he have to ruin everything?

"I'm just going to say goodbye to Winnie and Christopher, then we can go."

"Okay," Rodrigo said happily.

José walked into the kitchen, and she heard the murmur of voices underneath Rodrigo's recitation of how bad he was going to beat his brother at bowling.

A few moments later, José returned. "Let's go," he said to his brother.

"Bye, Lucy. I'll see you later."

"Have fun bowling," she said. "And José. Have fun on your date tonight."

A muscle flexed in his jaw but he said nothing, only ushered his brother out the door, leaving Lucy feeling this odd, empty ache inside.

It wasn't love, Lucy told herself sternly. What she felt for José was simply…admiration. Respect. Attraction. But not love.

She refused to let it be love.

CHAPTER TWELVE

"I HAD SUCH a wonderful time last night. It was just the best. Are you sure there aren't any more tickets available? I'd love to take my sister, who lives over in Hope's Crossing."

Abby, her arms full of grocery bags, shook her head at the woman in the expensive-looking down coat who had waylaid her as she walked out of the store.

"Winnie says all the tickets sold out the day they went on sale. I'm sorry."

"If you find out differently, please let me know. Maybe there's a waiting list or something I could put my name on. My schedule is pretty flexible."

A waiting list. That was a good idea, one she wasn't sure Winnie had thought about.

"I'll mention starting a waiting list to the Silver Belles."

"I would like my name at the top. Louise Arnold. My husband owns the real estate agency over on Pine Street. I would be a Silver Belle myself but I can't sing worth a darn. Last night sure made me wish I'd taken voice lessons or something."

"Thanks, Louise. I'll make sure to pass along to Winnie and the others how much you enjoyed your evening."

"So much. I've already told all my friends from out of town how wonderful it was. If Winnie opens up any other dates between now and Christmas, I'm sure she could fill them in a heartbeat, especially as it's for such a good cause."

"I'll tell them. Thank you."

Louise waved at her, climbing into a luxury SUV while Abby loaded her bags.

She would say the first ever Christmas at Holiday House had definitely been a success. Louise was the third person who had stopped Abby during her short shopping excursion to tell her how much they had enjoyed it.

Everyone had been so kind, treating her as if she alone had been responsible for the evening's success, merely because she had been the one who answered the door and took tickets.

Was everyone always this genuinely nice, or was her reception here because of her close connection to someone so obviously beloved as Winnie?

Leaving this place would be hard. In only a few weeks, she had come to love so many things about Silver Bells, from the gorgeous setting to the kind people to the historic architecture.

She could stay.

This wasn't the first time the idea had popped into her head. Christopher was already lobbying hard for that option. As before, she quickly pushed the possibility away. She was struggling enough not to make a fool of herself over Ethan. The smartest thing for her right now would be to go back to Phoenix, finish packing up their apartment and head straight to Austin to start her new life there.

The idea appealed to her about as much as trying to do a 360 off the ski jump in town.

Austin had history, too, and she was quite certain she would find the people there every bit as kind as those she had met here. She had a job waiting for her, an apartment already. She had investigated schools, neighborhoods, extracurricular programs for Christopher.

She had everything figured out, and she wasn't going to throw away months of planning simply because she had enjoyed this holiday break so very much.

With that thought firmly in mind, she drove through the picturesque streets toward Holiday House.

She reached the house just as a shiny blue pickup truck pulled through the gates heading out. José Navarro lifted a hand in greeting from the driver's seat and his brother, Rodrigo, waved with wild enthusiasm.

She waved back, feeling heartened as she pulled up to the house.

When she carried the groceries into the kitchen, she found Christopher eating a grilled cheese sandwich while Lucy entertained him and Winnie with card tricks.

They all greeted her. Lucy jumped up. "Can I carry in groceries for you?"

She held up the multiple bags hanging on each arm. "This is everything. I take it as a personal challenge to carry all the bags in one trip."

"Everybody needs a goal, I guess," Lucy said. She smiled, but Abby thought she detected shadows in her friend's expression. Maybe she was still just tired.

"Hey, Mom. Guess what?" Christopher beamed at her around a giant bite of sandwich.

"Finish what you're eating, then you can tell me."

He sighed but chewed several times and swallowed, then chased it down with a glass of water.

"Guess what?" he repeated. "My friend Rodrigo and his brother were just here. They're going bowling. Can we go bowling sometime? Maybe we could take my friend Dakota."

Everyone seemed to be Christopher's friend, which she found one of the best things about her son. She smiled. "That does sound like fun. We'll have to see if we can find time while we're here. I'll see if I can arrange it with Mariah."

She had started putting away groceries when she noticed Winnie wincing a little and flexing her fingers.

"Are you hurting? Do you need a pain pill? I was worried yesterday was too much for you."

"I am just fine. Don't worry about me."

"Maybe you should try to rest for a while before tonight. It's going to be another long evening for you, leading tour groups."

"I will," Winnie promised. "I need my strength."

"That reminds me," Abby said. "You are the talk of the town right now. While I was shopping, everyone had wonderful things to say about Christmas at Holiday House last night. I was even asked about a cancellation list."

Winnie's wrinkled features brightened. "Oh, that's a good idea. We had two people cancel yesterday and ask to come a different night. I had to tell them every night was full. I'll talk to the board members about figuring out a system to keep track of a waiting list."

They talked about the logistics of it for a few more moments and details they still needed to iron out. Lucy was uncharacteristically quiet while they talked.

As Abby finished putting away the last of the groceries, she saw Winnie wince again.

"You know, I can wake you when dinner is ready. I'm making more of that chicken enchilada soup you liked."

"That does sound good. All right. Only because you're making me," she said with a dour look as she rose and made her way down the hall to her room.

"Chris, it's rest time for you, too."

"I'm too old to take a nap. I'm five years old now."

This was not a new argument between them but one her son had yet to win.

"I've told you that you don't have to take a nap. You only have to play quietly in your room for a half hour. You can read a book or play with your toys. It's up to you."

She had been trying to keep some sort of routine while they were here in Colorado. She wanted to think it had been good for him. She *knew* it had been good for her.

"Only half an hour, right? Then I can come out again and play with Lucy?"

"Unless she has something else going on."

"I've got no plans," Lucy said. "I'm all yours."

Her son gave a heavy sigh and trudged off to their room as if he were carrying Santa's entire pack on his back.

After he left, Lucy cleared away the plates the three of them had been eating sandwiches from. "Don't tell me to nap. I've been sleeping for the past fourteen hours."

Though Lucy tried to make a joke, Abby could still see something was bothering her.

"Is everything okay?" she finally asked.

Lucy looked startled but forced a smile. "Sure. Everything's fine. Perfect. I'm home. What could be wrong?"

She obviously didn't want to talk about whatever was bothering her. Abby could wait. She had learned when they were roommates that Lucy sometimes needed to process things in her own way before she was ready to share.

"I'm so glad you were able to make it here a few days

early. Your grandmother seems overjoyed to have you back."

Lucy's face softened. "Thank you for taking such good care of her these past few weeks."

Abby poured a cup of coffee and sat across from her. "I enjoyed every minute of it, as I'm sure you knew I would. I can see why you've always raved about your grandmother. She is a remarkable woman." She paused. "You take after her in a lot of ways."

Lucy gazed at her and then, to Abby's total astonishment, she actually sniffled a little. What in the world was going on? Lucy *never* cried.

"She's pretty wonderful. I wish I could be a tenth the woman she is."

Abby touched her friend's hand. "Why do you always put yourself down like that? You're bright, beautiful, caring. Winnie's granddaughter, through and through."

"I love you, you know," Lucy said.

"I love you, too," Abby said.

"I don't have another friend I could have called at the last minute to help out with Winnie."

Abby didn't know why Lucy was in this strange, reflective mood. It was very unlike her.

"It worked out for all of us." She hesitated, then plunged forward. "We've had a wonderful time here in Silver Bells, but now that you're back, I was thinking maybe Christopher and I should take off and go home to Phoenix."

"No!" Lucy said, eyes widening. "You can't go already!"

"Winnie never really needed my help, at least not with her health. She has a vast network of friends who could have stepped in for the minimal care she needed, which was mostly helping her wrap up her arm so she could shower at night and helping her dress. She's become so used to the cast she doesn't need even that now. I was glad I could help get things ready for the Silver Belles' event, but that's all done now. Now that you're home, there's no real reason for us to stay."

"Other than I want you to! I was so looking forward to spending the holidays with you and Christopher. Can't you stay at least through Christmas?"

"That's another week and a half."

"Right. Not long at all."

What would she do here for a week and a half? Besides spend time with her son enjoying a winter wonderland.

"Winnie will want you to stay through Christmas. You know she will. And of course I want you to. Ethan probably does, too. You two looked like you were getting along great last night."

Abby could feel herself blush. How could she explain to Ethan's sister that he was the main reason she worried that she should leave now, before she did something completely stupid like fall in love with him?

"What's waiting for you in Phoenix now except moving boxes and an empty apartment? Would you rather spend the holidays alone with Christopher there or here in Colorado in this house you've decorated so beautifully for the season, being with people who love you? Namely me and Winnie."

At least she hadn't included Ethan among that number.

"You would break Winnie's heart if you left before the holidays," Lucy went on. "While you were out shopping, my grandmother mentioned at least twice how much she was looking forward to having Christopher around this year to brighten the season."

"I'm beginning to remember why I always hated arguing with you."

Lucy grinned. "Because I can get my point across in eight languages?"

"That, and you don't leave room for anyone else to get a word in edgewise. In all the years I've known you, you've never let anybody stand in the way of what you want. Even when they start out thinking they want something else."

She wasn't sure what she said but Lucy said nothing, only stared at her for a long moment with a strange look in her eyes.

"Thank you for that reminder," she finally said. "I needed it."

"Glad I could help," Abby said, completely baffled.

"So does that mean you're staying?"

Abby knew when she was beat. It didn't help that she had been thinking many of those same things. "Christopher has loved his time here. I suppose we can stay until Christmas. Everything you said is true. We will be going home to moving boxes, chaos and a solitary Christmas. While we do have good friends in Arizona, they're all busy with their own families this time of year."

Lucy looked delighted. "Oh, yay. I'm so glad. And trust me, Winnie will be over the moon. We're going to have so much fun. You'll see."

She didn't doubt she would have a good time with Lucy and with Winnie. Now, if only she could figure out how to keep from ruining everything by falling hard for Ethan.

Lucy rose from the table with an air of suppressed energy, as if she had come to a decision about something.

"I know you said it was time for Christopher to take a

rest and I know it hasn't been a half hour yet. But would you mind terribly if I borrowed him this afternoon?"

"You want to borrow my five-year-old? First, of course. Second, why?"

Lucy shrugged, avoiding her gaze. "I have been sleeping all morning and now I have a lot of energy. I need somewhere to put it. Rodrigo and José were leaving here to go to the bowling alley in town and Christopher wanted to go with them. Right now, that seems like a lot of fun. Would you mind if I take Christopher?"

"Now?"

"I know, it's a wild idea. We'll be back in an hour. Maybe an hour and a half. Bowling doesn't take too long. When we get home, he probably even would have time to rest before the big event tonight."

Abby didn't know what Lucy was doing, but she suspected it had something to do with José Navarro.

Was she a terrible mother that she loved the idea of having an hour to herself, with absolutely nothing to do but read the new paperback she had picked up at the supermarket?

"Sure. Knock yourself out."

Yes, she had told Christopher he had to stay in his room for a quiet half hour. But once in a while there was nothing wrong with breaking the rules.

SHE SHOULDN'T HAVE come.

Lucy stood just inside the bowling alley attached to one of the most popular pizza joints in town, wishing with all her heart she hadn't been so impulsive.

What was she doing here? What was she trying to prove?

She had been struck by what Abby had said about her powers of persuasion. Maybe in some corner of her mind, she thought maybe she could wield those powers against José and convince him to bend a little. Maybe they could forget this heat between them and just go back to being good friends. Even better, maybe they could just have a steamy holiday affair, get it all out of their system and then go back to being friends.

Okay. She wasn't thinking rationally. Now that she was here, she realized how impulsively shortsighted she was being. José wouldn't bend on this. She knew him well enough to know that. It was all or nothing for José Navarro.

She should just slip back out of the bowling alley, climb back into her rental car and drive back to Holiday House.

Except she had dragged Christopher into this whole thing, and he was looking around the bowling alley with wide-eyed excitement.

"I can't wait," he said. "I always wanted to go bowling."

She couldn't back out of it now. She might be a terrible person but she wasn't completely irredeemable. She could not offer a child a treat and then take it away simply because of her own poor decisions.

How could she deny Christopher something he was looking forward to, only because she had chickened out?

What was wrong with her? She was a freaking mess. José was right. She did not want him, but the moment she found out someone else was dating him all she could think about was kissing him again.

No. That wasn't right, either. She absolutely did want him, she just knew the two of them together would be disastrous.

He was a sweet romantic who wanted happily-ever-after. She, on the other hand, was the world's greatest cynic. Even her best friend said so.

She and José could never be together. She would break his heart and would wind up hating herself because of it.

So what was she doing here?

"Do you want shoes or not?"

The pimply-faced clerk behind the counter at the bowling alley was looking at her like she was a few pins short of a spare.

"Shoes. Right. I'm a women's size seven and a half. What shoe size are you, kiddo?" she asked Christopher.

He shrugged. "I don't know. I'm five years old. Is that my shoe size?"

"Take off your boot."

He sat on the ground, slipped off one of his cute little snow boots and handed it to her. "Looks like he's a youth size one," she said.

A moment later, the clerk handed her two pairs of oh-so-attractive bowling shoes. "You'll be in lane six," he said.

Lucy found a bench and helped Christopher into his shoes.

"Why do we have to wear special shoes?" he asked.

"Regular shoes might damage the floor," she said. "Plus, these are supposed to help you bowl better."

"Do they have magic powers?"

A legitimate question. "Not that I know of, but we'll have to see."

Soon they were both ready to go. They stowed their own footwear in a cubby, then selected a couple of balls she thought would be sized right for them before heading to their designated lane.

In some corner of her mind, she had been hoping she

and Christopher would be positioned on the opposite side of the bowling alley from Rodrigo and José, and the two Navarro brothers would never even know she had been there.

She should have known fate wouldn't be that kind to her. Lane six happened to be right next to their lane. Naturally.

Oh, this had been such a mistake.

With a sigh, she made her way over to their lane, which was already set up with bumpers for Christopher.

She had just set her ball into the return when Rodrigo spotted her. "Lucy! You came bowling with us!" Rodrigo hurried over and enveloped her in a huge hug, joy radiating from every pore.

José didn't look nearly as thrilled.

His mouth was set in a line, his eyes dark and cloudy.

"It sounded like so much fun that Christopher and I decided to come, too. You don't mind, do you?"

"No!" Rodrigo assured her. "But we're almost done. I won one game and José won the other one. He's really good."

Yes. She could attest to that, at least if she were judging the way he kissed.

"This ball is so heavy."

She glanced down and saw Christopher red faced, arms straining to hold the bowling ball.

"Sorry, kiddo." She quickly took it from him and set it on the ball return along with hers. "Should we bowl?"

He threw a fist up in the air. "Yes! Winner gets an ice-cream cone. That's what you said."

"That's right."

For the next while at least she was able to focus on Christopher as she taught him the basics of bowling—how to line up the ball and release it at precisely the right moment and with just the right momentum.

Each time his ball made any contact whatsoever with a pin, he jumped around as if he'd won an Olympic gold medal, which she found adorable.

She had just taken a turn when she heard a shout of happiness from the next lane over.

"Winner winner chicken dinner," Rodrigo crowed, dancing around his brother.

"You rocked it, dude," José said good-naturedly. "Somebody's been working hard on their bowling game."

"It's me." Rodrigo held up a hand. She had to smile. Rod was a lucky guy, actually. He was loved and supported by his family, who all worked hard to help him live his best possible life.

Differently abled people in some of the other parts of the globe where she had worked didn't always have the same opportunities, sometimes facing prejudice and even superstition.

"How's it going over here?" José asked, interrupting her thoughts. She was glad to see that he seemed to have put away his annoyance for now.

"Chris is a natural, aren't you, bud?"

"I knocked down six different pins on my first try!"

"Wow. That's terrific." José smiled down at the boy and she felt something catch in her chest.

"And on my second try, I knocked down two more. That's—" he counted on his fingers "—eight all together."

"Good job."

"Can we watch Lucy play?" Rodrigo asked his brother.

José looked torn. She could tell he didn't want to but he looked at Rodrigo then back at Lucy and Christopher and shrugged. "Sure. We still have a little while before I have to take you home."

This felt much worse, having him sit behind her when she tried to bowl. She was ultra aware of him, long legs stretched out as he talked to Christopher and Rodrigo, who were apparently the best of friends already.

Still, she managed to make it through the match with a respectable score. It wasn't as good as Christopher's, though, since he had the advantage of the bumpers, which were lifted for her.

Seeing the jubilation on his features took away any sting of defeat. "I won!" he exclaimed. "That means I get an ice-cream cone."

"You sure do. Let's put away our shoes and balls and we can go get one."

"I won, too. Can I have an ice-cream cone?" Rodrigo asked his brother.

"Sure," José said. He pulled a bill out of his wallet. "Here. Why don't you take Christopher over and the two of you can pick what you want."

The two walked to the concession stand, chattering about Christmas, from what she could tell.

As soon as they were out of earshot, José rounded on her.

"What are you doing here, Lucy?"

She had been asking herself the same thing for the past hour. "I told you. When you mentioned that you were taking Rodrigo bowling this afternoon, I thought it sounded like fun."

He looked around to make sure no one was around before he spoke in a low, intense voice. "You're not going to change my mind, Lucy. No matter what games you play. I'm not sleeping with you."

She yanked her boots on with more force than necessary. "Is that really what you think of me? I'm going to spend the entire holiday break chasing you all over town because I am desperate for a man?"

"No," he said quietly. "I think too few people have said no to you and you don't like it."

"Are you kidding?" she snapped, forgetting to keep her voice down. "People have been saying no to me my entire life."

No, Lucy, you can't stay in the same school two years in a row. You have to go back and live with your dad.

No, Lucy. You can't stay with your grandparents this year. We've decided to send you to boarding school.

No, Lucy. I didn't invite you to the wedding because my new wife doesn't like that you're older than she is.

"I'm sorry to be one more, then." He did look regretful. She thought for a moment he was going to reach out and pull her into an embrace.

She was relieved when he didn't. At least that's what she told herself.

"We're going to see each other again over this holiday season," he said quietly. "Silver Bells is a small town and we can't avoid it, with our families being so close. Can we both please try not to make this any harder?"

Christopher and Rodrigo returned at that moment, and she could do nothing but give a short nod.

As she bundled Christopher into her rental car to drive back to Holiday House, her throat felt tight and her chest ached. She told herself it was just residual exhaustion from two days of travel, but she knew better. She was grieving the loss of a dear friend and slowly coming to accept the hard, inescapable truth that she could do nothing about it.

CHAPTER THIRTEEN

"How did last night go?" Ethan asked his grandmother on a video call Sunday afternoon. "Was the second night as successful as the first?"

Winnie beamed at him. "Even better than Friday. We didn't have a single no-show last night. At the end of the night, we even had several people donate more than the original price of the ticket."

"That's great. People seem to be raving. I've had several comments at the hotel."

"And you were so worried about me. Maybe you should learn to trust your old grammy."

"You're not old. But you're probably right. I should."

"Probably?"

He smiled. "Definitely right. As always."

"Darn straight." As she tilted her head, the sunlight streaming into her room made her hair glow. "You're still coming for Sunday dinner tonight, right? You haven't even seen your sister since she got here."

"I saw her for a few moments when she arrived," he defended himself.

He would have stopped by last night, but he had been slammed with some last-minute problems at their Macau hotel that had kept him on the phone most of the night. Besides that, he had expected Lucy to be busy helping out with the fundraiser.

And, okay, he had been avoiding Abby.

He didn't like the way she and Christopher kept wriggling their way under his skin, no matter how hard he tried to keep them out.

He had a long tradition of coming for Sunday dinner with Winnie or taking her out to the hotel restaurant. That practice had fallen to the wayside over the past month since her injury.

"You shouldn't be fixing a big meal on the one day you have free from hosting your big event," he protested.

"I'm not fixing jack," Winnie told him with a grin. "Abby and Lucy put their heads together earlier and decided to try a recipe Lucy learned when she was in Morocco a few years ago. I think they're cooking it in a tangerine, somehow."

He did his best to hide his smile. "Do you mean a tagine? That's a casserole dish from that area of the world."

"Oh, you're right. That's what Lucy said. Tagine, not tangerine. And they're making couscous."

He did like Moroccan food. Lancaster Hotels didn't have property in the country, but he had visited a few times to check out other luxury hotels and found the country beautiful and fascinating.

"They said there will be tons of food. I think Lucy is planning on you being here."

Ethan shifted, torn about what to do. While he did want to see his sister and knew his time with her was limited, he knew spending more time with Abby and Christopher was dangerous.

It was hard enough now to think of them leaving town soon. Spending more time with them would only make their inevitable parting harder.

"I don't know," he hedged. "I have a lot on my plate today."

"Too much to even take time to have a meal with your family? You work too hard. Your grandfather would have been the first to tell you to slow down and enjoy life a little."

He sighed. "I'll see plenty of Lucy while she's home. Did she tell you she's agreed to work at the hotel all week as a translator? She'll probably be sick of me by week's end."

"You know that's impossible. Lucy adores you."

He adored her right back. Though separated in age by three years—and his only full sibling amid a sea of halves and steps—they had always been close. He didn't want to disappoint her. If that meant spending an evening with Abby and Christopher, he could probably manage it.

"Fine. Couscous sounds delicious. I should be able to break away. What time are you eating?"

"Seven."

"I'll see you then."

That gave him four hours to figure out how to protect himself from any further incursions by Abby Powell and her adorable son.

"You know I'm happy to help you cook," Abby said to Lucy as they worked together in the kitchen. "But I think Christopher and I should eat in our room."

Lucy gawked at her. "Don't be silly. Why would you even suggest that?"

Abby shrugged, feeling foolish. "I don't know. This seems like a family dinner for you, your brother and your grandmother. The first chance you've all had to really get together since you've been back in town. Christopher and

I really don't need to intrude on your evening. I know he can be a bit of a distraction."

"What's a 'traction'?" Christopher looked puzzled and intrigued.

Oops. She thought he had headphones in, watching his favorite PBS children's show, and couldn't hear her. That would serve her right for trying to use her son as an excuse.

She forced a smile. "A distraction is something that diverts attention away from something else. Like when you're playing with a ball and then see a truck and decide to stop playing ball and play truck instead. I just meant that instead of talking to each other, Lucy and Ethan might want to talk to you since they both like you so much."

"I like them, too. Ethan is my friend and so is Lucy."

"There. You see? We will both want to hang out with our buddy Christopher. And you, of course." Lucy said the last as if an afterthought, then grinned to show she was teasing.

"A family dinner isn't much of a family dinner with only the three of us. How can you resist the smell of that tagine? It's going to be epic. And I made enough to feed Winnie's entire choir."

Abby refrained from pointing out she and Christopher could still enjoy Lucy's food, just in the comfort of their own room.

"It does smell good," she conceded. "It's wonderful to see you have picked up a few culinary skills since we were living in the dorm together. As I recall, you could barely reheat a can of soup."

"I've lived in a few places over the years where it was either learn to cook or starve. I like to eat too much to starve so I adapted."

From Abby's perspective, Lucy had changed a great deal

from her old college roommate. She had to admit, Lucy had intimidated her at first. She had thought they would have little in common when they were fortuitously matched by the university's housing department.

From the first night, something between them had clicked. Perhaps it had something to do with the fact that they had both endured difficult, unorthodox childhoods. She didn't know. She only knew she cherished Lucy and felt so lucky to have her in her life.

"I'm setting five plates at the table. You have to join us."

Abby sighed, throwing up her hands both actually and figuratively. "See? It's utterly impossible to win an argument with you."

Lucy didn't laugh, as she expected. Instead, her friend's smile slid away, and for a moment she looked almost…sad.

The expression slid away so quickly Abby wondered if she had imagined it.

Lucy shrugged. "It's a gift. What can I say?"

"Too many things. That's the problem. And in any language."

"Ethan will be here in about a half hour, so we'll eat shortly after that."

She mentally braced herself. "Okay."

"That's not a problem for you, is it?"

"Why would it be a problem?"

Lucy shrugged. "I don't know. I just thought I sensed something weird between you the other night when I arrived."

"You didn't," Abby said briskly. "We had both had a long day. That's all."

"Ethan is my friend," Christopher interjected into the conversation. Apparently, he had given up watching his show and was now playing a game on his tablet and listening to the two of them talk. "He took us on the snow-tube hill and we went so fast you wouldn't believe it!"

"Wow! That sounds fun," Lucy said.

"Yeah. And he said he would take us skiing, except my mom's afraid of being too high up in the air. So Ethan said he would take just me and Mom could watch us from the log."

"The lodge, sweetie," Abby corrected gently.

"Right. The lodge."

"You should really take him up on that while you're here," Lucy advised. "My brother is an excellent ski instructor. He taught me when I was a little girl. I was just your age."

"You were five years old, too?" Christopher asked.

"Around that. Maybe a year or two older. I just remember that Ethan was three years older and already a good skier. I thought he could do anything." She grinned. "I'll tell you a secret. I still think he can do anything."

Despite all her self-talk about keeping boundaries with him, Abby couldn't help but be charmed to imagine a younger Ethan teaching his sister to ski.

"I like Ethan. He's my friend," Christopher said.

"You have good taste," Lucy said.

As the two of them chattered about the things they each liked about Ethan, Abby fought down a growing sense of dread.

She should have been more careful. She had been so busy trying and failing to protect her own heart that she hadn't given the care she should have to protect her son.

Christopher was so impressionable right now, open-hearted and loving. Her son clearly adored Ethan already.

She couldn't let the man become too important to either of them. Once she and Christopher left Silver Bells, what were the odds she would ever see him again? Probably not great.

Christopher already would have to leave Winnie, whom he loved. She hoped she hadn't doubled his pain.

"If Ethan's coming over, I'm gonna go get my digger. I told him I would show him when he came over again."

"You left all your trucks in the box by your bed, remember?"

"I remember."

Christopher scooted off his chair and raced to their rooms.

Lucy watched after him with an affectionate smile. "I sure love that kid of yours."

"What's not to love? I'm the luckiest mom in the world."

"I can't disagree." Lucy paused. "He's really taken to Ethan, hasn't he? And vice versa."

"Your brother made a strong impression on him during our outing on the tubing hill, probably because Chris hasn't spent a lot of time around men lately."

Lucy gave her a meaningful look. "You should really do something about that. Kevin has been gone two years."

She was half-tempted to tell Lucy about her disastrous dates and the humiliating nausea that had resulted, but it was too embarrassing. She'd already overshared with one of the Lancasters. She didn't need to tell the other one.

"I will," she finally said. "When I'm ready. I loved Kevin with all my heart."

"I know. And you were shattered when he died. I get that. But you don't have to love a man to date him. Why can't you just go out for fun and companionship?"

"Are you suggesting I should take romantic advice from the woman who self-identifies as the world's biggest cynic?"

"I believe in love for other people. How could I not? You and Kevin were sweet together. It was lovely to see two people care about each other so much."

"So why are you convinced that kind of love is impossible for you?"

Lucy looked down at the onions she was chopping for the couscous. "I don't know. I guess maybe some of us are programmed differently. We lack the necessary genetic markers that allow us to open our hearts to love."

"You think you're predestined to be unhappy like your parents were."

"I think the odds are good that I would screw up any long-term relationship," she said flatly.

Abby knew it was a mistake to ask, but she couldn't resist. "What about Ethan? He has the same genes, the same parental history. Are you saying you don't think he could ever fall in love?"

"I hope so," Lucy said, though she didn't sound entirely convinced. Which wasn't an answer at all, really.

Abby wanted to press her, but Christopher came back into the room before she could, his arms loaded with all his favorite diecast vehicles. "I brought my digger but I also brought my dump truck and the grader. Do you think Ethan will want to see the grader?"

"I wouldn't be at all surprised," Lucy said. "Now why don't you help us set the table, then you can go in and tell my grandmother that dinner will be ready in a few moments?"

"Okay," he said happily, and hurried to obey.

"HERE. YOU SIT by me."

Ethan had to smile at the boy's peremptory tone. Apparently, he was taking orders now from a little boy.

"Christopher. You're being bossy again. Remember we talked about how that's not good manners? When you would like someone to do something, you should always ask them, not tell them they have to do it."

Christopher gave a sigh that sounded put-upon.

"Ethan, you're my friend. Would you please sit by me so I can show you my digger and my grader?"

"I would be delighted. Thank you."

He sat beside the boy and pulled out his napkin, laying it carefully across his lap. He was charmed when Christopher immediately mimicked him.

He spent a few moments admiring the diecast vehicles and remembering his own vast collection when he was this age.

"Have you done anything fun this weekend?" he asked him.

"Yesterday I played with Lucy and Winnie while my mom went to the store and then I went bowling with Lucy and José and Rodrigo."

He raised an eyebrow at Lucy, who had just come in carrying a platter of olives and other vegetables. If he wasn't mistaken, she might have blushed a little.

"Did you?"

"It was my first time. I picked a green ball with glitter on it and then Rodrigo and me had ice-cream cones. Vanilla. That's my favorite."

"Mine, too."

"When we came home, I went outside with my mom and we played in the snow. We built a snowman."

He could picture it clearly, both of them laughing as they rolled the snow around the yard. He would have liked to have joined them.

"You built that snowman? Nice work! I saw him when I pulled up. He was huge. Bigger than me."

"And it was our very first time building a snowman, too," the boy informed him.

"You did an excellent job, both of you."

"I know."

"I loved seeing that snowman out my window this morning," Winnie said. "Thank you for putting him where I can see him the moment I wake up."

"You're welcome. My mom said when you look at the snowman, maybe you can remember us after we go back to Arizona."

"I won't need a snowman to remember you," Winnie said, her voice a little emotional.

The boy's words seemed to cast a pall over the entire meal. Ethan didn't like to think about it, either, but he also didn't want the meal his sister and Abby had prepared to go to waste. He carefully changed the subject.

"Explain to me how you've been in Thailand for a year, yet the first dish you make when you come home is a chicken tagine from Morocco."

Lucy looked sheepish. "I love Thai food. I really do. But I was craving chicken tagine and couscous the whole time I was there. This is mostly for my benefit."

"We're the lucky ones who get to enjoy it," Abby said. "This is delicious."

"Thanks." Lucy smiled, but Ethan knew his sister well enough to see the shadows in her eyes. She wasn't her usual cheerful self. Something was wrong. All his protective older brother instincts flared.

What was bothering her? He found it an interesting co-incidence that José had been acting like a bear caught in a trap all day, short-tempered and sour, which wasn't at all like him, either.

"The house seems so quiet without all the people and music and holiday cheer of the past two days," Winnie said.

"Don't worry. All of that will be back tomorrow," Abby said.

"Why aren't you doing your fundraiser on Sunday?" Ethan had to ask.

"Everybody wanted a day to rest their voices and be with their own families," Winnie explained. "It's such a busy time of year, it's hard to schedule something every single night. Maybe next year we'll start earlier in the season and only do it four nights a week or something."

"That makes sense."

"I can't believe we have already done it two nights and only have six more to go. Next Sunday at this time, we'll be all finished with them and will have money to start work on the adaptive lodge. It's going to be so marvelous to break ground for it in the spring."

His grandmother glowed when she talked about her latest pet project. Winnie loved helping other people. She always had. She was happiest when she was doing something to make the world better.

Too bad that altruistic, compassionate gene had completely passed over her son. Ethan's father generally only cared about himself.

"Do you think you'll make enough?" Lucy asked.

"Between that and the gingerbread contest next week

for Rodrigo's birthday, we should at least have enough for the initial construction. The endowment fund will help us with the continuing cost of running it and we should be able to supplement with the proceeds from future house tours. If we decide to continue them, anyway."

"Have you already chosen the site of the lodge?" Abby asked.

Ethan answered her. "This has been in the works for a while. We did the preliminary survey work last year."

He did not add that he had intended to have Lancaster Hotels donate the materials and labor portion of the construction costs. He hadn't even told Winnie that yet. He thought he would surprise her with it at Christmas.

"Speaking of the gingerbread contest next week, you're taking me again, right?" Winnie asked him.

"Of course. I wouldn't miss it."

"Ethan has been my partner at the annual gingerbread contest for years," Winifred told Abby. "Before this year and our own fundraiser here at Holiday House, that was always the highlight of the season for me. We can't win, unfortunately, since Lancaster Hotels always donates the grand prize. Personally, I don't think the rule disqualifying us is particularly fair, but I'm outvoted on that year after year."

Ethan laughed. "I don't think it would be a very good look if two Lancasters won a week's all-expenses-paid stay at one of their own hotels."

"Whatever," Winnie said. "If not for that rule, I'm sure we would have won the competition at least twice by now."

"Maybe we ought to sit this one out and simply enjoy the day, since you're on the injured list."

"Forget that! I've been working on designs all year long."

"Can I build a gingerbread house?" Christopher asked. "We did one at my preschool last year. I put crushed candy canes on the roof."

"I bet that looked great," Ethan said, smiling down at the boy. He shifted his gaze in time to see Abby looking at him with an odd, arrested look on her face.

She quickly looked away. "Maybe we can go watch."

"This is a pretty heated competition," Lucy said. "If you show up you have to come ready to throw down."

"Why do you want to throw gingerbread down? Won't it be ruined?" Christopher asked, looking genuinely concerned.

"It's a saying. It means come ready to do your best work. There is a kids' competition," Lucy said. "You should definitely join in the fun."

For the rest of the meal, they discussed the competition and the themes of previous years. The food was delicious and the company enjoyable, making Ethan glad he had let Winnie talk him into it.

Finally, after Lucy brought out a dessert of lemon cake she admitted she had bought from Emily Tsu's bakery, Abby slid her chair back.

"That was delicious. Thank you for including me, but somebody here needs to go to bed."

It was almost nine, Ethan realized with shock. They had been eating and talking for almost two hours.

"Not me," Christopher said sleepily.

"You've had a big day, sweetie. And will have an even bigger one tomorrow. Say good-night, and then we had better get you to bed before you fall asleep in the tub."

"I won't fall asleep because I'm not tired," he claimed, but ruined it with a big yawn that had the adults at the table all trying to hide their smiles.

"Come on," Abby said.

Christopher sighed. "Okay."

To Ethan's shock, Christopher threw his arms around his neck and hugged him. "Bye, Ethan. See you later."

Abby was frowning. Had he done something wrong? He couldn't help noticing that her frown seemed to ease a little as Christopher went around to Winnie and Lucy for hugs, as well. Was it only him, then?

After she left, he and his grandmother and sister stayed at the table a little longer, until he saw Winnie yawn, as well.

"Why don't you go to bed, Grandmother," he said. "I can help Lucy clean up."

"I'm not sure why I'm so tired," she grumbled. "I feel like I slept all day."

"You're still recovering from a major injury," Lucy said. "It's no wonder you're still tired."

"Take a little advice from your old grammy. It sucks to grow old."

Lucy hugged her. "I'll help you into your nightgown, since Abby is busy with Chris."

While the two women made their way to Winnie's room, Ethan rose and started clearing away the dinner dishes.

He was loading the last dish into the dishwasher when Lucy came out from their grandmother's room.

"I could have cleaned that up."

"I didn't mind. Thank you for dinner. It was delicious. Makes me wish again that we had a hotel in Marrakesh."

When she didn't respond by either word or gesture, he

had the feeling she had barely heard him. What was bothering her?

He finally decided to ask.

She looked surprised at the question. "What makes you think anything is wrong?"

"Maybe a wild guess. You just seem distracted and upset."

She shrugged off his concern. "Probably jet lag."

He didn't buy that was the only reason so he took a wild guess. "Did something happen yesterday at the bowling alley? Christopher said you were there with José and Rodrigo."

She froze, almost dropping the leftovers she was transferring to other containers. "We weren't there with José and Rodrigo. Technically, we went separately. I took Chris and José took Rod. We just happened to be assigned lanes next to each other."

He couldn't read her expression, which made him suspect he was right. Lucy was usually far more transparent. "And did something happen?"

She gave a laugh that sounded forced. "No, other than it was Christopher's first time and he still bowled better than I did."

"I can see where that would upset you greatly for thirty-six hours. I don't blame you a bit."

She made a face. "That's me. I'm as passionate about my bowling game as Winnie is about her gingerbread house."

"I'm surrounded by cutthroat competitors."

She smiled, though it still didn't quite reach her eyes. "I'm fine. You can stop worrying about me."

"Impossible. It's my job. It always has been, right?"

She let out a laugh that almost sounded like a sob and

hugged him. "I have the best big brother in the world," she said.

He wanted to ask her if her mood had anything to do with the tension he had sensed between her and José but had a feeling she wouldn't answer him honestly.

He wasn't sure he wanted to know, anyway.

He decided to change the subject. "I'm actually glad I had the chance to talk to you. You're still planning to help out at the resort this week, right?"

"Yes."

"Thanks for doing that."

"I don't mind. I still haven't heard exactly when I'll be needed yet."

"I'll have José get in touch with you."

If he had any doubt her strange mood had anything to do with José, the sudden tightness around her mouth would have confirmed his suspicion.

"Great," she said in a deceptively mild voice.

He decided to press forward on something he'd been thinking about for a long time, not sure if he would get the chance again during her visit home. "While you're here, will you do me one more favor?"

She looked suddenly wary. "If I can."

"Will you at least think about sticking around? You know we can always use someone with your vast language skills to help us out with translation services at the resort. And now that José is sticking around closer to home, I could use somebody to scout out new locations. Who better than my baby sister, who loves to explore new places and speaks about fifty-three languages?"

"Eight," she corrected. "With another six or seven dialects."

"Sorry. I always forget the dialects." He gave her a serious look. "I mean it. I would love to have you on board, Lucy. We make a good team. I know it's been important to you to go out and help the world. I respect that. I do. You've done wonderful work. But you could do good things at Lancaster Hotels, too. If you don't want to be involved on the business side, there's always plenty to do for our charitable arm."

"You know I'm not very good at staying in one place."

"I know that's what you've told yourself. But how do you know? You've been moving around constantly since college. Think about it, okay?"

"I like my life," she said.

"I know. But who's to say you wouldn't like your life as much or more if you stuck around where people love you?"

She didn't say anything, and he could only hope that meant she was absorbing his words as she said good-night and headed for her room.

WAS HE GONE yet?

Abby stood at the door of her room, hand on the knob as she debated whether it might be safe to go into the kitchen yet.

Before Christopher had fallen asleep, he had been almost inconsolable to realize he had left his favorite road-grader toy at the table. She had promised she would retrieve it and place it with the rest of his vehicles so he could find it first thing in the morning.

So why couldn't she make her legs cooperate to walk into the other room?

She knew why. She wasn't sure if Ethan was still there, and she didn't want to run the risk of facing him again.

She was such a coward.

She hadn't heard voices for several moments, since she had heard Lucy go down the hall to her room and her door close. A moment later she thought she heard the outside door close.

Okay. He was probably gone. She could do this. With determination, she turned the doorknob and walked out into the hallway.

The grader would probably be somewhere around the table. She flipped on the kitchen light and nearly screamed when a dark figure appeared in the doorway leading to the great room.

"Sorry. I didn't mean to scare you," Ethan said.

She willed her suddenly racing heart to calm down. "I didn't expect to see you. I thought I heard the outside door."

He gave her a long look, and she wondered if he could guess she had been avoiding him.

"I started to head out but then remembered that earlier today Winnie asked me to check on an electrical problem in one of the rooms on the second floor. I came back in like the dutiful grandson I am, then realized she didn't tell me which room. I was debating either trying them all or forgetting the whole thing. You don't know what she was talking about, do you?"

She could almost breathe normally again. "Yes. The power in the angel room keeps tripping. Every time it does, we have to reset the fuse in there. I wonder if it's an issue with too many Christmas lights overloading the circuit."

"That's a possibility. The electrical lines in this house were all upgraded during the previous renovation but can still cause issues. It could be a fire hazard. I better take a look. It might be a two-person job. Want to give me a hand?"

"I… Sure."

She didn't. She wanted to rush back into her room and shut the door. But she wasn't a complete coward. She could do this.

She followed him to the great room. The Christmas tree they had decorated, on a timer until midnight, still glowed merrily.

She couldn't help thinking about the first time he had kissed her.

"It looks pretty good from up here, doesn't it?" Ethan said as they reached the landing to the second floor.

She glanced over her shoulder. "Wonderful. I've never seen a prettier tree. Some nights I like to come in here by myself and just sit here with the fire in the hearth and the snow falling outside. I find great peace here."

He smiled a little. "I can see why. I could use a little peace. Maybe I need to sneak over in the middle of the night to follow your example."

"I'm sure Winnie would welcome you, as long as you gave her a little warning first."

"Right. I would have to tell her in advance or she would probably clobber me with the Tongan war club she keeps by the side of her bed."

"Her what now?"

He laughed. "You haven't seen her war club?"

"I can't say that I have. Why does your grandmother have a Tongan war club?"

"She picked it up at an estate sale somewhere because she liked the carving. She didn't pay much, but a friend who collects antiques persuaded her it might be worth something so she had it appraised. Turns out, it's rare and worth thousands of dollars, believe it or not, but Winnie doesn't care about that. She still keeps it stashed under her bed in case burglars ever come in to attack."

"Wouldn't a baseball bat work just as well?"

"Probably. But it wouldn't have the same panache. Why use a baseball bat when you can use a priceless Tongan war club?"

Oh, she adored Winnie. She would miss her so much. "Your grandmother in an amazing woman."

"I know. Believe me, I know."

At the angel room, she led the way inside and flipped on the lights. They came on for a moment then flipped back off again.

"Definitely overloading the circuit," he said. "Let's un-plug what we can, reset the fuse, then try again."

She started with the Christmas tree while Ethan worked on the other side of the room.

"I suspect this might be the problem," he said, pointing to an extension cord that had a second extension cord with three lamps plugged into it.

"I've talked to her about not using extension cords ev-erywhere," he said with a sigh, unplugging the lamps. "She's going to burn this whole house down."

He unplugged the second extension cord and the lamps. "I'll go reset the circuit breaker down at the end of the hall. Stick your head out and let me know if the lights come back on."

"Okay."

A moment later, the overhead chandelier came back on.

"Should I try to plug the tree back in?"

"How many extension cords did she use there?"

"None. It's a pre-lit tree with only one plug."

"Go ahead."

She bent down, found the outlet, and a moment later the lovely white angel tree came on.

"We're going to have to leave two of these lamps off. I think it's just too much with all of the other lights on in here."

He plugged only one lamp in, then went back to turn the light off and on. This time it worked perfectly. He turned it off and on again with no further problems.

"I think you did it. Good job," she said. "I don't know why we didn't think to check the extension cords."

He turned off the light for good and walked out into the hall, his features set with frustration.

"What would happen if a fire started up here and worked its way down to her bedroom when she is alone in the house again after Christmas?" he asked as they headed down to the great room. "She doesn't move very fast these days. I don't know if she could make it out."

She didn't want to think about that possibility. Nor did she want to think about Winnie being alone.

"I've offered to move in with her, but she doesn't like that idea, either," Ethan went on. "It wouldn't be a perfect solution for either of us since I travel so much, but at least it would be something."

"Maybe she could hire a companion."

"I've suggested that, too. I wish I could persuade Lucy to come home to stay, but even that wouldn't be the perfect situation."

"Winnie loves this place."

"I know. I get it. But even before she was hurt, Holiday

House was too much for her to take care of by herself. I wish I could help her see that."

"This isn't just a house to her, though, is it? This is Winnie's whole identity. She's spent her entire adult life in this house. Sixty years. She has cared for it, remodeled it, raised her son here and, if I'm not mistaken, largely raised her grandchildren."

"True enough."

"Now that she's coming to an age when the demands of caring for it are becoming too much, I wonder if she is struggling to figure out her new place in the world. If she's not Winifred Lancaster, owner of Holiday House of Silver Bells, who is she?"

He stared at her, the lights of the Christmas tree reflected in his eyes. "You might be right."

"I don't know the answer, though. I'm sorry."

"Thank you for being a sounding board, anyway." He looked out the big windows to where the outside lights he had fixed twinkled against the darkness.

"It's snowing again," he said. "Which reminds me. When can I take Christopher skiing? I've got some time Wednesday afternoon. Would that work?"

She wanted to tell him no day would be good, but she knew she was being selfish. She didn't want to go skiing, but it was unfair to deprive her child of something because of her own fear.

"I think Wednesday would work. That's very kind of you. Thank you."

"I like Christopher. He's a great kid. His enthusiasm for life is contagious."

"It's hard to have a bad day when he is always reminding me of how beautiful and exciting life can be."

"He's right," Ethan said gruffly. "It can be."

The silence stretched between them, suddenly crackling with awareness.

He wanted to kiss her again. She didn't know how she knew—it was something in the slant of his mouth, the heat in his eyes. She caught her breath. She should walk away right now, just whisper a quick good-night and slip back to her bedroom where she was safe.

"Abby. You should probably go to bed." His voice was a rasp that seemed to shiver down her spine.

"I know," she whispered, though she couldn't seem to make herself move, her heart pounding again and everything inside her waiting for the delicious magic of his kiss.

At last, at long last, he released a breath that sounded like a sigh and pulled her into his arms.

HE SHOULDN'T BE doing this.

Ethan knew the moment his mouth touched Abby's again that he was making a mistake.

Every time he kissed her, he only ended up wanting more.

She was so soft and sweet and she made tiny, sexy little sounds when he kissed her, which he found intoxicating.

He wanted more than kisses. That was the problem. He wanted to find an empty room in the house, and spend the night discovering new and creative ways to elicit more of those sexy sounds.

She fascinated him on so many levels. She was kind, compassionate. A caring woman with a huge heart, as he saw in the way she interacted with her son and the patience she used with Winnie. She could also be brave, facing with courage and strength the kind of pain that would have destroyed a weaker person.

He admired and liked her more than any woman he had met in a long time. That didn't mean he wanted anything more than kisses with her.

Abby deserved a man who was free to give her all the love and affection she could ever want, someone with the same capacity for love that she had.

That man wasn't Ethan. Hadn't he already demonstrated that clearly? He never let his heart get involved. That's what the woman he had once intended to marry had told him, anyway. A year away from Brooke had certainly proven her right. He hadn't loved her. He was probably incapable of love. That part of him may have been damaged irreparably by his parents and their endlessly bad romances.

He didn't want to hurt Abby. She had suffered enough. But, oh, it was hard to do the right thing.

For a little bit longer, he allowed himself to savor her mouth, the softness of her arms around him, the curves of her body against him. He dreaded the moment he would have to stop.

He finally knew he couldn't put it off any longer. He slid his mouth away from hers and dropped his arms to the side.

When he spoke, he used a deliberately casual tone.

"Sorry. Looks like we got a little carried away again."

She blinked for a moment, looking dazed and aroused. "I...guess we did. We seem to do that when we're alone together."

"Maybe we should be more careful not to find ourselves alone together."

He saw heat flicker in her eyes for only a moment before she blinked it away. "Good idea. Fortunately I won't be here much longer. We only have to make it through Christmas and we should both be home free. Good night, Ethan. If you'll excuse me, I have to go find a toy grader."

As he walked out into the cold December night, Ethan knew he had handled that poorly.

He should have been honest with her, but how did a guy tell a woman that he suspected something inside him might be broken?

By the way. I know we're only kissing here, but in case you wanted something more, don't look for it here.

It sounded ridiculous, even to him.

So now what? He couldn't avoid her. She would be staying with his grandmother until after Christmas. He was supposed to take her and her son skiing in a few days.

No matter. He would simply be as polite to her as he was to Mariah Raymond, Emily Tsu and all the other Silver Belles.

No matter how difficult.

CHAPTER FOURTEEN

THIS WAS CERTAINLY awkward.

For the past half hour, Lucy had been doing her best to interpret a small billing dispute between the front-desk staff and a guest from Japan who spoke and understood English but preferred to have a translator along just in case.

The billing dispute wasn't the problem. They were close to resolving it to the satisfaction of everyone, until the man asked to speak to management—which meant José.

Lucy had been working at the resort for three days and hadn't seen him except from a distance during that time.

As she was working mostly with guests and tour operators, staying under the radar hadn't been difficult until now.

Mr. Aiko, it turned out, only wanted to thank the hotel management for the wonderful stay he and his family had enjoyed. He asked Lucy to explain to José that he was part owner of a group of hotels across Asia. He had heard good things about the Lancaster properties and wanted to check them out himself.

"Thank you very much," José said. "We would love to return your visit and see what we can learn from you. Which of your hotels would you recommend?"

They discussed visits and exchanged contact information, then Mr. Aiko and José bowed to each other, the guest thanked Lucy for her help and then left her alone with José.

She knew she should slip out the door of his office, as well, but she admitted she was starved for the sight of him.

She missed her friend. She missed taking in a few ski runs together at the end of the day or hanging out in the hotel bar, listening to the live entertainment. She missed having Sofia's delicious tamales that she spent all day cooking or going ice-skating together at the park.

"How was your date the other night?"

The moment she asked the question, she wished she hadn't. She should be trying to find some kind of common ground to regain what she could of their friendship, not jumping in with a question destined to antagonize him.

A muscle seemed to tighten in his jaw. "It was good. Quinn is a lot of fun to be around."

Lucy could be fun. She was a good conversationalist, she could tell jokes in many languages, she knew how to belly dance.

She let out a breath, reminding herself that, despite the distance between them right now, he was still her friend and she wanted him to be happy. She hadn't had the opportunity to meet Quinn yet as their paths hadn't crossed, but others seemed to like the woman.

Not that she had said anything outright to anyone else about her, but there was a chance Lucy might have unobtrusively steered a few conversations in that direction.

"Great. I'm glad to hear it."

"Are you?"

"Yes. You're my friend, José. I care about you and want you to be happy. If you like this Quinn person, I think that's great."

"I hear a definite *but* in your voice."

She should walk away right now. She had no business

pushing things between them when he had made his point clear. A wise woman would smile, say good afternoon and go back to work.

When had she ever been wise?

Right now, she wanted to lock his office door, sidle around his desk and splay her hands across that broad, gorgeous chest of his.

She did one of the three, closing his door and locking it behind her.

"I just…can't forget that kiss in Thailand," she said, her voice husky. "No one has ever kissed me like that. Ever."

He gazed at her for a long moment, his pupils widening and his breathing suddenly ragged. Finally his mouth tightened.

"I'm not doing this with you, Lucy."

He sounded weary, and she suddenly felt like a stupid, cruel girl, poking a bear with a stick.

"Doing what? You started it when you kissed me."

"And you ended it when you made it clear you don't want the same things I do. It's not enough for me anymore to be friends with you, content to wait in the nice, safe box you have shoved me into. Your good buddy José, fun to FaceTime when you're bored or hang around with for the week or two out of the year when we get together." He shrugged. "I want forever and you don't. It is as simple as that. We have a basic disconnect we can't get past."

Lucy hitched in a breath, feeling perilously close to tears. What was *wrong* with her? She never cried. They were angry tears, she told herself.

"We only have a disconnect because you insist on being a…a typical obstinate, arrogant male who has to have things your way."

He shook his head. "I refuse to sleep with you unless we're actually dating with an eye toward a future together, and that makes me an arrogant male. Really?"

She knew he was right. If their roles were reversed and she was on the outside looking in, she would consider a man who only wanted sex without commitment an ass.

She knew she was in the wrong. That was what kept her tossing and turning each night since she had come home. She told herself it was jet lag, but she knew better. It was confusion, guilt, pain.

She couldn't hurt him. That was the overriding emotion taking center stage right now.

"You're asking the impossible of me, José," she finally said quietly. "I am not capable of giving you what you want. A commitment. You know the chaos I came from. You saw it from the outside. My parents were a mess. The boyfriends, the girlfriends, marriages and divorces, with new people coming in and out of my life. All because of love. If I had a quarter for every time one parent or the other would tell me he or she was in love, I could buy my own ski resort."

"Your parents were and still are two childish, irresponsible people who should never have brought offspring into the world. Their core problem is that they have no idea how to be happy, how to think about someone else's welfare before their own. You and Ethan are not your parents. You don't use people like they do."

He circled the desk and sat on the edge of it, legs outstretched and his hands resting on the edge behind him.

"I think you're using Rick and Terri and the wreck they've made of their lives as an excuse. A crutch. I think you know in your heart what you truly want, you're just afraid to reach for it."

She wanted to reach for him. The urge to throw her arms around his waist and hold on forever was so powerful she almost gave in.

But then what? He would end up hurt, and she would end up hating herself.

"I think you don't know what you're talking about," she snapped, fumbling behind her for the door lock and stomping out before he could respond.

So much for scintillating conversation, she thought as she hurried back to her temporary office, hot, angry tears burning in her eyes.

She shouldn't have said anything. She didn't know how it was possible, but instead of clearing the air between them she had only managed to make everything so much worse.

"YOU DON'T HAVE to do this," Ethan said Wednesday afternoon. "I can take him on the lift by myself."

Abby was so very tempted, her fear ballooning as she looked at the ski lift overhead. "I know. But I've come this far. We did fine on the bunny slope. I might as well go on an actual ski run."

For the past hour, she and Christopher had been receiving private lessons from a man who obviously knew what he was doing on the slopes—and looked gorgeous doing it. He had a lean, natural grace that somehow didn't surprise her. She *was* surprised by how much she enjoyed his lessons.

He was patient, encouraging, knowledgeable. Somehow in the space of an hour, Ethan had done a marvelous job of teaching them the basics of skiing—a nervous woman afraid of heights and a five-year-old boy who had never been on a ski hill.

Christopher was a natural. Abby, not so much, but she thought she could possibly make it down the most basic hill without falling more than two or three times.

"I honestly don't mind taking him by myself," Ethan pressed. "You can watch from down here or even go into the lodge."

"I know. But someday, when you're not around to take us, he might want to go skiing again. I would like to be able to say I had at least tried it."

He gave her that unreadable look again, the one that made the butterflies jump around like crazy in her stomach. "All right. If you're sure, we can all ride the lift together."

They got into the fairly short line and a moment later reached the front. "Okay, just ski to the line and the chair will come and scoop you up. Christopher in the middle. That's it."

Somehow she made it on without panicking, but the moment the lift chair headed away from the ground and up the small hill, Abby's stomach seemed to plummet.

This was insane. Who invented this? No human should ride something like this without seat belts or anything. She was going to fall out. Or, worse, Christopher was going to fall. She clutched his arm so tightly, he scowled at her.

"Mom. That's too hard," he said.

To her relief, Ethan pulled down a safety bar and then reached an arm out and grabbed her arm. "I won't let you fall," he said quietly.

It was as if she had taken an instant anti-anxiety pill. Her breathing seemed to slow and she could feel calm wash over her. She could do this. Ethan would be there to make sure nothing happened to her.

Dismounting the chairlift at the top was a little tricky, but she managed to stay upright and didn't humiliate herself.

Christopher skied off as if he had been doing this forever. She remembered Winnie saying that younger children often took to the sport far more easily than older people.

Ethan guided her over to the top of the slope. "This is no different from what we've been doing on the practice slope. Remember what I taught you. We'll take it slow. Go ahead. I'm right behind you."

Christopher didn't wait—he immediately started down the hill. If she didn't want her son to ski down this big mountain by himself, she would have to follow. She drew a deep breath and launched herself down the mountain.

This was no different from the tubing, she told herself. Except she was standing up on thin pieces of wood and trying to keep her balance at a high rate of speed.

She tried not to think about what she was doing. Instead, she leaned into the moment.

She wouldn't believe it possible, but after the first four or five turns, she got into the rhythm of it. If she only focused just ahead of herself on the hill and didn't look all the way to the bottom, she didn't even remember that she was afraid of heights.

At the bottom, she almost forgot how to stop until she saw Christopher snowplow. Her son was a natural.

"So?" Ethan asked once they reached the bottom. "What did you think?"

Christopher seem to bubble over with excitement. "That

was so fun. It was more fun than tubing. Can we go down again? Can we please?"

Ethan grinned. "I'm game for it. What about you, Abby?"

She wanted that feeling again, that heady sensation that she was leaving her troubles at the top of the hill.

"Sure. Let's go again."

He grinned at her, his teeth flashing white in the sunshine, and she felt a giddy hitch in her stomach.

Apparently, the man didn't even have to kiss her to set off fireworks inside her.

She had worried things might be weird between them on this ski outing after the way things had ended the other night, with that intense, almost tender kiss and then the abrupt ending.

She shouldn't have worried, with Christopher there. He treated Ethan like his new best friend, and his happy mood seemed to set the tone for the whole afternoon.

"Here we go. We're almost to the top," Ethan said. "Get ready."

This was the part she didn't love, that moment when a skier had to leave the relative safety of the ski lift to depend on his or her own hard-fought ability to stay upright on the snow.

She imagined there was probably a metaphor in that for her life, but she didn't have time to figure it out before Christopher took off down the mountain again with a cry of glee.

"The kid is a natural," Ethan said with a laugh when they all reached the bottom again.

"I was afraid of that." Abby wasn't able to keep the glum note out of her voice.

As she might have expected, he caught it. "Why is that a bad thing? I would have thought you'd be happy."

"How often will I be able to take him skiing once we've resettled in Texas? Ski resorts aren't exactly a dime a dozen there."

"You can always come back to Silver Bells to visit Winnie and Lucy during ski season. You know Winnie would love to see you."

Could she? Once she left town, would she feel comfortable coming back to visit? If she were only likely to see Winnie and the other Silver Belles, yes.

Once she left, she intended to do her best to forget about Ethan Lancaster and all these feelings he sparked in her.

After two more runs, her calves ached in the hard boots and she was ready to stop and go inside for a mug of cocoa to warm up, but Christopher's enthusiasm hadn't flagged yet.

At least he would probably sleep well that night.

"Can we go one more time?" he pleaded.

Ethan must have seen her exhaustion. He placed a hand on her arm. "I'll take him. Go warm up in the lodge. You can cheer us on from inside."

She wouldn't argue with that. She left her skis on the rack, as she had seen others do, and made her way into the lodge, where she grabbed cocoa and then stood at the wide window. It was easy to find Christopher since his coat was red and his hat was a bright purple.

The two of them looked so natural together, she thought as she watched. They had a rapport that touched her as much as it worried her.

She didn't want her son to be hurt when they left town and Ethan no longer played a part in their lives. She could only hope it wasn't too late.

CHAPTER FIFTEEN

IF SHE HAD any doubt the people of Silver Bells loved the holidays, the town's annual gingerbread competition quickly put that to rest.

Sunday afternoon, Abby looked around the large ballroom at the Lancaster Silver Bells, where three dozen teams worked feverishly around small tables. Each table held supplies for the gingerbread houses. Squares of gingerbread, fondant, gumdrops, pretzel sticks. Anything one might need to decorate an elaborate gingerbread creation.

Winnie had explained the rules to her earlier in the day. She knew the teams could plan their creation ahead of time but couldn't do any work until they arrived. They had a two-hour time limit to create, and the winners were chosen by the pastry chefs at the three Lancaster hotels in town.

At the front of the ballroom, a jazz combo played holiday tunes beneath a banner that read Happy Birthday and Joyous Holidays, Rodrigo.

"You really do this every year?"

Winnie looked positively gleeful, as she had since they'd walked in fifteen minutes earlier. "Oh, yes. We have since Rodrigo was about twelve or thirteen. It used to be a small event, family and friends only. In the years since, it's grown and grown until it has become one of the most fun traditions we have around here. Visitors make an annual trip of it. And the competition can be fierce, I'll tell you. The grand prize is airfare plus a week's stay at any Lancaster property in the world, and all proceeds benefit our family foundation, which is funding the endowment for the accessible lodge."

Silver Bells just might be the most festive town around anywhere. When she had agreed to help Winnie for these few weeks, she had wanted Christopher to experience a white Christmas. She just never expected she would come to love the place.

"Are you ready to get to work? I am."

"I'm sorry you're not eligible for the grand prize."

"Doesn't matter. We can still win the random door prizes that are donated by local businesses. I've got my eye on a free session of hot yoga."

She smiled, adoring Winnie as much as she loved Silver Bells.

The woman had become so very dear to her over these past weeks. Winifred Lancaster had endured great pain, losing the husband she loved, two children in infancy, having her only remaining son make a mess of his life.

She was a great example of resilience and strength, and Abby wanted to be just like her someday.

Maybe without the pink hair, which would clash horribly with her normal auburn coloring.

Whenever she thought about how much she would miss the woman when she left town, Abby's chest felt tight.

She hadn't realized how much she had been yearning for the influence of mature, wise women until this time she had spent with Winnie. Most of her friends in Arizona were her contemporaries. Nurses she worked with or other parents with children Christopher's age.

Winnie offered a long-range view that helped Abby put everything into perspective.

"You're entering Christopher, right? You won't be disqualified from winning."

"Can we, Mommy?"

"Sure," she said on impulse. "Let's go enter."

A few moments later, after paying the entry fee, she and Christopher were set up at a small table with supplies to build their own house.

She enjoyed listening to the music and talking to Mariah Raymond and Dakota while the boys worked on their respective houses.

"I'm building a dinosaur to go on the lawn," Christopher said.

"Good job," she said, smiling at the gumdrop-and-pretzel creation that did indeed look like a little T. rex. She wasn't sure what a T. rex was doing on the lawn of a gingerbread house, but who was she to question artistic license?

She was helping him shape the long tail when she heard a deep voice.

"There's my favorite ski buddy. I've been looking for you."

Her heart started pounding, and she glanced up to find Ethan heading toward their table.

"Ethan! Hi! Look. I'm making a dinosaur."

"Wow. That's terrific. Almost good enough to eat." He winked, which made Christopher giggle.

"Don't eat my dinosaur. If you do, we can't win."

"Need help?"

"I can only have one grown-up helper. That's what the lady said," Christopher said regretfully. Abby had a feeling that if she hadn't been there first, he would have thrown her under the bus in a heartbeat as long as it meant he could have Ethan's help.

"Looks like you're covered, then."

"Mine is almost done," Christopher said. "Look. I made a car in the driveway. And I have a guy on a sled that I made out of pretzels."

"Perfect. You're really good at that."

"I know."

Ethan smiled. For an instant, their gazes locked and she thought she saw something there, a strange mix of hunger, longing, regret.

He looked away before she could be certain she hadn't imagined it.

"Since you don't need my help, I guess I should go see if anybody else does," he said. "I'll see you both later."

Before she could stop him or at least encourage him to wipe the frosting off his hands, Christopher reached out to give Ethan a hug, which left a green smudge on Ethan's fitted dress shirt.

"Oh, no. I'm so sorry," she exclaimed, reaching for a paper towel and dabbing at it while her son, oblivious, went back to his work.

"I'm not worried. It will wash out. I'm just glad he's having a good time."

She looked around the crowded ballroom at the convivial atmosphere. "How could he not? Everyone is so kind here."

"Silver Bells isn't a perfect town by any means, but people here are pretty decent, for the most part. No doubt you will find Austin the same."

"I'm sure you're right," she said.

He looked as if he wanted to say something but seemed

to change his mind at the last moment. "Well, good luck with the gingerbread house. I'll be rooting for Team Christopher."

"Thanks."

The moment he walked away, a crowd seemed to converge around him. It was obvious as she saw him here among others in town that Ethan was well liked and well respected. She wouldn't have expected anything else, she thought. She certainly liked him and respected him.

"I saw that."

Abby looked away from Ethan's retreating back to find Mariah watching her, a speculative look in her eyes.

"Saw what?" Abby tried to sound innocent.

"You told me there was nothing going on between you and Ethan. That didn't look like nothing."

She could feel herself blush and knew instantly that Mariah noticed that, too. "Ethan has become a friend over the past few weeks. That's all."

"Honey, I wish I had a friend who looks at me like he looks at you."

"You're imagining things."

Mariah just gave her husky laugh and went back to helping her son. The other woman was someone else she would miss when she went to Austin.

Abby had made many cherished friends in the few short weeks she had been here. The Silver Belles had embraced her as an honorary member despite her lack of singing skills.

Perhaps she ought to try to join some other kind of group like this when she moved. If one didn't exist, she could always start it.

Somehow Austin no longer held the appeal it once did. She would find her enthusiasm again, she told herself. It was only a matter of time.

How HAD ONE woman and her son managed to become so very important to him in only a few weeks' time?

As Ethan made the rounds of the ballroom, greeting friends and neighbors and guests of the hotel who had decided to join in the fun, his attention seemed to constantly shift back to the other side of the ballroom, toward Abby and Christopher.

He couldn't quite believe they had only been part of his life since Thanksgiving.

She was leaving soon. Christmas Eve was only four days away. Winnie had told him, rather tearfully, that they would be leaving the day after Christmas.

They had less than a week together.

Already, his world seemed a little more gray when he thought about them leaving.

"Ethan! I wondered if I would see you here today."

Jolted from his thoughts, he turned toward a table where a group of women were working on a gingerbread house built around an "Under the Sea" theme, apparently.

It took him a moment to place the woman who had called out to him. Her name was Cora Parker and she was a cousin to Brooke, his former fiancée.

She was married to a police officer in the next town over, he remembered. In the year of his engagement, he and Brooke had attended two or three of the same social occasions with Cora and her husband.

"Cora. Hi. Nice to see you again. Your team's creation is looking great."

"This is my bunco club. We did this last year and had so much fun, we decided to come again."

"It looks good. I like the octopus there."

"Thank you."

She took a step toward him with an expression that instantly put him on edge. That feeling was confirmed when she reached out and placed a hand on his arm.

"How are you?" she asked in that overly solicitous tone that people usually reserved for the recently bereaved.

"Fine," he answered a little warily. Why wouldn't he be?

"I never had a chance to talk to you after…well, after things went south," Cora went on in a low voice. "I just want you to know that Jim and I both think Brooke was crazy to break things off with you. Oh, I know you said in the letter you both sent out right after you broke up that it was a mutual decision, but I don't think anybody missed putting two and two together when four months later she marries somebody else and has a baby less than a year after that."

Ethan could feel himself go rigid, annoyed with Cora for bringing this up now, amid the festivities for Rodrigo's birthday.

He felt the usual sting at the reminder of Brooke and the life she had so quickly gone on to build without him, but he could acknowledge that sting wasn't hurt but injured pride.

He hadn't loved Brooke, as she had so accurately pointed out when she ended the engagement.

Her words seemed to ring through his memory.

Something is broken inside you, Ethan, she had said, tears streaming down her cheeks. *I thought I could live with a man who doesn't love me as much as I love him. I know you care about me but not the way I need. I told myself you would let me all the way into your heart eventually. But we're supposed to be married in a month and nothing has changed. I can't take the risk that nothing ever will. I deserve better.*

She must have found what she needed in Marcos Palmer, the professional basketball player she had married only months after she was supposed to marry Ethan.

He had seen pictures of them in various tabloids, and she had glowed in a way she never had with him.

"Brooke and I had an amicable separation," he said carefully now to Cora, though he wanted to tell her none of it was her damn business. "I'm glad she found happiness with Marcos."

"He's nice enough, I guess. And their baby girl is adorable, at least the pictures I've seen. But I still think it was wrong, what she did to you."

He didn't want to be having this conversation with a woman who was a virtual stranger to him. "Thank you for your concern," he said as calmly as he could manage, "but I wish your cousin nothing but the best."

He started to ease away, hoping that would be the end of it, but Cora apparently wasn't done causing trouble.

"Did you know she's coming to town to spend the holidays with her folks?"

Great. Now he could look forward to more gossip and more of those pitying looks. He gave a forced smile.

"That's terrific. There's no better place to spend the holidays than here in Silver Bells. I hope your family has a joyous season. Give her my best if you see her, won't you?"

Cora seemed a little deflated by his reaction, as if she were hoping for more drama. She must be one of those people who loved to make trouble, stirring pots that had long ago gone cold.

He wasn't about to give her the satisfaction of a reaction. "Will you excuse me? One of my staff members is trying to get my attention."

It was a lie but gave him the excuse to turn his back and walk over to José, who was talking to one of his sisters. When he reached them, he stopped to chat to give his lie the ring of truth, all while his thoughts raced.

He had accepted over this past year that he and Brooke would have made each other miserable. He would have been constantly disappointing her. If they had married, they likely would have ended in divorce. At least they hadn't had kids who would pay the price for his poor choices.

His gaze shifted again to Abby. She was smiling down at something Christopher had said. The light hit her just so, making her face glow with life and grace. He felt a hard tug in his chest, an ache he didn't want to feel.

She was leaving soon. As much as he would miss her, it was for the best.

Something is broken inside you.

He didn't know if that was true or not. He only knew he had already hurt Brooke. He didn't want to do the same thing to Abby and Christopher.

He deliberately turned away, hoping this ache would go away as soon as they left Silver Bells.

ORDINARILY THE TOWN gingerbread contest was Lucy's favorite event of the year.

This year, it was torture.

Oh, she and Rodrigo were having fun building their house. He had come prepared with drawings he had obviously been working on for a long time, and they now had a two-story masterpiece that looked like the house in the Disney movie *Up*, complete with hundreds of little gumdrop balloons.

It was gorgeous, if she did say so herself. It made her want to climb inside and float away.

Rodrigo was having the time of his life, greeting many friends who stopped by to offer him birthday greetings. Even people who didn't know him stopped to wish him well.

Rodrigo was one of the most popular people in town. People loved his cheerful attitude and the way he embraced each day with joy.

As always when she came to the gingerbread competition and saw the outpouring of affection for her friend, part of a group historically marginalized, she thought her heart would burst.

How she loved Silver Bells and the good people here. Before she was in high school, her visits with her grandparents had been limited to a few weeks every summer and six months during one glorious year when her parents had been fighting over custody.

Unlike most custody disputes, her parents hadn't been fighting because each of them wanted her and Ethan with them. Of course it wouldn't be anything as straightforward as that. Instead, Rick and Terri both happened to be involved with someone new and wanted honeymoon time. They had each wanted the *other* parent to have custody.

She had probably been ten, Ethan thirteen. In the end, Winnie had stepped in and they had been gloriously happy at Holiday House for several months. That had been a short-term solution, and they were soon back to being traded back and forth like Christmas fruitcake.

Winnie had also finally put her foot down a few years later, when Ethan was a senior in high school and Lucy just starting. Her grandfather had just died and Winnie claimed she needed company in the big house.

"Also, it will do them good to stay in one place for a change," Winnie had said.

Oh, how she had loved that time, when she and Ethan lived with Winnie during the school year and had to deal with their parents' endless drama only in the summer.

When people asked her where she was from, she always told them Silver Bells, Colorado. This place called her home, no matter where else she was living.

Rodrigo and his family were part of the reason for that.

"Hey, Lucy, look at where I'm putting the chimney."

"Looks perfect, Rod," she said. She and Ethan had often talked about how wonderful it would be if everyone in the world had someone like Rod in their lives, someone who embodied pure, unspoiled love.

"Our house is cool." Rodrigo beamed from ear to ear. "We always have the best one."

"You rocked it, as usual. Every year, our house looks better and better."

He beamed at her. "I'm glad you're here, Lucy," he said. "Everything is always more fun when you're here."

She smiled, touched to her soul. "Thank you, dude. Being with you is the best part of my whole year."

Though they were working hard on their gingerbread house, Rodrigo insisted on stopping construction so he could hug her, sugar-sticky hands and all. She laughed, hugging him back. When she looked up, she saw José standing a short distance away, watching them.

His expression made her shiver—until Lucy realized he was standing next to Quinn Bellamy, who was smiling up at him and chattering about something Lucy couldn't hear.

José and Quinn hadn't come together, Lucy knew that, but they had connected shortly after José arrived with his sister, and Quinn hadn't wandered far from his side.

She seemed very nice, with a cheerful smile and kind eyes. Lucy wanted to hate her, but she couldn't. If the woman could make José happy, how could she dislike her?

Lucy might know that rationally, but she was a horrible person, apparently. She wanted to throw a bowl of frosting in her face.

She forced herself to turn her attention back to their house, working with Rodrigo to add final touches while the swing combo, made up of many of Winnie's old friends, played "Jingle Bells" and "Rudolph."

Finally it was time for the prizes. She wasn't eligible to win, which was fine with her. She traveled enough. She didn't need another excuse.

Claiming the privilege of the birthday boy, Rodrigo always gave out the prizes to the winners, and he had a particularly good time handing them out tonight.

She was thrilled when two middle-aged sisters won the grand prize with a gorgeous gingerbread ski lodge complete with a little ski lift made out of fruit leather.

"Looks like we have a tie in the under-ten category. Christopher Powell and Dakota Raymond. Can you come up here?"

Christopher and Dakota raced up hand in hand to receive a stocking each filled with what looked like candy and little Christmas toys. The boys danced around in excitement, much to the enjoyment of the crowd.

"And that concludes another year of our special Birthday Party Gingerbread Competition. Feel free to walk around and admire everyone else's creations. See you all next year."

"I'll be thirty years old next time," Rodrigo said, shaking his head in disbelief. "I'm old."

She had to laugh. "I'll be thirty in February so I'm even older."

"Old lady," Rodrigo teased.

She felt old, suddenly. Thirty was a pivotal year. She had spent her twenties doing what she wanted, going where she wanted, exploring the world, having fun.

Somehow it didn't seem enough anymore. Maybe it was time she shifted focus.

"Your gingerbread house is amazing, as always," Sofia, Rodrigo's mother, said, admiring their display. "How do you do it, year after year?"

"It's not me. As always, Rodrigo is the creative genius behind this operation."

His mother smiled broadly, hugging him. "Thank you for being his partner again."

"Are you kidding? It's the highlight of my year. I wouldn't miss it."

Sofia smiled and patted her hand. "You're a good girl, Lucy. Once I had hoped maybe you and my José would... Well." She shrugged. "A mother hopes. It's not to be. But you should know I would have been happy to have you for my daughter."

For a moment, Lucy didn't know what to say, emotion clogging her throat. When had she ever heard her own mother say anything remotely close to that?

"That's very sweet of you, Sofia," she finally managed.

Sofia looked embarrassed. "Do not tell José I said anything like that to you. My son, he already thinks I interfere too much in his life."

"I won't," she promised.

"Now, I can take Rodrigo home with me. *Mijo*, where is your coat?"

"I put it under the table so I wouldn't lose it." He reached under the table and pulled it out with a triumphant noise.

"Are you sure? He's my date. I don't mind taking him home."

"No, no. We're going to walk around and admire all the gingerbread houses, and then his sisters want to have cake and ice cream at home."

"I like cake," Rod informed her.

"Good thing," she said, helping him with his zipper. "I'll see you later, dude. Happy birthday. Thanks for the fun day."

"Bye, Lucy. I love you."

"I love you right back."

This of course necessitated another hug. Anyone in Rodrigo Navarro's life had to put up with plenty of hugs, which she had never found a hardship.

She cleaned up the remains of their gingerbread frenzy, then did her part to help clean up other tables with a few other lingerers.

"You don't have to do this. We have a crew standing by to clean up."

Somehow her path had led her to José. Had that been accidental, or had her subversive subconscious led her toward him?

She shrugged. "I don't mind. I'm not washing fondant out of the carpets or anything, only throwing away some trash. It's always such a fun day, isn't it? And for a good cause."

"Rodrigo loves it. We hear about it all year long. Thanks for being his partner."

"It's absolutely my pleasure."

"I know. Which makes it mean even more."

She felt that ache in her throat again. What was happening to her? She had cried more since coming back to Silver Bells than she remembered doing in years.

"You're helping with the wedding this week, right? The one with the Russian woman whose family speaks no English?"

"Da." She answered in Russian. It wasn't among the strongest of the languages she knew but was one of her favorites.

"The wedding is Tuesday evening, but the bride and her family are all arriving first thing tomorrow."

"Yes. I'm going to the airport with the limousine to pick them up."

"That's perfect. Thank you."

Lancaster Hotels was all about service. She would have been happy to help anyway since Katya Morozov was marrying a good friend of hers from high school, Daniel Fox.

"I have a dossier on the Morozov family in the office that might be helpful, if you have time to pick it up now so you can look it over before you go to the airport."

Of course he did. The Lancaster staff was nothing if not thorough. "That would be great."

She followed José out of the ballroom and out to the elevators that led to the administrative offices.

Was he enjoying his job? she wondered. She knew José had pulled back from his responsibilities as Ethan's second in command so that he could focus more on helping his family.

He could have any job he wanted, at Lancaster or anywhere else.

"Quinn seems very nice. What is this? Your fourth date? Fifth? You must be getting serious."

The only sign he gave that he was annoyed was a slight tension in his long hands as he pulled out an ID card and used it to swipe into his office.

"Today wasn't a date," he said as he opened the door for her. "We were both working. She was at the gingerbread competition because her job includes event planning. If it had been a date, don't you think I would have taken her home?"

To her house or yours?

Lucy bit her tongue to keep from asking the question or from pointing out that his non-date had managed to somehow still touch him frequently every time they were together. A tap on his shoulder to direct his attention somewhere, a hand on his arm when she was making a point.

Not that Lucy was noticing or anything.

She couldn't say that either without revealing she had been watching them together most of the afternoon.

"Sorry. I didn't mean anything. I guess I just...wanted to say that I'm glad you two seem to be hitting it off."

"Are you?"

She blinked at his harsh tone, so unlike his usual easygoing nature. "What do you want me to say? I want you to be happy, José. She seems very nice. That's all I meant."

"She is very nice. But she's not you."

She gazed at him, struck speechless by the raw emotion in his voice. His words seemed to twist through her, leaving her breathless, achy.

"José."

That was all she said. Only his name. But in a moment, he was kissing her again, with all the heat and emotion she had remembered from their kiss in Thailand.

His mouth was sweet, like raspberry candy. She couldn't get enough. She wrapped her arms around his neck and returned his kiss with the hunger that had been growing inside her since that first kiss between them.

This was José. Her friend.

And the man she cared about more than anyone else she had ever known.

She wanted the kiss to go on forever. Here, in his arms, she could forget all the reasons they could never have more than this.

He was the one to break the kiss. He dropped his arms to his sides and backed away from her, swearing in Spanish.

She couldn't seem to catch her breath, and her thoughts flew in a thousand directions. Why couldn't this be enough? They would be amazing together. She knew they would. Every time they kissed, she thought she would implode.

"I didn't mean for that to happen," he finally said hoarsely. His beautiful mouth was now set in a harsh line. The eyes that could look at her with such warmth and humor and joy were so dark she couldn't read his expression.

She missed him so damn much. Her friend.

"Why did you have to change everything?" she asked before she could stop herself.

His mouth thinned even more, if possible. "It was time to stop pretending these feelings haven't been growing between us for a long time, Lucy. Maybe forever. We can't go back now."

She had known it, but hearing his words made her ache even more.

"Fine. Let's go forward. Let's sleep together and see what happens."

For just a moment, she thought she might have pierced through. Heat flared in his eyes and he almost took a step forward. She held her breath, everything inside her frozen in anticipation.

Finally he shook his head. "I want all or nothing, Lucy. I know how you work. It's always been entirely too easy for you to walk away before your heart can get involved. You just pack up your suitcase and take another job somewhere else."

He made her seem horrible, someone who crushed men's hearts for the fun of it.

She wasn't like that at all. The exact opposite. She went to great lengths not to hurt people, always walking away before things could grow too serious.

"I love you, Lucy Lancaster. You're smart, funny, giving. I fall in love with you all over again every time I see you being so sweet and kind to Rod."

His words made her throat ache again. She wanted to stand here and soak them all deep into her soul. At the same time, panic flared and she wanted to run out of the room and keep going without looking back.

"I want you like I've never wanted anything in my life. Like I know I will *never* want anyone or anything else. But I have too much on the line here. I want a future with you. Everything."

She felt shaky inside, wanting so badly to reach out and take the precious gift he was offering her.

No. She couldn't. Love was a trap that made otherwise rational people do cruel, terrible things to each other.

She would destroy him, like a tsunami washing away everything beautiful in its path.

She picked up the dossier on the Russian bride and her family and clutched it to her like a shield. "You're asking too much from me."

A muscle flexed in his jaw. "Did you ever think that maybe you're not asking enough of yourself?"

She was going to cry. She could feel the tears burning. Not here. Not in front of him.

"I'll be here first thing to go to the airport with the limousine," she said, hoping he didn't hear the quaver in her voice.

"Lucy."

She wouldn't look at him. If she did, if she saw the love she heard in his voice, she would probably do something ridiculously stupid like throw the dossier into the air and jump back into his arms.

"Good night."

She walked out of his office, down the elevator and out the lobby before the tears came, freezing on her face the moment they hit the air.

CHAPTER SIXTEEN

MONDAY—THE DAY AFTER the gingerbread competition—was the last night for Christmas at Holiday House. They were supposed to end Saturday, but the Silver Belles had voted to offer a bonus night for those who had to cancel for some reason or couldn't obtain the earlier sold-out tickets.

Abby wasn't sure if she was relieved or upset that the event was drawing to a close as she helped Emily Tsu set out the final batches of cookies for attendees to enjoy while they listened to the choir's final new numbers.

The great room looked charming and warm, the fairy lights on the mantel twinkling above the dancing fire. The tree she and Ethan had decorated towered above the last tour group, its ornaments gleaming in the firelight.

She couldn't imagine a more festive setting, especially with the light snow falling outside the big windows and the choir's lovely arrangement of "Still, Still, Still" ringing through the room.

She had created such wonderful memories here in a relatively short time. She was quite sad that tonight was the final evening of the fundraiser.

After the choir's stirring final number, the guests lingered, sipping hot cocoa and talking to the choir members. Finally, the last guest was ushered out the door, leaving only the remaining Silver Belles.

They all seemed to breathe a collective sigh.

"I can't believe we pulled that off," Mariah Raymond said, shaking her head.

"Not just pulled it off," said Vicki Kostas, holding hands with her wife, Kathleen. "We rocked it. People will be talking about Christmas at Holiday House for years."

"I just have to say one thing," Winnie said, picking up a mug filled with mulled cider and holding it up in the air. "When I had this idea, I truly didn't know how on earth I could pull it off. I shouldn't have worried. Not for a moment. I should have known I would have help from the most amazing group of people I've ever known. Thank you all so very much for your support and encouragement. We couldn't have done this without each and every one of you."

They all raised whatever mug or wineglass they were holding and saluted each other.

"I have one more person to thank, someone who came in at the last minute when I was at my lowest point and rescued everything. Abigail, come here, please."

Touched and embarrassed at the same time, Abby would have preferred to slip down the hallway to her room, but she couldn't disappoint Winnie by doing that.

She stepped forward as the Silver Belles clapped hard for her. She had come to admire and respect these women and men, who had given up their time, resources and talents for something they cared about.

"You really did save the day," Winnie told her later when they were finally alone with Lucy in the house. "We would have had to cancel the whole thing if you hadn't come to our rescue."

"I seriously owe you," Lucy chimed in. She smiled, but it didn't come close to reaching her eyes.

Something was wrong with her friend. Abby didn't

know what, but Lucy hadn't been herself since the night before. She had come home from the gingerbread house contest late and had barely said two or three words to them before escaping to her bedroom. She had been gone early that morning and probably would have slipped back to her bedroom if Winnie hadn't insisted she join them for the final night of tours.

Abby wasn't the only one who saw it. She saw Winnie give her granddaughter a worried look.

Both of them were waiting for Abby to respond, she realized. "It's been a joy," she finally said. "I don't know when I've enjoyed a holiday season more."

"I had fun, too," Christopher said, sporting a chocolate mustache from what was probably his third cup of cocoa for the night.

Abby couldn't have imagined a better Christmas season for him. From tree trimming to gingerbread competitions, skiing to building snowmen. He had experienced everything she might have dreamed for her child.

"Christmas itself is going to feel anticlimactic, I'm afraid," Abby said.

"We won't let it," Winnie vowed. "It will be joyful this year. Not only will I have both Ethan and Lucy to share it with me but now you and Christopher. I can't tell you how excited I am to have a child in the house again on Christmas morning. Won't it be wonderful, Lucy?"

Lucy jerked her attention away from the fire she had been gazing into. "Absolutely," she said. "Completely wonderful."

Abby wondered if her friend even knew what she was agreeing to.

"Abby and I have been working on a plan for Christmas

Eve and Christmas Day, just like I had for Thanksgiving. A schedule, meals, timing of things. That sort of thing. But we can save that for another night, shall we?"

Winnie yawned hugely, which made Christopher smile until his smile turned into a yawn, as well.

"I don't know about you girls, but I'm exhausted. I feel like I showed every Coloradoan through my house."

"Not everyone. Just most of them," Lucy said with a smile that looked strained.

What was bothering her?

"I can help you to your room and then get Christopher settled."

"Take care of your boy," Winnie insisted. "I'll be fine. I don't need your help. We can talk more in the morning."

"I'm helping with the wedding tomorrow, remember?" Lucy said.

Winnie looked intrigued. "Oh, yes. The Russian bride that nice boy Daniel Fox is marrying. I didn't have a chance to ask you how things went today."

Was the wedding the reason Lucy seemed in such an odd mood?

"Good. I met Katya's family and helped them get settled. We then took a sleigh ride this afternoon up to the frozen waterfall. They said it reminded them of home."

"I want to go on a sleigh ride," Christopher said, looking enthralled at the idea.

Abby rolled her eyes. They had done every possible Christmas thing but that.

"We might be able to arrange that before you go back to Phoenix," Winnie said. "I'll see what I can do."

She turned back to her granddaughter. "What a lucky break for Ethan and José that you have been able to help them out with such an exciting event. I do believe that this proves my point. You're needed here. You should think about coming home for good."

Lucy seemed to bite her tongue. This was obviously not a new conversation between the two of them and not one Abby thought her friend would appreciate. Lucy was happiest when she was exploring new things and meeting new people.

Lucy didn't argue with her grandmother, though. "Sleep in tomorrow. You've certainly earned it," she said. "You and Abby can figure everything out for Christmas and just tell me what you need me to do for Christmas Eve and Christmas Day. I'm good at pad thai and cinnamon apple pumpkin pie. And of course couscous."

"Duly noted," Winnie said. "Good night, my darling loves."

Christopher chuckled at that. Despite all the sugar he'd had that evening, he looked like he was going to fall over.

"I'm going to put him to bed, and then I'll come out and straighten things up out here," Abby said. "You've had a long day and need to sleep."

"No doubt. But I can fold up tables and chairs at least."

As Lucy didn't seem like she was in the mood to argue, Abby let it rest.

When she returned to the great room after helping Christopher into his pajamas and reading him a quick story, she found Lucy sitting in front of the fire, a wine bottle on the table in front of her.

"Look what I found in the kitchen. I think Mariah left it. I'm having some. You in?"

Abby wasn't much of a wine drinker, or any alcohol,

really. It made her too sleepy. But she sensed Lucy needed companionship, so she poured a little into a glass.

"What's going on? What's wrong?" she finally asked after Lucy had poured a healthy portion for herself and downed it in almost one swallow.

"What makes you think something is wrong?"

She wanted to remind her friend that she rarely drank in college and was already on her second glass in five minutes.

On the other hand, she and Lucy hadn't lived together in years. People changed, picked up new habits. Maybe Lucy liked to party and had managed to hide it while living overseas.

"I don't know," she said slowly. "You've been acting off all evening. Last night, too, actually. Are the Russians being too hard on you?"

"Not at all. They're fine. The bride, Katya, is very sweet. She's so in love with Daniel and just wants the whole thing over with."

"Are you sure something else isn't troubling you?"

Lucy said nothing for a long time, taking another healthy sip of her wine.

"Why do some people have to be so difficult?" she finally blurted out.

It was a rhetorical question, one Abby really couldn't answer. "Sometimes I find the most difficult patients are really only scared."

"Or sometimes they're only being stubborn," Lucy muttered.

"Maybe. In my experience, those who fight the hardest usually have the most to lose."

Lucy sighed and sipped at her wine. "Or sometimes they're only being stubborn," she repeated.

"Maybe."

They talked philosophy for a few more moments, until she could see Lucy's eyes close and her head begin to sag against the sofa cushions.

"Speaking as a medical professional and as your friend, you need to put the wine away now and go to bed," Abby said. "That's my prescription for you right now. Sometimes the best cure for dealing with difficult people is a good night's sleep."

"I will after this glass."

"Okay. I'm going to bed. Good luck with the wedding tomorrow."

Lucy made a face. "You know how much I love weddings," she grumbled.

"Fortunately, it's not yours. Good night."

LUCY SWALLOWED ANOTHER mouthful of wine, barely even tasting it as she watched Abby make her way down the hall to her room, where Christopher was sleeping.

She had no reason to be feeling sorry for herself right now. She had made her own choices in life, her own path. She wasn't selfish. Between the peace corps and the NGO where she had worked, she wanted to think she had made a difference in people's lives.

She should handle her life with the kind of grace and dignity that Abby did. Abby had lost the love of her life to a violent crime. Instead of curling up and feeling sorry for herself, she was still compassionate, still kind. Abby was courageously embracing new opportunities.

Lucy, on the other hand, felt as if she fumbled her way through life, messing up constantly and coming up short.

The main constants in her life were Ethan and Winnie. And José.

She had lied when she told Abby and Winnie that her day had gone well.

Oh, her translation duties had been fine. The Russian family was big, gregarious, charming. They were in love with everything about Colorado, wearing oversize Stetsons and boots and quoting John Wayne in Russian. Daniel might as well have been John Wayne himself to them.

The bride, Katya, was truly sweet, though a few times throughout the day Lucy had suspected she might be suffering a little attack of nerves.

No, that part was fine. But Lucy had seen José twice that day in passing as she went throughout the hotel.

She hadn't spoken with him, but even those brief glimpses left her feeling as if she had been gouged by a hundred sharp knives.

She hated knowing she had ruined their friendship.

His words seemed to ring through her head in a constant refrain.

Did you ever think that maybe you're not asking enough of yourself?

He wanted her to be someone she wasn't. How completely unfair of him. She couldn't help the awful childhood cards she'd been dealt. It wasn't her fault her parents were serial cheaters who jumped from romance to romance.

José came from a warm, loving family. His parents had adored each other, his sisters were happily married. He couldn't understand the dysfunction and the chaos.

She sighed. She couldn't sit here drinking all night. She

had a wedding the next day, where she would have to smile and be pleasant while she translated all the romantic, sweet events of the day for Katya's family.

After that was Christmas with Winnie and Abby and then she would grab her backpack, hop on an airplane and go back to Thailand and her students, to a place where no one expected her to be something other than what she was.

CHAPTER SEVENTEEN

THOUGH SHE HAD only had two glasses of wine, Lucy woke the next morning feeling hungover, her head fuzzy and her stomach in knots.

She wanted so badly to pull the covers over her head and stay in bed. Everything ached, mostly her heart. She couldn't stop remembering those moments in his office after the gingerbread contest. The raw emotion in his voice, the pain in his expression.

She's not you.

She didn't want to remember. She wanted to pretend the whole thing was a bad dream. Climbing out of bed and standing in the shower didn't make anything better, but at least she felt clean.

She had brought nothing appropriate for a winter wedding among the few clothes she had carried with her from Thailand. Fortunately, the bulk of her clothes were still in her bedroom closet at Holiday House. She stood in front of it, looking for something that might work. She finally settled on a simple deep green dress she thought looked good with her dark hair.

None of the attention would be on her, anyway. Everyone would be looking at Katya.

No one was around in the kitchen, not even the corgis. Grateful she didn't have to make small talk with her grandmother or Abby or, worse, evade any other probing questions, she had coffee and a piece of cinnamon toast before heading to the hotel.

Her day was busy from the moment she hit the Lancaster Silver Bells. She helped while Katya's mother and sisters had their hair done, while they dressed, while her father talked to the caterer and the florist. She noticed Katya growing increasingly pale as the day progressed and tried to convince her to eat something.

Finally it was time for the wedding. Daniel's local friends and family filled up most of the chairs in the lovely room being used for the wedding.

Lucy helped Katya's father have a conversation with Daniel's father about the reception later, then went to see if Katya's mother needed any help with anything.

She found the women in the hot, stuffy dressing room set aside for them. It smelled of hair spray and perfume and Katya's six female relatives were talking loudly and laughing about a story one was telling about her own wedding.

Katya stood alone, slightly apart from them. She looked ethereally lovely in a richly embroidered dress trimmed in fake fur. Her slender features were pale, tense, and she looked poised for flight.

Lucy wasn't sure what to do. She was here as a translator. That was all.

She had already asked if Katya would be kidnapped by her family, as was tradition in Russia, so that her groom could pay a "ransom" in challenges. Katya had told her Daniel had already paid his ransom when he had visited her in Russia and asked her to marry him.

After two days of helping with the wedding party, she knew Katya's and Daniel's romantic story. They had met in Italy when both were tourists there and had fallen head over heels, changing all their travel plans to spend a glorious two weeks with each other. For three years, they had carried on a long-distance relationship, meeting where they could, until Daniel had finally flown to Russia to ask her to marry him.

They really were lovely together. Except right now Katya looked as if she was going to be sick.

"Are you all right?" she asked Katya in Russian. Though she knew the other woman's English was good, Lucy thought she might find Russian more comforting as she prepared to take this big leap into marriage.

"Da. Nyet." Katya heaved in several shallow, rapid breaths and Lucy panicked, worrying she was going to hyperventilate.

"You need some air," she said on impulse. She knew there was a balcony along the corridor just outside the room. It was locked, but she was a Lancaster and knew one of the doors had a trick handle that unlocked with the right amount of pressure.

Grabbing her by the elbow, she steered her out of the room to the balcony where immediately the cold Colorado air and the gorgeous view of the mountains seemed to calm her a little. At least her cheeks took on a little more color.

"What's wrong?"

"I don't think I can do this."

Lucy looked at her, alarm bells ringing. "Do what?"

"Marry Daniel. I can't. I have to take this off." She tried to yank off her engagement ring. "I can't marry Daniel. He deserves a better wife than me."

She started pacing the balcony, trying to pull flowers out of her bouquet.

"Let me get your mother," Lucy suggested, completely out of her element here.

"No! My mother would never understand. She would yell at me in Russian and tell me I was shaming the family. Then she would cry and tell me how much my father has paid for the wedding and for our tickets here and how she came all the way across the world to be here so I could marry my American cowboy."

"What about...about Daniel's mother? Carol is very nice. I've known her for years."

Katya looked completely miserable. "She is nice. And his father is very nice. I don't want to hurt any of them."

Lucy had one job here. To help this wedding go off without a hitch, and so far she was failing miserably.

"It's normal for brides to be nervous. I would guess all brides are, a little. It's a huge commitment, merging your life with someone else's."

"I can't do this to him."

"Do what? You love Daniel and he clearly adores you. You two belong together. You're perfect for each other."

Was she really giving a bridal pep talk—in Russian, no less—to a woman she had just met yesterday? Could her life become any more surreal?

"He could marry anyone. Yesterday at the rehearsal, I heard something. His cousin said Daniel should have married the girlfriend he had before me. She was beautiful and rich, from a powerful family."

"But he didn't, did he? He wants to marry you."

Katya started to cry, big noisy tears that made her makeup run. Lucy wanted to go find someone else, anyone else, to deal with it but was afraid if she left, Katya might disappear into the winter evening.

She grabbed Katya's cold, trembling hands in hers, squeezing them tightly. "All you have to do is ask yourself one question. 'Will my life be better if I marry Daniel or if I don't?' It's as simple as that."

The trembling of her fingers seemed to still slightly, so she pressed on. "You love Daniel, right?"

Katya gave a tiny nod. "With all my heart."

"He loves you the same way. You two are wonderful together. Everyone can see it. One stupid cousin doesn't matter."

She met the other woman's gaze, still holding her hands. "Do not let your fears stand in the way of your happiness. If you're willing to let those fears be more important to you than the love you feel for him, then I would have to agree with what you said before. He *does* deserve someone better."

She could feel Katya wavering. "It's going to be okay. You love each other. What else do you need?"

Katya sniffled a little. "I do love him. I don't want to live without him."

"There you go. That's all that matters. Now, you've got people who want to celebrate with you. Let's go inside and have your mother help you straighten your veil, and we'll try to fix your makeup and your bouquet a little."

"Okay."

"We're good, right?"

After a moment, Katya nodded and let Lucy lead her back to the dressing room. When she stepped back out into the hall, she cringed a little inside when she saw José looking gorgeous in a well-fitted charcoal Italian suit that showed off his gorgeous physique. Worse, he was heading straight toward her.

She was quite certain she didn't have the energy for a confrontation with him right now. She almost slipped inside the dressing room, but he caught up with her before she could do more than take a step in that direction.

"I saw you out on the balcony with Katya. She looked upset. Is everything okay?"

She nodded. "A few last-minute jitters, but I think everything is under control now."

He looked shocked that she had handled the crisis by herself. Lucy didn't blame him. She couldn't believe the things she had said to Katya about love and fear.

She was even more shocked that they still resounded through her with the ring of truth.

At that moment, Katya came out of the dressing room with her mother and sisters behind her. All had been set to rights and she looked stunning, with a new peace about her that had been missing for two days.

She came to Lucy and kissed her on the cheek.

"Thank you," she said in Russian. "Thank you for being so wise and for reminding me that love is the most important thing of all."

Lucy couldn't look at José, grateful he didn't speak the language, as Katya glided down the hall.

LUCY WASN'T SURE how she made it through the rest of the wedding ceremony and the long hours of partying afterward. It helped greatly that José seemed to disappear after the ceremony itself, presumably to handle some other crisis at the hotel or one of the others in town.

The wedding itself had been beautiful. The groom had cried, which had made Lucy want to cry, too. Afterward, Katya and Daniel's families both proved language barriers were irrelevant when it came to dancing and drinking and having a wonderful time to celebrate the bride and groom.

By the time the last of Katya's family left the ballroom and Lucy's services were no longer needed, it was after midnight and Lucy was exhausted. Her brain ached from trying to remember vocabulary she hadn't used in a long time, and her feet hurt from dancing with Katya's three brothers and her uncles, who were all delighted to tell her stories about home.

She couldn't wait to go to her own home, slip off her heels and collapse on her bed.

First, she had to retrieve her coat, which she had left hours earlier in the closet outside Ethan's office.

She headed for the elevator to the Lancaster Hotels administration offices, waving to Jolene Turner, who had worked at the front desk forever.

When she reached the offices, she couldn't help noticing a light was burning in José's office and his door was ajar.

Unfortunately, she had to go past it to grab her coat. Through the sliver of light, she could see his head bent over a laptop as he worked on something, his tie loosened and his hair falling into his eyes.

She fought the urge to slide into his office and push that hair out of his way.

Not her place, she reminded herself. She had made sure of that.

Tears welled up as she stood there outside his office, the emotions of the past two days hitting her all at once. What was *wrong* with her?

Love.

She loved him.

The answer seemed to settle over her like a soft snowfall.

This ache in her chest had to be love. It was the only explanation that made sense. She loved him. She had loved him for a very long time.

In her shock, she must have made some sound. Or perhaps he merely sensed her presence. He lifted his head, his gaze going instantly to her. In that second, she saw raw, unfiltered emotion in his expression.

Instead of making her want to flee, she wanted to sink into his arms, to tell him she was so sorry.

He rose and came out into the hallway.

"You're leaving? Is the wedding over?"

She, who was fluent in eight languages and understood several more, could only nod.

"That's a long day. Thank you for helping out."

She managed to find her voice, though it sounded hollow, rough. "I was glad to do it."

"What happened today with the bride? You said she had last-minute jitters?"

Lucy let out a breath. "Yes. She overheard something one of Daniel's cousins said, and it made her fear the marriage was a mistake and one day he would regret marrying her."

"How did you bring her around?"

Her face felt hot suddenly. She wanted to give him some trite answer, but she couldn't do it.

She wanted to tell him the truth.

She looked away. "I reminded her how much Daniel loved her and couldn't wait to marry her. Everyone could see that. And I asked her if her life would be better or worse if she swallowed her fears and took the chance on love."

"You did?"

At the shock in his voice, she turned to meet his gaze.

She didn't know what he saw in her expression, but an instant later he breathed her name in a low voice, and then he was reaching for her.

His kiss was fierce, almost desperate.

"You win," he said on a groan. "I shouldn't have pushed you so hard. I was wrong and I'm sorry. I'll take whatever I can have with you. If that's only a week a few times a year and phone calls and video calls the rest of the time, I don't care. I love you, Lucy. I've been miserable without you."

She kissed him back just as fiercely, just as desperately.

"I have to tell you something else I told Katya today," she finally said.

He eased away, watching her with so much emotion in his dark eyes that she wanted to cry all over again.

"I told her that she couldn't let her fears get in the way of something beautiful and right." She gave him a solemn look. "As I said those words, I felt like the world's biggest hypocrite because that's exactly what I have been doing. I've been running for a long time, much longer than that last night in Koh Samui. I've been terrified that if I let someone into my heart, I would turn into one of my parents."

"You aren't your parents, Lucy."

"I know. I realize that now. My parents are selfish and irresponsible. I'm not like them in other ways. Why have I been so convinced I could be like them when it came to love? Why couldn't I just as easily be like Winnie, who loved my grandfather from the day they met until he died fifty years later? Longer, even. She still loves him. For eternity, she says."

His arms tightened around her, and she thought she heard him hitch in a breath.

"I choose Winnie and Clive, José. I want to be like them.

And I choose you. Always you. I love you. Like Winnie loved my grandfather. Like your mother loved your father. I want the same thing you do. A future together. I don't know if I'm any good at love but…but I would like to try. With you."

"You're good at everything you try. Scuba diving. *Muay Thai*. Speaking Russian. Why do you think being in love would prove any different?"

She laughed. "That is an excellent point. I'm probably going to be fabulous at it."

"I have no doubt whatsoever."

He pulled her into his arms once more, this time for good.

CHAPTER EIGHTEEN

CHRISTMASTIME SEEMED TO spin past faster and faster every year.

Ethan had no idea where the time went, but on the day before Christmas Eve Ethan drove through the crowded downtown of Silver Bells, trying to find a place to park.

He was so behind this year. While he had ordered several gifts in November for Winnie and Lucy and a few of his good friends, he hadn't made time to pick them up yet.

Now he had a few other last-minute things he had been thinking about for Christopher and Abby. He wanted something for them to remember Silver Bells.

Finally, a big SUV flashed its brake lights and backed out in front of him. He immediately pulled into the spot and turned off the engine.

A light snow fell as he headed into the fray of busy sidewalks and crowded stores, all filled with last-minute shoppers like him. Everyone seemed to become a little more desperate as the clock ticked down.

This was his penance for not taking care of things earlier, Ethan thought as he stood in a long checkout line at one store after another, then waited again to have things gift wrapped before heading to the sporting goods store for something else he wanted to get Christopher.

In a window display outside, his attention was caught by a BMX bike similar to the one he used to have. Christopher would love that, he thought, and could surely find places to ride it in Austin.

His chest ached every time he thought about them leaving.

He was going to miss them both so much. Christopher had brought so much joy and laughter into his life.

And Abby. How had he made it all these years without the sunshine of her smile?

Both of them would be gone soon. She was leaving the day after Christmas, which gave him only a few more days to store up memories of them.

He opened the door to the sporting goods store and had just headed down the aisle toward the bikes when someone jostled him.

"Oh. Excuse me," a woman said.

Ethan turned around and nearly dropped his bags.

The woman had a baby carrier over one arm and a bunch of packages over the other…and a huge diamond wedding ring on the hand where his own engagement ring used to be.

"Ethan!" Brooke Fielding Palmer exclaimed.

"Hello. Someone mentioned you were coming back to town for the holidays. How are you?"

At one time, she was his future. She was as lovely as ever, her makeup perfect, her hair looking salon-shiny. But he didn't feel a single thing.

"Good. So good. This is my daughter, Mia."

The baby was beautiful, with round cheeks, huge dark eyes and curly dark hair pinned back with a pink bow.

"Hi," he said softly to the child, who looked far too small and fragile to be out in the cold, even with her quilted wrap and little beanie.

"How are things?" he asked. "How's life being married to an NBA player?"

She gave a bright smile that looked genuine, he was happy to see. "Great. Really great. Mia has made something that was already good into something fantastic. I feel so blessed."

"I'm glad." He was, he realized. He had wondered how he would react to seeing her again, if he would feel hurt or betrayal or sadness. He felt none of those things. Only a strange sense of…relief.

He didn't have time to examine it.

"What about you? I see you have a bag there from a women's boutique. Does that mean you have a special someone?"

Ethan looked down at the hand-painted scarf he had picked out for Abby, nestled against an exquisite jeweled Christmas tree ornament created by a glass artist of some renown.

"This is for a…friend."

"Oh." She looked slightly disappointed. After a moment, she reached out and touched his arm. "I'm actually really glad I bumped into you. I feel like I owe you an apology. It's been bothering me for a long time. I can't tell you how many times I've started to text you or even call you, but I didn't know exactly what to say or where to start."

"You don't owe me any apology."

"I do. I should never have said such harsh things to you when I gave you back your ring. I cringe every time I remember them."

"You only said what you had been thinking."

"The thing is, I had been having doubts for several months. Not just about you but about me, too. I was afraid to admit I might have made a mistake when I agreed to marry you. It was easier to blame you than it was to face that. Because of my cowardice, I waited too long and made everything so much harder than it should have been."

Her little girl made a cooing sound and blew a bubble.

He looked at the baby and then back up at Brooke. "We wouldn't have made a good match, would we?"

She shook her head a little sadly. "On paper, we should have been perfect together. You are a terrific guy and I did love you. But no. We weren't a good match. We would have made each other crazy within a year. I need to be needed and you...you don't really need anyone."

That wasn't true.

A month ago he might have agreed with her. Not now.

An image of Abby's sweet smile and warm green eyes flashed in his head. He remembered her courage as she faced the ski slopes, her exhilaration despite herself, the tenderness of her kiss.

He needed her, more than he ever believed it was possible to need another person.

That she happened to have a son Ethan also already cared about deeply was simply a bonus.

"You don't hate me, do you?" Brooke went on, her voice hesitant.

Being liked had always been the most important thing to Brooke. It was the reason she was obsessive on her social media properties.

"Not for a minute," he said honestly. "I always only wanted the best for you. I'm glad you found it with Marcos."

"Thank you for teaching me some important lessons about myself, things I think I had to learn about who I was and what I needed before I could be in a healthy enough place to meet and fall for Marcos. If not for you, I wouldn't be as happy as I am now."

"Glad I could help," Ethan said with a wry smile.

She gave him a radiant smile. "I'd better go. Marcos couldn't find a place to park, so he just went around the block a few times while I ran in to grab something for my little brother."

"Give him my best. And to your family."

Except your cousin Cora, who is an interfering busybody, he wanted to add, but politely refrained.

After she left, Ethan finished his shopping, aware of the strangest feeling, as if a huge weight the size of Powderhorn Mountain had just lifted from his shoulders.

Only until this moment did he realize how much baggage he still carried over the end of his engagement.

Now that it was gone, now that he had come to see the breakup not as some kind of failure on his part but the best possible outcome for both parties, he felt a strange kind of peace.

One thing still puzzled him. Brooke had said she had learned things about herself after their engagement ended. Could he say the same?

Where was he now that he hadn't been a year ago?

In love, he realized with a jolt.

He was truly in love.

This wasn't something he had to convince himself he felt. The difference between what he had once thought he felt for Brooke and what he now felt for Abby was like the difference between the bunny hill and the resort's most technical black diamond run.

He loved her.

What was he going to do about it?

On impulse, he hurried back into the store and bought one more thing.

He was putting them all into the hatch of his SUV just as he heard someone call his name.

"Ethan! Hi! What are you doing in town?"

He whirled around to find his sister smiling at him with the brightest expression he had seen on her face in days.

"Are you really Christmas shopping on the day before Christmas Eve?" she teased.

Could she see the box with the BMX bike that he would be putting together tonight? Or the other gift that was completely an act of faith?

"A few last-minute things."

"Anything for me in there?" She pretended to look over his shoulder.

"I'm not telling. Stop snooping." He closed the hatch and to distract her, he pointed to a steakhouse nearby. "I was thinking about grabbing a bite to eat at the Branding Iron. Want to join me?"

He hadn't spent enough one-on-one time with his sister since she had been home, and she would also be leaving in a few more days.

She hesitated. "I'm actually…with someone. I decided to pop into the bookstore for a minute while he parks the car."

"Anybody I know?"

To his astonishment, her face flushed and she looked away. What on earth? Lucy *never* blushed.

"Um. Yes—" she started to say. Before she could finish, José, his best friend and most trusted associate, came up behind her, wrapped his arms around her and hugged her tightly, with an intimacy that was obvious for everyone to see.

José. And Ethan's baby sister.

He couldn't say he was completely shocked. He had known something had happened between them after José's most recent trip to Thailand, where he had met up with Lucy. He had been looking for some sign between them, but hadn't seen anything since Lucy had come back to town.

Apparently he hadn't been looking hard enough.

José froze when he spotted Ethan over Lucy's shoulder, and for a moment they all stood locked in an awkward tableau.

"Well," Ethan said. "This is new."

José stepped away from Lucy and scratched his face. "I wanted to tell you today, uh, but we decided we should both talk to you about it together."

"Now is as good a time as any," Lucy said brightly. "Here's the thing, Ethan. I'm in love with José and apparently I have been for a long time—I was simply too stubborn to admit it. When he came to Thailand a few months ago, things changed between us. It took me a little longer than it should have to realize how I felt, but here we are."

In love. Lucy, who had spent her entire life claiming she would never be foolish enough to fall in love. Who had made it very clear to everyone that she would never let herself become vulnerable and stupid like their parents.

Lucy was in love with Ethan's best friend.

"It wasn't just Thailand," José said quietly. "Feelings have been growing for a long time. It was easier for both of us to pretend otherwise. Until I couldn't pretend anymore."

The emotion in his voice came through loud and clear,

as did the tender look Lucy gave him. Their hands were entwined, and they didn't look like they wanted to ever let go.

He didn't know what to say. On reflection, though, he couldn't think of anyone better for his sister. The very things that made José such a valuable part of Lancaster Hotels were also what made him perfect for Lucy. He was patient, calm, loyal, with a deep core of compassion and kindness.

Exactly what she needed.

Perhaps now his sister might consider sticking around Silver Bells for five minutes.

He gave Lucy a tight hug and felt her sag with relief, almost as if she had been worried about his reaction.

"This is great news," he said firmly. "Wonderful news. I'm thrilled for you both."

"Thanks." Lucy hugged him back. "I'm sorry," she whispered. "I really didn't mean to spring it on you like this."

"No problem. Have you told Winnie yet?"

"No. I'm going to take her aside tomorrow morning," Lucy said.

"You know she and Sofia are going to think this was their doing."

She laughed. "We can let them think that."

"Do you want to join us for dinner?" José asked. "We had reservations for two but I'm sure they could add another plate to our table."

He shook his head, needing a little time to adjust to the idea of his sister dating his best friend. "You go on. I'm good. I've still got a few gifts to deliver and a few more to wrap. Have a great evening."

He waved them off and climbed into his vehicle as the snow began to fall in earnest.

Lucy. In love.

He honestly never thought he would see the day. She had been claiming forever that she wasn't programmed to fall in love.

Their parents' marriages and divorces had damaged her far more than they had Ethan. She had been younger, for one thing, subject to three more years of vicious custody fights while Ethan had been in college.

The experience had hardened something inside her. He never thought she would soften enough to fall in love.

What would this mean for Lucy's future? Would she go back to teaching overseas? It would be great to have her closer. He had been trying for years to convince her to take a position with Lancaster Hotels. He would love it if she agreed to take more of a role.

They could figure that out, he supposed. She didn't need to make any decisions right now about the future.

Ethan dropped gifts off to his personal assistant and to his current chief operating officer and their spouses, as well as a few other friends.

By the time he drove back through the brightly decorated town toward his empty condo, he was aware of a vague sense of loneliness.

Seeing Brooke and her baby, and then Lucy and José, all so happy with their lives, left Ethan feeling strangely hollow inside.

He didn't want to go home, to face that beautiful, sophisticated, empty space that didn't even have a Christmas tree.

He wanted to go to Holiday House to see his grandmother. But more than that, he wanted to see Abby and

Christopher. He ached for them. Her smile, so full of joy and life. Christopher's hugs and the generous affection he freely gave that made Ethan feel like he could do anything.

How had they become so very important to him? Not important. That was too mild a word. They were *necessary*, as vital as water and air and nourishment.

He was in love with her.

Love. The word that Brooke said he wasn't capable of. She was wrong. So wrong.

If Lucy could be brave enough to reach for her happiness, what was stopping Ethan?

He wanted forever with Abby and Christopher.

The realization seemed to seep through him.

He loved her.

A year ago, he had been upset about the end of his engagement, yes. That had been his pride only. It was nothing compared to the deep despair that filled him whenever he thought about Abby and Christopher leaving.

How could he persuade her to give him a chance?

She was leaving in three days. She had her future mapped out. A new job, a new life in Austin. New opportunities for Christopher.

Ethan had to somehow convince her to throw all those plans out the window and take a chance on him.

He had no idea if he could accomplish that. He only knew he had to try.

CHAPTER NINETEEN

"I CAN'T WAIT for Santa to come! When will he be here?"

Abby exchanged a look with Winnie. They had heard that question at least three times an hour since Chris woke up that morning.

"Later tonight. We're having dinner first, then we'll play games and go to church. Then when we come home, you'll go straight to bed. After that, Santa *might* come," she said.

"You'll have to leave cookies and milk," Winnie said. "Don't forget the cookies. I have it on good authority that Santa loves chocolate chip cookies."

That was certainly true. Abby could use a cookie right about now.

"I loooove Christmas Eve," he said, dancing around the kitchen and stopping to impulsively give Winnie a hug.

The older woman hugged him back, her eyes suspiciously bright. "Same here," she said. "What's better than family, friends and food?"

Abby couldn't think of a single thing.

"I'm so glad you persuaded José, Rodrigo and Sofia to come to dinner," Winnie said to Lucy, who was shredding lettuce for a salad. "What time do you think they'll be here?"

Lucy's expression went soft, something Abby had seen frequently over the past few days, ever since her friend had made the shocking admission that she was now seeing José.

"Soon. Rodrigo had a few gifts to deliver to his friends and his girlfriend, and then they're coming straight here."

Abby still wanted to shake her head when she saw that lovestruck look in her friend's eyes.

Lucy and José. She still couldn't quite believe it, considering all the years Lucy had claimed she would never fall in love.

She was so happy for her. José seemed like a wonderful man, and it was clear he was completely in love with Lucy. The two of them seemed perfect for each other.

"What else can I do?" she asked Winnie.

"You're the one with the list. What's left?"

She pulled out the spreadsheet she, Winnie and Lucy had worked out to schedule all the meal tasks so that everything finished at roughly the same time.

"We only have to put the rolls in when people arrive and then we'll be ready to eat."

This seemed so much like the first week she had been here at Holiday House, when she and Winnie fixed Thanksgiving dinner for Winnie's friends.

That seemed a lifetime ago.

"Isn't the holiday season an interesting thing," Winnie said, as if she read Abby's mind. "It starts with a big meal on Thanksgiving and then we have another big meal on Christmas Eve."

"With lots of music and friends and fun in the middle," Lucy said with a smile.

"And skiing and snowmen and tubing," Christopher added his two cents.

It really had been a joyous season, one she would remember forever.

Oh, how she would miss these women, this town, this house.

"Where is Ethan?" Christopher asked, which was his second favorite question of the day, right behind the one about Santa.

"He'll be here," Winnie assured the boy. "He said he would be late. He's working on a project he said isn't quite done yet."

"On Christmas Eve?" Lucy asked with a puzzled look.

Winnie shrugged. "I don't know. He said he would be here as soon as he could."

The doorbell rang at that moment and Abby's heart jumped. She hadn't seen Ethan since the day of the gingerbread contest, and she missed him far more than she should.

It couldn't be him. He didn't ring the bell at his grandmother's house.

"I've got it," Lucy said, wiping her hands on a dish towel and hurrying toward the door.

"Hola. Feliz Navidad," a voice boomed out happily.

"Rodrigo!" Christopher exclaimed, running toward the door.

The rest of the Navarros soon followed, and the house was filled with laughter, music and conversation.

She was pulling the plump, delicious-smelling rolls from the oven when she heard Ethan's voice. She whirled around, and for a moment it was as if everything else faded away and the two of them were alone in the kitchen. He gave her a long, glittery look, and then Christopher let out a sound of delight and jumped into his arms.

"I've been waiting and waiting for you," he exclaimed.

Ethan jerked his gaze away from Abby to focus on her son. "Sorry, bud. Merry Christmas."

Abby, flustered, her heart aching, was distracted and burned her hand pulling out the rolls.

"Run it under cold water," Sofia said immediately.

"It's just a little burn. I'm fine," she protested.

"Do it," Sofia ordered. "You're a nurse. You know how a little burn can get infected."

Abby sighed but obeyed, and Lucy and Sofia took over in the kitchen, ordering the men to help them transfer dishes to the dining area.

She didn't have a chance to talk to Ethan alone. For one thing, Christopher didn't want to leave his side. For another, he seemed distracted.

The meal was perfect, the company wonderful. Sofia told stories about her childhood Christmases growing up in Honduras. After dinner, they all worked together to clean up and then played Christmas charades and what was apparently a Lancaster tradition—Christmas bingo—with silly prizes that had everyone laughing.

Through it all, Ethan seemed to be avoiding her. He seemed on edge, in a strange mood Abby couldn't interpret.

After a delicious dessert Sofia had brought, a cake filled with dulce de leche, Winnie announced it was time for church.

They went to an evening service where Eli Shepherd spoke about finding faith and joy amid the inevitable hardships of life. Children of Silver Bells then gave a lovely Christmas pageant.

"That's my friend Dakota!" Christopher said in a loud whisper as a familiar-looking sheep walked past, giving him a surreptitious wave.

She felt ridiculously close to tears, for reasons she couldn't have explained, as Ethan drove her, Winnie and Christopher back to the house.

They took the long way so that Christopher could look at all the festive lights in town one more time. By the time Ethan drove up to Holiday House, her son was drooping in his booster seat, the excitement and anticipation of the day finally taking a toll.

"I can carry him," Ethan offered.

He scooped up her son, who immediately wrapped his arms around Ethan's neck and held on tight.

Abby wanted to do the same. Those tears burned again but she blinked them away, not wanting to ruin the peace of the evening by giving in to her sadness about the pain she knew hovered around the corner.

"I have to put out the cookies for Santa," Christopher said. "I can't forget."

He quickly put the cookies on a plate and took the cup of milk she poured to the table near the tree in the great room.

"Can I have a story?" Christopher asked.

"You do know Santa can't come unless you're asleep," Winnie said.

"A short one," he countered.

"I wouldn't mind a story," Winnie said. "How about *The Night Before Christmas*?"

Abby sighed. She didn't want the evening to end, either. "Pajamas first, then a story."

By the time he had changed into his red-striped footie pajamas, Christopher had found a second wind. She knew from experience it wouldn't last long. When he crashed he was going to hit hard.

They returned to the great room where they found Winnie sitting on the sofa with her corgis snuggled around her. Ethan sat in a chair by the fire, his expression unreadable.

They took turns reading *The Night Before Christmas*, to Christopher's rapt attention. When it was over, he gave a happy sigh.

"And to all a good night," he repeated softly, which made Winnie smile.

"Okay. Bed now, honey."

He nodded, too tired to argue. Christopher went to Winnie, working his way through the corgis to hug her.

"Good night, darling. Merry Christmas," she said.

Next, Christopher went to Ethan and threw his arms around his neck. "Merry Christmas, Ethan. I love you."

His words seemed to pierce what was left of Abby's control, and one of those tears that she had been fighting all evening spilled over.

Yes. Her son loved Ethan. And so did she. Somehow he had become so dear to her over this wonderful holiday season in Silver Bells. How would she ever be able to walk away from this place to build a new life in Texas, when all the people she loved were right here?

She wouldn't steal the joy and wonder of Christmas by worrying about that yet. She had another thirty-six hours to savor this season here at Holiday House.

As she expected, Christopher fell asleep quickly, almost before she pulled the blankets up to his chin. She was tired, too, but knew she couldn't sleep yet. She still had to put the gifts she had bought him under the tree.

When she walked into the great room, arms laden with gifts, the room was lit only by the fire in the hearth and the gleaming lights on the tree.

Ethan still sat in the chair by the fire. Her heartbeat

seemed to accelerate, especially when she realized he was alone.

"Where's Winnie?" she asked.

"She said she and the corgis were going to watch the BBC comedy Christmas special that she watches every year, and then she was going to sleep. Lucy texted that she was going to José's and we're not to wait up. Apparently they have Christmas gifts to exchange."

Was that why he seemed so tense? Did he have a problem with the new relationship between his sister and his good friend? She didn't think that could be it. Ethan adored Lucy and would want her to be happy.

"She said she would be late but gave strict orders not to let Christopher open any presents until we wake her up."

She smiled a little at that, then realized what else he had said. He had used *we*. "You're not going home?"

He looked surprised. "Didn't Winnie tell you? I'm staying in my old room upstairs. I wanted to be here to enjoy Christopher's Christmas morning, too. Having a child around makes everything seem more magical, doesn't it?"

Another tear slipped out and she wiped it away, hoping he wouldn't see. "Oh. That is so sweet of you."

"Can I help you put his gifts from Santa under the tree?"

"I… Yes. Of course. I brought some of them, but I have a few more in the closet of the room next to ours."

"I can get them for you."

She quickly arranged the gifts she had brought in a suitcase from Phoenix and others she had purchased in town. She also put a few small wrapped toys in the stocking Christopher had hung near the mantel.

A few moments later, Ethan carried out several more

boxes she had wrapped for her son. "Is this everything?" he asked.

"Yes. I think so."

He placed them under the tree, then stood back to admire the festive room.

"I have one more gift I thought you could give him from Santa. I hope that's okay."

"Okay," she said warily.

Ethan walked outside and returned a moment later carrying a set of Christopher-sized skis, a helmet, boots and poles.

"I went with the same sizes of the ones we rented the other day when we went, but we can always trade up for a bigger size if you want."

She stared, not sure what to say. "That's wonderful," she finally said. "What a kind and generous gesture. I'm not sure where we'll be able to use skis in Austin, but thank you."

He gazed at her for a long moment and she had the oddest feeling that he was nervous. Ethan Lancaster, the CEO of a vast luxury hotel group, seemed uncertain for the first time since she had met him.

"I have something else."

"For Christopher?"

"Sort of. And for you."

His odd mood made her even more wary.

What was going on?

"Have a seat," he said, gesturing to the sofa in the great room. Baffled, she complied and watched as he turned on Winnie's big screen. For the first time, she noticed a laptop on the chair where he had been sitting. He opened the laptop and an image was immediately cast to the big screen.

It showed a town she easily recognized as this one, surrounded by soaring mountains and blue sky.

A title read *Things to Love in Silver Bells*.

She gave him a confused look. "What is this? Some kind of tourist bureau ad?"

"I know how much you like lists. So I made one for you."

"You did?"

"Yes. I wanted to show you all the reasons why you should think about staying in Silver Bells."

"Staying."

Did he know how very much she wanted to do just that?

"Austin is great, I'm sure. It has good people, a great music scene, a lot of historical sights. But Silver Bells has a lot to offer, too."

She looked at the computer and then back up at the screen. "Winnie said you were working on a project. Is this why you were late tonight?"

To her astonishment, Ethan shifted, color climbing his cheeks. "Do you want to see the rest?"

He wanted her to stay? He must. Why else would he have spent time working on a very polished presentation aimed at persuading her to do just that?

It even had music, she realized. A soft, jazzy version of "Silver Bells." While the music played, images flashed on the screen.

Excellent schools, the first slide said, along with images of children playing in the snow and what looked like a stock image of a teacher in a classroom leading a discussion.

It stayed on the television for a moment before fading to another slide that read *A thriving business district*, accompanied by pictures of the downtown area of Silver Bells, crowded with shoppers.

Recreational opportunities, read the next one, followed by pictures of skiers, the tubing hill, hikers, a lake in summer.

Kind neighbors. The screen flashed to various pictures of the Silver Belles in the choir robes they had worn for the tours of Christmas at Holiday House.

Career opportunities. The next slide showed at least a dozen medical facilities, all with nursing positions available, circled in red.

"Where did you find all those positions?"

He shrugged, again looking embarrassed. "I reached out to people I know in the medical community and had them forward me any possible jobs. You wouldn't have any trouble picking one if you decide to stay."

"Why would you do that?"

He didn't answer, only looked at her for a long moment and then hit the next slide. She had a hard time dragging her gaze away from him to read it, but when she did, her breath seemed to catch.

People who love you, it read.

The next slide featured an image of Winnie surrounded by the corgis, Rodrigo at his gingerbread birthday party with frosting on his cheek, Mariah and Dakota in parkas and beanies, then Lucy, holding hands with José and smiling at the camera.

He had gathered all these pictures, put this all together. He must have asked people to pose for him. Did they know what he was doing?

What a wonderful man. A sweet, thoughtful, wonderful man.

She couldn't seem to catch her breath, feeling the hot trail of more tears sliding down her face. Finally Ethan clicked to progress the slide show one more time, and the next image made all the other thoughts fly out of her head.

It was a picture of Ethan gazing at the camera, his features serious, his eyes intense.

People who love you.

She looked at the image on the screen and then at the man beside her.

"What...what does that mean?"

He looked down at her, that unreadable expression shifting to one she recognized now.

Tenderness.

"You're going to make me say it, aren't you?" he said gruffly.

"Yes," she answered, sounding as breathless as she felt. "Yes, I think I am."

He smiled a little and took a step toward her.

"I love you, Abby. There. I said it. For a long time, I've worried that I wasn't capable of love, that my heart was somehow closed off permanently."

He cleared his throat. "I didn't realize how wrong I was until you and Christopher came to town."

He reached for her hands and tugged her closer to him. "I love you, Abby. I wasn't looking for it, but you showed up with your big heart and your sweet smile, and I fell hard."

"Oh, Ethan."

He paused. "It would be easier for me if you would consider staying here in Silver Bells, but if you have your heart set on Texas, we can figure out a way," he said quickly. "I don't know if you know this, but we actually have a Lancaster hotel in Austin. I could work out of there as easily as I work out of the Lancaster Silver Bells."

He would leave this place he loved, his grandmother, his sister, to follow her to Texas? If she had any doubt as to his sincerity, which she didn't, it would have disappeared in that instant.

She could feel more tears slip out and was touched beyond words when he wiped them away.

"I didn't mean to make you cry. Is it too soon for you? I know how much you loved your husband. I would never want to compete with that. I might not be him, but I would still be willing to love you and Christopher with all my heart, if you give me a chance."

How was it possible that she had been lucky enough to be loved by two such amazing men? She sniffled a little and reached for his hand.

"I did love Kevin. He was a very good man and so many parts of him live on in Christopher. But love is a funny thing, isn't it? When you open your heart to it once, it becomes that much easier to open it again."

"I wouldn't know," he said. "This is the first time I've ever been in love."

"This is the second time for me," she told him. "And I have a feeling it's going to be amazing."

She reached on tiptoe and kissed him, feeling the wonder and the magic of the moment sparkle through her like new snow in morning sunlight.

He kissed her softly, tenderly, his gaze locked with hers. She wanted to memorize every moment of this. The firelight casting shadows on his face, the snow falling softly outside and especially the joy that seemed to soak through all the lost and lonely places inside her.

Soon they were cuddled together on the sofa, and she didn't want this Christmas Eve to ever end.

"It's past midnight," he said sometime later, when they were both breathing hard and the lights on the tree had begun to blur. "Merry Christmas."

She kissed him again, her heart overflowing with love and the joyful promise of many more beautiful Christmases to come.

* * * * *

Ranch manager Annie McCade thought her twin niece and nephew could join her at the Angel View Ranch for Christmas with her absent employer being none the wiser. But when the ranch's owner, Tate Sheridan, shows up out of the blue, Annie's plans are upended. Soon she finds herself helping Tate make a Christmas to remember for his grieving and fractured extended family.

Turn the page for a preview of
New York Times *bestselling author RaeAnne Thayne's heartwarming Christmas romance,*
Sleigh Bells Ring*!*

CHAPTER ONE

THIS WAS WAR. A relentless, merciless battle for survival.

Backed into a corner and taking fire from multiple fronts, Annelise McCade launched missiles as fast as she could manage against her enemies. She was outnumbered. They had teamed up to attack her with agile cunning and skill.

At least it was a nice day for battle. The snow the night before hadn't been particularly substantial but it had still left everything white and sparkly and the massive ranch house behind her was solid and comforting in the December afternoon sunlight.

A projectile hit her square in the face, an icy splat against her skin that had her gasping.

At her instinctive reaction, giggles rang out across the snowy expanse.

She barely took time to wipe the cold muck off her cheek. "No fair, aiming for the face," she called back. "That's against the rules."

"It was an accident," her six-year-old nephew, Henry, admitted. "I didn't mean to hit your face."

"You'll pay for that one."

She scooped up several more balls as fast as she could manage and hurled them across the battlefield at Henry and his twin sister, Alice.

"Do you give up?" she called.

"Never!"

Henry followed up his defiance by throwing a snow-ball back at her. His aim wasn't exactly accurate—hence her still-dripping face—but it still hit her shoulder and made her wince.

"Never!" his twin sister, Alice, cried out. She had more of a lisp so her declaration sounded like "Nevoh."

Alice threw with such force the effort almost made her spin around like a discus thrower in the Olympics.

It was so good to hear them laughing. In the week since they had come to live with her temporarily, Annie had witnessed very little of this childish glee.

Not for the first time, she cursed her brother and the temper he had inherited from their father and grandfather. If not for that temper, compounded by the heavy drinking that had taken over his life since his wife's death a year ago, Wes would be here with the twins right now, throw-ing snowballs in the cold sunshine.

Grief for all that these children had lost was like a tiny shard of ice permanently lodged against her heart. But at least they could put their pain aside for a few moments to have fun outside on a snowy December day.

She might not be the perfect temporary guardian but it had been a good idea to make them come outside after homework for a little exercise and fresh air.

She was doing her best, though she was wholly aware that she was only treading water.

For now, this moment, she decided she would focus on gratitude. The children were healthy, they all had a roof over their heads and food in their stomachs and their fa-ther should be back home with them in less than a month.

Things could be much, much worse.

"Time out," Henry gasped out during a lull in the pitched battle. "We gotta make more snowballs."

"Deal. Five-minute break, starting now."

Annie pulled her glove off long enough to set the timer on her smartwatch, then ducked behind the large landscape boulder she was using as cover and scooped up several snowballs to add to her stash.

The sun would be going down in another hour and already the temperature had cooled several degrees. The air smelled like impending snow, though she knew only a dusting was forecast, at least until the following weekend.

She didn't worry. Holly Creek, Wyoming, about an hour south of Jackson Hole in the beautiful Star Valley, almost always had a white Christmas.

Annie's phone timer went off just as she finished a perfectly formed snowball. "Okay. Time's up," she called. Without standing up, she launched a snowball to where she knew the twins would be.

An instant later, she heard a deep grunt that definitely did not sound like Henry or Alice.

Annie winced. Levi Moran, the ranch manager, or his grizzled old ranch hand, Bill Shaw, must have wandered across the battlefield in the middle of a ceasefire without knowing he was about to get blasted.

"Sorry," she called, rising to her feet. "I didn't mean to do that."

She saw a male figure approach, wearing sunglasses. The sun reflecting off the new snow was hitting his face and she couldn't instantly identify him.

"No doubt," he said, wiping snow off his face with his sleeve.

She frowned. This was definitely not Levi or Bill.

He stepped closer and Annie felt as if an entire avalanche of snow had just crumbled away from the mountain and buried her.

She knew this man, though it had been nearly two decades since Annie had seen him in person.

It couldn't be anyone else.

Dark hair, lean, gorgeous features. Beneath those sunglasses, she knew she would find blue eyes the color of Bear Lake in summertime.

The unsuspecting man she had just pummeled with a completely unprovoked snowball attack had to be Tate Sheridan.

Her de facto boss.

The twins had fallen uncharacteristically silent, wary of a tall, unsmiling stranger. Henry, she saw, had moved closer to his twin sister and slipped his hand in hers.

Annie's mind whirled trying to make sense of what she was seeing.

Tate Sheridan. Here. After all this time.

She shouldn't be completely shocked, she supposed. It was his family's house, after all. For many years when her father was the ranch manager, the Sheridans had trekked here annually from the Bay Area several times a year for the Christmas season, as well as most summers.

His younger sister had been her very best friend in the world, until tragedy and pain and life circumstances had separated them.

She had wondered when she agreed to take the job if she would see Tate again. She hadn't truly expected to. She had worked here for nearly a year and he hadn't once come to his grandfather's Wyoming vacation ranch.

How humiliating, that he would show up when she

was in the middle of a snowball fight with her niece and nephew—who had no business being there in the first place!

"What are you doing here?" she burst out, then winced. She wanted to drag the words back. It was his family's property. He had every right to be there.

"I might ask the same of you. Along with a few more obvious questions, I suppose. Who are you and why are you having a snowball fight in the middle of my property?"

"You don't know who I am?"

Of course he wouldn't, she realized. And while she thought of him often, especially over the past year while living at Angel's View once more, he probably had not given her a moment's thought.

"Should I?"

It was stupid to feel a little hurt.

"Annelise McCade. My dad was Scott McCade."

He lifted his sunglasses, giving her an intense look. A moment later, she saw recognition flood his features.

"Little Annie McCade. Wow. You're still here, after all this time?"

She frowned. He didn't have to make it sound like she was a lump of mold growing in the back of the refrigerator. She had lived a full life in the nearly two decades since she had seen Tate in person.

She had moved away to California with her mother, struggling through the painful transition of being a new girl in a new school. She had graduated from college and found success in her chosen field. She had even been planning marriage a year ago, to a man she hardly even thought about anymore.

"Not really *still* here as much as here again. I've been away for a long time but returned a year ago. Wallace… your grandfather hired me to be the caretaker of Angel's View."

She saw pain darken his expression momentarily, a pain she certainly shared. Even after two months, she still expected her phone to ring and Wallace Sheridan to be on the other end of the line, calling for an update on the ranch he loved.

The rest of the world had lost a compelling business figure with a brilliant mind and a keen insight into human nature.

Annie had lost a friend.

"I'm sorry for your loss," she said softly.

"Thank you." His voice was gruff and he looked away, his gaze landing on the twins, who were watching their interaction with unusual solemnity.

"Are these yours?" He gestured to the children and Annie was aware of a complex mix of emotions, both protectiveness and guilt.

The children shouldn't be here. She had never asked permission from anyone in the Sheridan family to have the twins move into the caretaker's apartment with her.

She deeply regretted the omission now. While it was a feeble defense, she hadn't really known whom to ask. No one in the Sheridan organization seemed to be paying the slightest attention to any of the goings-on at a horse ranch in western Wyoming that represented only a small portion of the vast family empire.

Annie knew she was in the wrong here. No matter what uproar might have been happening during Wallace's illness and subsequent death, she should have applied to someone for permission to bring the twins to live with her here.

Instead, she had simply assumed it shouldn't be a problem since it was only a temporary situation and the children would be back with their father after the first of the year with no one in the family knowing they had been here at all.

"Not mine. They are my niece and nephew. Wes's children."

Tate and Wes were similar in age, she remembered, and had been friends once upon a time, just as Annelise had been close to Tate's younger sister Brianna. The Mc-Cades lived on the ranch year-round while the Sheridan children only visited a few times a year, but somehow they had all managed to have a warm, close bond and could always pick up where they left off when the Sheridans came back to the ranch.

She could only hope Tate would remember that bond and forgive her for overstepping and bringing the children here.

"Henry and Alice are staying with me for a few weeks because of a…family situation."

"Our mommy died last year and our daddy is in the slammer," Henry announced.

Annie winced, not quite sure where he had picked up that particular term. Not from her, certainly. She wouldn't have used those words so bluntly but couldn't deny they were accurate.

Tate looked nonplussed at the information. "Is that right?"

"It's only temporary," she told him quickly. "Wes had a little run-in with the law and was sentenced to serve thirty days in the county jail. The children are staying with me in the caretaker's apartment through the holidays. I hope that's okay."

Tate didn't seem to know how to respond. She had the impression it was very much *not* okay with him.

"We can talk about it later."

Annie frowned, anxiety and nerves sending icy fingers down her spine. She didn't like the sound of that.

What would she do if he told her she had to find somewhere else for the children to spend Christmas? She would have to quit. She didn't want do that as she enjoyed working here. But what other choice would she have?

"Why don't we, um, go inside," she suggested. "We can talk more there."

"We won, right?" Alice pressed. "We hit you like six times and you only hit us twice each."

Her priority right now wasn't really deciding who won a snowball fight. But then, she was not six years old. "You absolutely won."

"Yay! That means we each get two cookies instead of only one!"

Annie had always planned to give them two cookies each, anyway. She was a sucker for these two. The twins knew this and took full advantage.

"Kids, why don't you go change out of your snow stuff and hang out in your room for a few moments," she said when they were inside the mudroom. "I'll be there soon to get your cookies."

The twins looked reluctant but they went straight to her apartment through her own private entrance, leaving her alone with Tate.

Drat the man for somehow managing to seem more gorgeous in person than he looked on-screen.

A few years earlier, Tate had appeared in a public television documentary. Annie must have watched that clip of him at least a dozen times, seeing him help villagers dig a well in Africa.

He had looked rugged and appealing on-screen, even tired and sweaty. Seeing him now, dressed in jeans and a luxurious-looking leather coat, made her feel slightly breathless, a feeling she wasn't happy about.

"You obviously weren't expecting me."

The understatement of the month.

"No. I'm sorry. Maybe I missed an email or something."

Earlier in the year, Wallace would text her about once a month to tell her and the housekeeper/cook, Deb Garza, that he would be flying in for a few days, when he was arriving, what time to pick him up and how long he would stay.

That had been his pattern early on, anyway. Then he caught pneumonia in late spring and never seemed to bounce back. He seemed to be a little stronger the last time she spoke on the phone with him in October and he had been planning to come during the holidays but a heart attack had claimed him out of the blue only a few weeks later.

"We must have had a miscommunication," Tate said with a frown. "I thought my grandmother was sending word we were coming and she must have thought I would inform you."

"We?" Was someone else here that she hadn't seen yet?

"The rest of my family. I'm the advance guard, so to speak, but they're all showing up by the end of the week."

Annie gaped at him. "The rest of your family?"

"The whole lot of us. My grandmother Irene, her sister Lillian, my mother, Pamela, and her husband, Stanford. And my two sisters."

"Both of them? Even Brianna?"

"Yes. That's the plan. You were always good friends with Brie, weren't you?"

"That was a long time ago. Another lifetime. I think the summer we were eleven was probably the last time I saw her."

The instant she said the words, she regretted them. Both of them knew what had happened that terrible summer.

Brianna and Tate's father, Cole Sheridan, Wallace's son, had fallen down a steep mountainside to his death while horseback riding with his children.

The tragedy had lasting ramifications that rippled to this day.

"Yes. Everyone is flying in Friday. I offered to come out early to make sure the house was ready for company. Things have been so hectic I guess I just assumed my grandmother would have informed the staff, like my grandfather used to do."

"What staff?" Annie could hear the slight edge of hysteria in her voice. "There is no *staff* except me, Levi Moran, the ranch manager, and a ranch hand, Bill Shaw."

Tate frowned. "What about the housekeeper and cook?"

"Deb Garza used to fill both of those roles, but after Wallace got sick and stopped coming to Angel's View, she decided to retire. She moved down to Kemmerer to live with her sister. Your grandfather told me to hold off hiring anyone to replace her for now. We have a cleaning crew that comes a couple times a month to keep the dust bunnies under control but that's it. I take care of the rest."

Tate sighed. "That's going to be a problem, then. I have four days to get the house ready for Christmas and no idea how the hell I'm supposed to pull that off."

Don't miss Sleigh Bells Ring
by RaeAnne Thayne,
available wherever
HQN books and ebooks are sold!

Get 4 FREE REWARDS!

We'll send you 2 FREE Books plus 2 FREE Mystery Gifts.

Both the **Romance** and **Suspense** collections feature compelling novels written by many of today's bestselling authors.

FREE
Value Over
$20